Proceed with Caution

Ford Brothers Series

Sandra Alex

Keep in touch with the author by subscribing. Please
visit www.sandraalexbooks.com for details.

ISBN 978-1-989427-07-1
ISBN 978-1-989427-08-8

Chapter 1

Julia

"Tube Top Tuesdays!" I bark. "Are you serious?" My face turns as red as a tomato as Mary holds up a hanger, draped with a multitude of different colors of tube tops. Covering my heated cheeks, my expression says I am half aghast, and half *'are we really going to do this?'*. "You've GOT to be kidding! I'm NOT wearing one of those!"

"We're ALL wearing one!" Mary insists, tossing each one on her bed. We both giggle over the AC/DC playing in the background. Her house is empty for the next five minutes, when we expect the other two of our work girlfriends to arrive.

"I wouldn't be caught dead in one."

Mary feigns a glare. "And you're not wearing those glasses, either."

"Really?" I place my hands on my hips. "And how do you suppose I'm going to be able to see? Or shall I just walk into the walls?"

Shrugging, she tears off her white t-shirt, braless underneath. Her jeans remain as she wiggles into a flamingo pink tube top. As she tugs it into place, her pert breasts sitting perfectly under the elasticized garment, she mirrors my defiant stance. "See? Not so bad."

I must admit, with the tight blue jeans, the tube top is hot on her. "Now you try one." Mary glances at my red denim skirt and decides on a white top.

Modesty getting the better of me, I turn my back and lift my cream linen shirt, and then unfasten my bra. "Oh, for Chrissake!" she steps in front of me and helps me wiggle into the top. "Perfect. Your nipples show just enough."

Through bulging eyes, I watch Mary pull my spectacles off and place them on her dresser. "Now for makeup."

"I don't wear any."

"That's the problem. It's...what...twice a year your man goes away on business? You're wearing makeup. AND you're ditching the rock." She points at my engagement ring as I mentally tally the two jars I have in my head: one for Mary being a good influence, the other for her being a bad influence. The bad influence jar is about to overflow. "We're straightening this hair, too." She picks up a handful of my long brown curls that extend three quarters down my back. Straightened, I'd be sitting on it.

"That's going to take hours." I pull a strand of her short black hair, almost envious.

"Not with four of us at it."

Six minutes later we hear voices downstairs. "Up here!" Mary yells over the music as she draws a thin black line across my upper left lid.

"Where's Chris?" Misty asks Mary as she opens the bedroom door. Mary's bedroom boasts a four-poster oak bed tall enough that you have to get on your tippy-toes to get on it. The matching oak dresser and chest of drawers are thoughtfully placed in the small room so that one can enter and exit the room without challenge. Her iPhone sits in a cradle on the nightstand with a small speaker attached, playing music almost too loudly.

"Fishing." Mary answers as she dabs the eye shadow palette and blots it onto my lid.

"I brought wine and glasses, girls!" Karen calls as she comes in behind Misty. Misty and Karen are both single, and Mary has been living with Chris for nearly a year.

Finishing with a dab of red lip gloss, Mary stands back and observes my painted face.

"Wow, you look awesome!" Misty compliments as she hands me a glass of wine.

"Thanks. I feel like I'm about to wake up in a grocery store wearing nothing but this tube top."

"Pick which one you want." Mary gestures towards

the bed, at the leftover tube tops. "And then come help me tame this mane." She lifts my hair again. "You guys remember the straighteners?"

Misty plugs hers into the outlet above Mary's dresser and touches up her mid-length red locks. Karen tosses back her wine and picks out a flaming red tube top to go with her leather skirt. "Girl, you look hot!" Mary whistles at Karen.

While nervous, I can't help feeling liberated. John rarely goes away and when he does, I have to go with him. This once a year trip is paid for by the company and therefore no spouses are allowed. Despite his distaste, he went. Our wedding is still two years away, only because his company is rumored to be relocating, and he doesn't want us to settle until that is over with. Luckily, I'm not in a rush. Frankly, I hesitated when he knelt in front of me and asked me to be his forever. If it wasn't for my father, I would never have said yes. Dad told me that John had asked him for his blessing first, and the warning not to disappoint did not fall on deaf ears.

Gregory Abbott's mission in life is to marry off his daughters to well bred men, and I'm no exception. We haven't even started planning our nuptials yet. But with money, timelines are a moot point. John's said more than once that we'll have a spontaneous destination wedding if he has his way about it. But we'll see. If John knew what I was up to tonight, I don't even want to say...John hates Mary, and has warned me to avoid her, but what can I do? I work with her. Mary, Karen, Misty and I all teach at the same school, and have for the last two years.

My phone rings from the other side of the room, inside my purse, announcing that it is John. Hearing it, Mary gives me a warning look. "Ignore it, babe. This is our night." the 'bad influence' jar tips over inside my head. I'd heard it beep ten minutes ago but I hadn't said anything. John is likely flipping out back in Toronto, where he flew for work. A mere two-hour plane ride away, and I can still feel his seething glare. I'll pay dearly for that when he gets home.

The Florida summer heat is almost too much to bear. Thankfully, we're all wearing next to nothing when we hit the hottest club in town. Mary has been wanting to check it out for months, but John would never let me go. "Here. Give me this." My bossy girlfriend slides the one and a half carrot solitaire diamond ring off my finger and places it in her jewelry box. "You're single tonight. You'll have way more fun that way." Inside my head, the jar falls off the counter and onto the floor. For this, I'll pay.

An hour later we arrive at *'Proceed with Caution'*, the newest, hottest club in Florida, that just opened six months ago. They opened with promotional nights where ladies have no cover charge, this one entitled 'Tube Top Tuesdays'. The place is crawling with people and it's only ten o'clock. As we enter the club, a pack of four gorgeous men are standing by the door, leering at all the women who arrive sporting tube tops. One is particularly delicious in jeans that hang so sexy on his toned hips. His sandy blonde hair is swept back in a Patrick Swayze look. "He's cute." Karen comments, leering back at him.

"I bet you're not that impressed." Misty says to me. "What with the Adonis you have pining for you."

Rolling my eyes, I adjust my tube top, which is surprisingly comfortable and staying in place. Looking down, I can see that the makeshift pasties I applied earlier using toilet paper are working. You can't see my nipples at all, and Mary is none the wiser. "Let's get wasted." Mary announces, grabbing me and Misty by the arm, as we follow Karen to the bar.

"You'll thank me for tonight." Mary says after she orders two white wines. She speaks over the din of music. "You look so hot and sexy; the men will be lining up for an ounce of your attention. You haven't lived until men worship you." The oval dance floor congregates the whole first floor except for the bar off to the side, and a couple of tables peppered towards the entrance. Patrons are lined up in three layers waiting for booze. A second floor, with a wraparound balcony for accessing upper offices and a second set of washrooms, has people lined up end to end, leaning on the handrail, watching dancers from their Birdseye view.

The sexy male bartender, who could pass for Channing Tatum, hands us our drinks with a wink. "See? What did I tell you?" Mary brags. "Let's go shake it up." She wiggles her eyebrows.

I begin to wonder if this escapade is about dancing and having a girls' night out or picking up guys. Then I observe the four of us, clad in the least amount of material, and I inwardly nod. We aren't even on the dance floor yet and a pack of guys are following us, one of them trying to grind me from behind. "You go girl, uh huh." Mary coaxes as the guy remains glued to my side like a hopeless magnet. He is only semi-cute, but evidently, he fit Mary's bill.

A popular song comes on and the dance floor is suddenly jammed. Karen takes our drinks and places them on the ledge over the handrail while we dance. The magnet guy is apparently a boob man, as he's moved on to a girl who looks like she shoplifted two watermelons. The music is pumping, and the alcohol starts to seep in just enough to help me relax. Mary and Karen are grinding together as two guys watch from behind the railing.

A blonde, thoroughly inked, approaches me with a toothy smile. Smiling back, I continue dancing as he inches his way closer. He is cute, with a baby face and blue eyes. My guess is that he has a fake I.D., and that he has the ink to appear older. Not completely through his pubescent years, I surmise he can't even grow a beard. But he isn't being vulgar with his moves; his hands stay above my belt and away from my chest.

"What's your name?" he shouts over the music.

"Julia." I answer, unsure why I give him my proper

name.

Lifting his left forearm, he shows me his bicep, which boasts a tattoo with 'Julia' on it. Impressed with himself, he smirks. "It's a magic trick."

Squinting, because my glasses are on Mary's dresser, I look closer. Sure enough, my name is etched on his skin. "So you use that as a pickup line?"

He shrugs. "Kinda."

"My real name's Linda."

The song changes and the dance floor thins out some. Magic Man picks up on the joke and chuckles. The song is slightly slower, not quite a ballad, but slow enough for sexier moves. "What's your name?" I ask as he places his hands on my hips and lifts his hips from side to side with my motion.

"Rick."

"I'm going to get more drinks." Karen shouts to us, winking at me. She mouths to me. "He's cute."

Smiling, I let Rick close the gap between us as his hips rise and fall with the rhythm. His breath is minty, and his cologne is heady but not overpowering. "You smell nice." I say. "What're you wearing?"

Leaning in, his cheek brushes mine as he answers that he's wearing some men's fragrance brand that I wouldn't remember. Karen delivers the drinks and I take a sip of mine, suddenly feeling very brave. "What are *you* wearing?" Rick asks me.

"Nothing." I answer, which he takes as flirting, I'm guessing, because he moves closer, draping his arm under my hair and pulling me to him. As I'm enjoying the proximity to him, with this stranger who is being semi-gentlemanly with me, something catches Karen's eye and she whispers to Mary.

Mary lifts on to her tippy toes, searching for something. When her eyes widen, I pull away from Rick. But it's too late.

Cutting in front of Rick, Mary stands in front of me, so we are face to face. Karen shooes Rick away, but he can't get away before he's grabbed by another man's barbaric grip. "Party's over." Mary's gaze on mine is firm, almost protective. There, in the middle of the dance floor, with a cold, cutting glare in his eyes is John, my fiancé.

What I do next is impulsive and life-altering.

It's the smartest thing I've ever done to date.

...and the stupidest.

Chapter 2

Colton

Gripping the man by the scruff of his shirt, I look him in the eye. His eyes are glassy with booze, and his breath smells like a brewery. Before I can lift my tightened fist towards his face, he passes out. Releasing him, I watch him slither to the ground like a large garbage bag full of old clothes. As he lies flat on his back on the floor, I catch my breath and rake a hand through my mussed hair. "Anyone know how to get in touch with Maggie?" Maggie is Ralph's wife, the man who lies completely pickled on the floor of Mingles, the bar I work at.

"I've got it, Colton." Liz, one of the waitresses, offers. "Are you okay?"

Moments ago, Ralph had called Liz over for another beer, but she told him he'd had enough. She'd cut him off ten minutes ago when he downed his fifth bottle. Not liking the answer, Ralph first threatened her, and then when she turned her back to serve the customers behind him, he shoved her. Offering her my hand, I help her to her feet, and she dusts off her apron. "I'm fine. It's Maggie I worry about. Hope he doesn't go pushing her around like that at home."

"Hey, Colton!" My younger brother Wade calls me from the stage, where he is playing the guitar and singing lead vocals. "Can we start up again?" Wade and his band had paused during the confrontation.

Lifting my thumb into the air, I see Wade nod once and the music starts again. "You're sure you're alright?" I ask Liz.

"I'll have a bruise on my ass tomorrow." She sighs and waves her hand as she lifts her serving tray off the floor. "Someone want to get me a mop?"

One of the other waitresses brings over a mop and bucket while I begin stalking the bar again. An older woman, maybe in her fifties, is giving me bedroom eyes.

"Hey, sailor. You got anyone warm to go home to tonight?" She has bleached blonde hair with caramel roots, and caramel colored teeth to match.

"Oh, hey, Colton don't go home with no one." Cheetah, one of the regulars at Mingles, says. He's sitting at the table across from Brown Teeth. "I think he's either a sissy-boy or he's shell-shocked." Cheetah and his trailer trash friends laugh.

"He's not gay, that I can tell." Brown Teeth argues. "See how he walks? Straight as a pin? And his pants aren't tight enough."

Watching Cheetah, I feel my nostrils flare. It isn't so much his comments that bother me, it's the fact that I can see through the corner of my eye that one of Cheetah's friends is stealing Liz's tips off her tray as she delivers drinks to another table. This exchange is a diversionary tactic that I've gotten used to. If I had my way about it, I'd ban Cheetah and his gang from Mingles, but his Uncle keeps our liquor license. It was Cheetah himself who nearly made us lose it, after bringing in a pack of minors without identification.

"Well, he's shell-shocked then."

Brown Teeth gives me a once-over. "You serve in the military?" she asks as though it's complimentary. "A marine? Na, I'll bet you were on the front lines. With all that muscle and ink and all." She clucks her teeth like a hen. I try to ignore them while I walk towards Liz and motion to her that somebody is taking her tips. The guy is ninety-five pounds soaking wet. He takes one look at me up close and his face goes pale. Liz holds her hand out and he gives it back to her immediately.

"He don't like talking about it." Cheetah continues. "He's too sensitive." He says in a sing-song voice, trying to get under my skin. I walk away and scan the room. Everyone seems to be having a good time. Wade punches it up a notch with a more upbeat tune and the small dance floor fills up with about twenty people. Mingles is around two thousand square feet, with a bar on the longest wall at the entrance, the dance floor, and twenty small, round tables scattered around the dance area. Wade has been playing exclusively at Mingles for the past two years. The music is soft and hard rock, and the place is packed every Thursday through Saturday. It is the most popular bar in North Carolina, if we keep the fights to a minimum. Me and Bingo, the three-hundred-pound bouncer who mans the entrance, and two other bouncers who are scattered through the bar, keep the place as peaceful as possible.

"Yo, bro!" Wade calls as the band takes a break from their set. "You want a beer?"

"No, man. Still on duty, thanks."

Wade is my doppelganger, except that he's two inches shorter and has darker hair like my dad. I inherited my mom's dirty blonde locks. We are the youngest of five boys, Jack, Garrett, and Dalton being the three older boys. Wade is five years my junior. Our brothers don't live far from here; in South Carolina. "Well, I'm having one, and I'm still on duty."

Taking a pull from his beer, he speaks softer, with the pre-recorded music playing lower through the small speakers flanking the dance floor. "Why didn't you smack that guy out?"

Giving him a 'how-stupid-are-you?' look, I lean my shoulder on the wall and cross one leg over the other. "You know why, moron. Ralph's just a drunk. He won't hurt anyone."

"I'm not talking about Ralph, stupid. I'm talking about Cheetah."

I roll my eyes as a woman walks by me, towards the washroom, and winks. Wade follows her gaze as he sizes her up. "Great rack."

"Cheetah I'd never touch on account of Paul. We would lose our license in a heartbeat if I ever showed that loser what I really thought of him."

Bingo opens the door and motions to me to come over. Maggie has arrived and needs help bringing Ralph to her car. Me, Bingo and Wade carry the intoxicated man out, while the other two bouncers keep watch. "I promise you I'll keep my eye on him. Lord, he must have walked from home. We had a big fight and all. It's my fault. I'm sorry, Colton."

"It's okay, Maggie. Make sure he sleeps on his side and keep a garbage can next to him." I advise.

"You didn't have to hit him, did you?"

"No, Ma'am. But he gave Liz a good shove."

Her look is apologetic. "Please tell her I'm sorry. I'll make it right, I promise."

Ralph is lengthwise in the back of the car as Maggie slides into the driver's side. As we watch Maggie pull away, I see a car pull up with Florida license plates. "I'll head back in." Wade says. "You alright?"

"Fine. I'll be in in a minute." I say, waving him off. Bingo has already returned to his post at the front door. The small, red Ford Focus makes a round in the parking lot and comes to the entrance.

A brunette rolls down the window and asks, "I'm sorry to bother you, but do you work here?" The woman is tanned, with long brown hair and glasses. She doesn't have that flirtatious glint in her eyes that most women do. Her gaze is sincere, almost worried. She looks like an angelic librarian. For as long as I can remember, no woman has stirred my insides the way that this beauty is. After what I've been through in the last five years, I thought I'd never be able to feel real attraction to anyone again.

"Yes, I do. Can I help you?"

"Is Liz in there? There's no parking and I didn't want to park in a fire zone."

"She is. Can I get a message to her?"

"If you wouldn't mind. Can you tell her that Julia is here and that I'll meet her in the parking lot when she's done? She said she was finished at one and it's almost that now."

Liz doesn't drive and she usually gets a ride with Nelly, one of the other waitresses. "Sure, I can tell her."

"Thanks."

As I walk back into the bar, I quickly approach Liz.

"There's a girl named Julia outside waiting for you. She wanted me to tell you that."

Relief washes over Liz's face. "Oh, thank God. Her phone must have died on her way here. I haven't heard from her all day."

A question is burning inside me, but I don't dare ask.

"I'll go clear out my till." Liz sets down the last of the drinks on the tray and begins walking towards the cash register at the bar. I follow her. "You sure you're okay? I mean, from Ralph pushing you?"

"I told you I'm fine. That's the least of my worries right now, Colton." She swiftly places the bills and loose change that remains in her apron into the cash drawer. "I don't want to burden you with my troubles, but I'll tell you, I'm in a real pickle right now."

The question still burns in my mind.

I watch her count her tips and put them in her handbag, which she keeps below the bar.

Wade is playing a soft ballad. Lord knows where he got the pipes he has. Neither of my parents could sing, and I couldn't sing my way out of anything. He was inspired by anyone from Jeff Healey to Blue Rodeo and anything in between. Some day he'll be a star, I'm sure. He's worked long and hard enough. Talented? He certainly is.

Liz adds her numbers to the ledger and slides her purse over her shoulder. "Thanks for earlier, with Ralph, I mean."

"No problem. You better get on out there to Julia. She's waiting for you, and it's late. You girls be careful getting home."

"We will. Thanks." She says as I watch her walk out of Mingles.

I've served in the military and fought battles I never dreamed I'd have the balls to fight. I've got all the tattoos and muscles I'd ever need in the world and I haven't got the courage to ask a simple question.

...who is she?

***

It's just past two in the morning. All hands are on deck to clean up the bar, including me. Despite my burning eyes and aching feet, I mop the spilled beer and spirits off the dance floor, while the other waitresses wipe down the tables. Wade and his bandmates are packing up their instruments, and Blake, the bartender, is wiping down the bar and taking inventory of alcohol, when the phone rings. "It's for you, Colton." Blake shouts.

I don't make a habit of carrying my cell phone on me at work, so if anyone needs to contact me, they have to call the bar. "This is Colton." I answer.

"Hey, Colton. Sorry to bother you. It's Charles."

Charles, my neighbor, is an older gentleman. Widowed, he lives alone, and he often watches my place for me while I'm at work. "Listen, that pack of crazy ones are lurking around your place again. They're carrying on just like the last time. Thought I'd let you know."

"Thanks, Charles. I'll be home shortly anyhow."

"I know as much. Just wanted to give you a heads up."

"Appreciated."

I hang up the phone and don't see Wade. "Yo, Blake. I gotta hit the road. Tell Wade for me, alright?"

"Will do." Blake is drying a glass. He nods once.

As I salute everyone on the way out, I see Wade loading his truck. "You outta here, brother?"

I sigh, placing my hands in my pockets. "Something like that. Seems Cheetah's up to his old antics over at my place again. Charles just called me to let me know."

Chuckling, Wade shakes his head in disbelief. "Lord, I don't know who's more of a fool. Him for keeping on trying to mess with you, or you for still working at this low-down place for so long. Tell me, brother, why don't

14

you call it quits and get the hell out of here? You've got clowns following you and harassing you day in and day out, and for what? Set yourself free, man, and go do something you love."

Clapping Wade on the shoulder, I say. "Little brother, when you're done here, so am I."

"I don't see no record deal coming my way, do you?"

I shrug. "You never know."

As I begin walking towards my car, Wade takes my arm. "Hey, you're not going to do anything stupid are you? With Cheetah, I mean."

"Na. I just don't want him scaring Charles or the horses."

Giggling, Wade leans in. "You're not going to do the same thing you did the last time, are you?"

As I walk away, I wink. "Like I said. You never know."

Chapter 3

Julia

The drive to North Carolina is beautiful, despite the circumstances. As I say goodbye to palm trees and fry-an-egg-on-the-sidewalk-hot temperatures, I realize, sometimes in life you have to weigh the odds. After receiving a distressed call from my sister, I had to go. Dad gave me the same advice he gave Liz thirteen years ago when she left: leave and forget about support. Somehow, poverty seemed trivial compared to what my sister was going through. She needed me, and ironically, I needed her, too.

As I drive, I think about the movie Frozen, and how those girls were there for each other. That's like Liz and me. We manage to remain close, even though we live four hours away from each other, and she's been disowned since she decided thirteen years ago to elope and keep the baby born out of wedlock. Mom left when we were kids and married some Puerto Rican. We've barely heard from her since. Dad never remarried, but then he's married to the business, which is half the reason I'm guessing why Mom left. Granny Abbott helped raise Liz and I when Mom flew the coop for Puerto Rico. Granny died a few years ago.

Liz made some bad choices in life, especially when she met Grant. Expecting, she had to sacrifice her education in exchange for motherhood, which is why she was stuck waitressing at a bar for a living. Grant never encouraged her to go to school and do something any better. Then again, he never made much more than minimum wage with the mediocre jobs he had over the years. Her pride, and my father, never let me pitch in and help, even though I had more than I ever needed. This whole situation was kind of the straw that broke the camel's back. Enough. It's time to help her.

Pulling up to Mingles, I can see what she means by it being a very happening place. There is not one parking spot to be found, and I've driven through the lot twice. What is not very encouraging is the scene I witness upon my arrival. Two men are stuffing another man, who is as limp as a dead goldfish, into a small sedan. Great. The woman who is on the sidelines looks as impressed as I feel. Lucky her. She gets to take the drunkard home. Just when you think *your* life is the pits...

After doing another round in the lot, the dial-a-ride is gone, so I reluctantly pull up to the front door, where one of the men remains. He looks like he's going to ask me for identification. Nervous, I roll down my window to speak to him. The portico is well lit, and the double doors in front are wide open. Music pours out from inside the bar. Few people are milling around outside. The man who approaches my window is wearing a dark purple t-shirt with the Mingles logo on it, so I know it's safe to talk to him. Leaning over so he can hear me over the din, I can see many tattoos bordering the cuff of his t-shirt. He has big blue eyes and lashes that go on and on. His full mouth frames a good set of white teeth. Wavy, dirty blonde hair, kept longer front and back, borders his face perfectly. A thin line of sweat beads across his forehead, causing stray hairs to curl.

His smile seems perfunctory but well-mannered, and his speech is smooth and genuine. Although he isn't as big as King Kong standing at the front door, this man has large, corded arms, and his shirt hangs over his well-toned chest, just level with his pant line. He's tall and lean but looks imposing. When I ask him to get a message to Liz, he obliges immediately. I watch him walk into the bar with a strong, confident gait. He probably makes a fantastic bouncer. Nobody would want to mess with him.

I remain in that spot, since there aren't any others, until I see Liz approaching the door. Happy to see her, I leap out of the car and give her a big hug. "Sorry I didn't call. My phone died just as I left West Virginia. I couldn't find the charger, I left in such a rush."

"That's okay, I'm just glad you're here." My kid sister says. Her blonde hair is slicked back into a pony tail, which hangs just below her bra line. She has on a dark purple shirt with the Mingles logo on the left breast, and a pocket on the right. Her purple linen pants are soiled in the seat. Faded pink lipstick shines dull on her mouth, and she's broken a nail. "I know." She sighs, "I look like hell. Had a bad night. Some drunk shoved me to the ground." She feigns a smile as she walks to the passenger side door and slides into the car. "I got some great tips, though. Fifty bucks."

Ten minutes later we pull up to her rental home. Quaint and cute, she has flowers in pots lining her windowsills that flank double-paned glass windows on either side of the front door. The door to the bungalow has a half window and is painted a teal blue color, matching the windowsills and frames. The roof is dark grey, and a chimney is clear from the back. There is a single car garage and there are no cars in the driveway. "Nathan's probably still up."

"You let him stay up this late?"

She lowers her gaze. "He's thirteen, Jules. Did you go to bed before two o'clock in the morning when you were thirteen?"

"Well...yeah."

"That's because you were a nerd."

I give her a playful shove. "Give me a hand with my bags."

The house is quiet except for the faint sound of music coming from the back. The home is open concept, with the eat-in kitchen directly to the left, and the living room on the right. A round, wooden table for four sits in the centre of the galley-style kitchen. A television set in between a set of two bookcases is displayed on the long wall in the living room. In front of the television is a three seated couch, a loveseat, and an end chair. Beyond the living/dining and kitchen area is a hallway that leads to the back rooms. We set my bags down at the front door. "Nate?" Liz calls. "I'm home.

I've got a surprise for you." She winks at me and mouths, "he doesn't know you're here."

Nate walks down the hall, unimpressed, as though the last time she'd announced a surprise, it turned out to be a set of dish towels. His dark brown hair is a mess of curls. He keeps it short, almost bald in the back and sides, and too long on top. It looks like it hasn't been brushed in a couple of days. Nate is tall, at least a head taller than Liz, and very slender. If Granny Abbott were alive, she'd be force-feeding him her famous homemade bread. When he sees me, he forces a smile, "Hey Aunt Julia. What are you doing here?"

"I have the summer off, so I came for a visit." I lie.

He gives me a hug, or half a hug. It is him draping his arm over my shoulder and leaning over me. He barely touches me. "I'm going to bed." He says to his mother, and she playfully pats his behind.

"You hungry? Want some tea?" Liz asks, forever the hospitable.

"No, I'm fine. Where am I sleeping?"

"Well, you can sleep with me, or you can take the couch. Whatever you like. I need to have a shower. Make yourself at home; you know where everything is."

Leaving me at my resources, I search through my bags and find my phone charger, stuffed in between my toiletry case and my shoes. After plugging in my phone, I pull my toiletry case out, looking for my toothbrush. As my knuckles brush past my toothpaste, I knock into a soft velvet box. Opening it, I remember that I brought my engagement ring. The Rock, as Mary calls it, sits pretentiously in the case, as though laughing at me. This jewel is way more than I asked for, and so not me it's ridiculous. Granny Abbott bought me a birthstone ring when I was ten; dainty and delicate, I loved it more than any other jewelry I'd received since. It still sits on my right ring finger. It's been sized a few times since age ten, but it is still as beautiful as the day I got it.

The Rock had been appraised at twenty-five thousand dollars, for insurance purposes. The princess cut and clarity are impeccable. I slide it in my back pocket, with an idea in mind, as I grab my toothbrush and paste and get ready for bed.

Thirty minutes later, Liz and I lay in her bed, sleep betraying us. We laugh at some old jokes, and then Nate knocks on the door and asks us to be quiet. He planned on going to school, after all, but Liz said it was unlikely.

"Does Nate know Grant's gone?"

"He'll figure it out."

"Liz. Don't you think you owe him an explanation?"

"About the same one I got, yes. What do you want me to do? Make something up? I'm not going to lie to my son."

"Well, of course you're not going to lie to him, I'm not saying that. But at least tell him what you know."

Sighing, exasperated, Liz flops her head on the pillow. "Now I understand why certain people don't get involved with the opposite sex."

"What do you mean?"

"I threw away thirteen years for Grant. Let's not even get into what happened with you and John, and just about everyone I know at work has some story about getting shafted by a member of the opposite sex."

"We really need a new set of friends." I tease. "Hey, let's be gay."

"Stop." She laughs.

As I lay on the bed in my clothes, I feel the velvet box poking into my butt. "You ever want to do something more with your life? Like go to school? You always talked about getting into culinary arts. Do you ever think about that anymore?"

She blows a puff of air out. "Yeah, right. Remember, you're the one that got all the money to go to school. You're the one who's the teacher." She lifts a defensive hand. "I'm not blaming you or anything. I made my own bed and now I've got to lie in it, I get that. But...getting an education isn't an option for me. Especially now with Grant gone. I don't even know how I'm going to pay for this place."

"Well, you have a roommate now. I can help pay the bills."

"Thanks. And I'm not too proud to ask for it, either." She elbows me.

Reaching into my back pocket, I hand her the ring box. "What's this?" she gasps, feigning excitement. "Oh, is this a gift? Like the fake ring you gave me when you were eight? When you asked me to marry you after Desmond, that kid you had a crush on, rejected you?"

I'd completely forgotten about Desmond. "No, just open it."

Sitting up, she opens the box. "Um, I've seen this before. Why are you giving me your engagement ring?"

"It's worth about twenty-five grand. I want you to take it and go to school."

Her eyes widen. "What? Are you serious?"

"I'm completely serious. You deserve an education and a proper job, too. You'll probably have to stay at the bar for a while or get another job for a while to pay the bills, but I want you to have a great job like I do."

"Oh my God! You're the best!" she leans over and hugs me tightly. "I can't believe this!"

Her smile is contagious. "It's nice to see you smile again."

"Thanks."

It's time to change the subject. "So, you wanna be gay with me? We can form like the new 'Gay Team', you know, instead of 'A-Team'?"

She rolls her eyes. "It's relationships. They suck."

"They do suck."

"This guy at work, he gets hit on every night...I mean EVERY night, by multiple women, sometimes even men," she chuckles at herself, "he never goes home with *anyone,*" she slices a hand through the air, "Never gets involved. I hear he's a basket case, so that's moot, but whatever, he stays away. That's what I should do."

The voice inside my head says *don't ask. Don't ask about Eyelashes, whose body I haven't been able to get out of my mind for the last hour.*

"I feel bad for him, kind of. Not sure why he's even working there, really."

"Why do you say that?"

Sighing, Liz drops back down on the pillow. "Oh, who knows. I don't want to get into it right now. I'm beat. Good night." she says and turns off the light.

As I turn over in bed, fully dressed, I'm biting my tongue with a burning question.

...How come you've never told me about him before?

Chapter 4

Colton

It's the bucket laying on the ground by the stables that gives it away, proving how stupid Cheetah and his three-cent-cigar loser friends truly are. The bucket had been filled with cold, cooked oatmeal and placed on the top of the stable doors, rigged to fall onto the head of any intruder. The stupid part was that I'd done the same thing the last time we had a run-in with him and his friends. My stable and my house are booby trapped in several places. Overhead cameras catch the idiots on tape every time. The tapes make for great entertainment with guests, but Wade and Charles get the biggest kick out of it.

The ranch, when I found it, had been abandoned. It was nothing but a pile of wood put together like matchsticks. With my brothers' help, six months later, it was what it is today. Maya and Rebel, my horses, are mother and son. I bought Maya from a friend of Charles, and then I bred her, and Rebel was born. With four other stalls, I can have myself a team of horses, but so far, I don't have the time to care for them. I ride as often as I can, but it's never enough.

Maya and Rebel are down for the night. The drive-by oatmealing didn't seem to disturb them. They didn't even stir when I entered the house. Setting my keys on the console table by the front door, I walk over to the fireplace and toss in a log and some kindling. It was when I put the kettle on for tea that I heard a recognizable knock at the front door.

"Sorry for the disturbance earlier." I say to Charles as I open the door and let him in.

"It's no trouble." The old man says. "I won't stay a minute. Just wanted to make sure that the horses were okay."

"They're fine. Sleeping. I suppose they're getting used to these clowns passing by. They'd sense if there was trouble. I don't think there's much of a threat there."

"Nah. They're just drunks." Charles giggles. "One of them tripped..." he motions with his fingers, "on the damn oatmeal. Funnier than hell. He slid on his ass like he was Bambi learning how to walk. Right up in the air and then down, flat on his fanny." The old man lets out a belly laugh, his face red. It's infectious. We both stand there laughing like Charles had just told the best joke.

"We'll have to watch the video tomorrow."

"Yeah, we'll have to." Charles is still laughing, shaking his head as he turns towards the door.

"See ya, Charles."

"Yeah, see ya, Colton."

✳✳✳

Sipping my tea, I hear the phone ring. I know it can only be Wade at this hour. "What's up, bro?" I answer.

"Have we got some cool footage to watch tomorrow?"

"Looks like. Charles got an eyeful." I look at my watch. "You got company, or are you...um...done?" I half-joke. Wade does well with the ladies. Most nights he goes home with someone from the bar.

"Na, I'm alone. I was going to hit on that chick we saw earlier by the bathroom; the one with the smoking hot rack. But I saw her leave shortly after. Slim pickin's tonight."

"My heart bleeds."

"I bet it does. Hey, um, Bingo says you were talking to some girl outside the bar tonight. What's going on there? I didn't know you talked to girls."

"Very funny. She was there to pick up Liz. I went to give her the message."

"Was she hot?"

Suddenly, I feel irritated. "She's off bounds, little brother. You know the rules. No sleeping with coworkers or anyone who's got any connections with coworkers."

"I believe those are *your* rules, not mine."

"Your rules are you don't have any rules."

"And you've got too many rules, big brother. That's why you haven't been laid in...oh, God, how long has it been?"

"Wade..." I warn.

"You haven't slept with anyone since...well, since Pam left, have you?"

"You're on thin ice, Wade."

"It's true, isn't it. That woman wrecked you for other women. She was either really hot in bed, or really bad in bed." He keeps prodding and teasing. If it wasn't for the fact that the kid had been there for me at a time when I needed him the most, I'd knock his head off.

"Wade. Quit acting like a bratty little brother and shut the hell up. Isn't it past your bedtime?"

"Fact is, you're afraid, aren't you? You're afraid of getting hurt again. You're afraid to find another perfect woman, make a life with her, only to find out that she doesn't want what you want, and that she told you that she wanted the same things you did just to string you along. Isn't that the truth? You can't trust women anymore because of Pam."

Pam *was* perfect. Beautiful, successful, sweet and kind to all. I was lucky to have even met her. I was lucky that she loved me, warts and all. Messed up and hopeless, if it weren't for Pam and Wade, I wouldn't be here today.

"She never lied to me."

Wade guffaws. "She lied through her teeth." His voice raises an octave. "She lied through her teeth, and you know it."

"Why are we talking about this...now? It's almost two o'clock in the morning. We're both tired." *And the truth is, I don't want to talk about this...ever.*

"Always an excuse."

"Wade, I have to go. Come over tomorrow and we'll watch Cheetah and his stupid-ass friends slip in oatmeal."

"Fine. But we're not through."

"Fine."

The truth is, in the ten seconds that I'd spoken to Julia, knowing nothing about her, except that she was from Florida, something deep inside me opened up. I'm not saying I believe in love at first sight, because I'm no fool. I've never believed in that. But if given the chance, I'd want to speak to her again. Something in me senses that she is someone I'd like to get to know a lot better. That's more than I can say about any other woman I've known since Pam. Not sure if it is in her cadence, or the way that she addresses me without the typical leer, but something about her makes me want to reach out to that part of me that has been asleep since Pam left.

Should I break my own rule and reach out to her? Should I take a chance and take the plunge?

...who is she? And what is she doing to me?

Chapter 5

Julia

Two Weeks Later

"And you wore this out in public?" Liz asks as she scrolls through pictures in my phone from 'Tube Top Tuesdays'. "I wouldn't be caught dead wearing that."

"That's exactly what I said to Mary. I didn't want to wear the thing, but she made me."

Pressing her lips together, avoiding a smirk, I know Liz doesn't believe me. "Okay, I caved. Mary is a bad influence and it's probably not a horrible thing that I'm four hours away from her right now."

Liz's cell phone rings from her purse and she picks it up. A brief conversation ensues, and she doesn't look impressed.

"What's up?"

"Nelly's sick. I lost my ride."

"I can drive you."

"Are you sure? I don't like you coming out that late to get me."

"Oh, and you think I'm okay with you working all hours of the night in that place?"

She clucks her tongue and chooses not to pursue the argument. "You decide how long you're staying?"

"Are you trying to get rid of me already?"

Rolling her eyes, Liz places a hand on her hip. "I'm just asking because I can make up the spare room for you. It's small; I used to use it as a laundry room, but it'll be yours. No offence, but I always hated sleeping with you. You snore."

"And you're a bucket of roses, too. Blanket hogger."

Giving me a slap on the rear end, she walks past me. "Nate's school is hiring if you're interested. I'd check with him first to make sure that you're not disobeying some cardinal teenage rule about relatives working in close proximity to your hangout. He's not there much, so I'm not sure if he'll care or not."

It bothers me that Liz is so cavalier about her son. She lied and told him that Grant had gone to visit a sick Aunt in Raleigh, instead of telling him the truth. Does she think Grant is coming back? Is she too ashamed to tell him what's going on? I'm not sure and I don't want to press. I've made headway with her; she applied to the local college for the fall term, and she seems rather excited about it. I am too.

"Give me a hand with the extra bed in the basement." Nate is out with friends, so he can't help her. "There's a spare dresser down there, too. I used it when Nate was a baby. We can clean it up and it'll be like new."

"Sounds good. I'll give you some money towards bills, too."

"You paid for the groceries. You're good."

"Don't argue with me. Remember, I get benefits while I'm off during the summer. I can afford to help you and I'm going to."

"Have your friends from work asked what you're up to?"

That is a topic I don't wish to cover. There is a lot Liz doesn't know about what happened before I left, and now isn't the time to share. "They know I'm here. Mary's away with Chris, anyway, for summer vacation."

The basement is what I would call an organized mess. It is clear that Grant left a bunch of stuff down there; half the area is his things, half is Liz's things, based on marked boxes. A small area holds Liz's exercise equipment: a recumbent bike, a set of dumb bells, and an inversion table. There is a tube television against the main wall, adjacent to the equipment. An old crib is disassembled and leaning against the wall, along with a folded stroller and a bundle buggy. "I use that when I go shopping." She points to the wire bundle buggy with worn wheels.

"You know something? I need to teach you how to drive. If you're going to go to school, you've got to have a way to get there, and I'm going to be working all day, so there's no way I can take you."

"I could never afford a car, anyway, Julia, so the point is moot. I pay Nelly fifty bucks a week to drive me. With her shifts, she should be able to pick me up, and I can take a bus there."

"What are you so afraid of?"

"I'm not afraid, I just never had the time or a reason to learn. And I could never afford it, so why bother?"

"Well, what if you *could* afford it?"

She shrugs as we approach the small, single bed and frame that is leaning up against the wall with the crib. "Maybe I would, maybe I wouldn't."

I smile. "Your first lesson is tomorrow."

***

"How about I French braid your hair for work tonight?" I ask Liz as she applies makeup in the bathroom. Nate is wolfing down a sandwich as he walks down the hallway towards his bedroom. "Remember? Like when we were kids?"

Liz pauses from applying mascara and shoots me a glare. "Newsflash...I hated that."

"You...did...not!"

"Yeah I did."

Her blonde hair is tied up in a messy bun. Only my sister can pull off making a messy bun look nice. With my jungle hair, I don't stand a chance. My buns are more like mammoth Kaiser rolls and look ridiculous.

"Hey, I know this is a shot in the dark, but, with Nelly sick we're short-staffed. It's Saturday night and we could use some help. You don't have to have your server's license or anything if you're just delivering the drinks or cleaning off tables. Would you mind?"

"Oh my God, Liz, I have no idea how to do that! I'm so clumsy...more drinks will end up on the floor than on tables!"

She waves at my comment. "Please...do you know how many drinks *I* spill? It's not rocket science. Plus, the tips are great on Saturdays. Please?" She doesn't wait for a response. "I have spare shirts in my second drawer."

***

We arrive at Mingles early so Liz can give me a crash course in waitressing. There is nobody there except for King Kong, who is setting up for the band. "Oh, God, I can't do this!" I whine as I practice carrying beer bottles on a tray, starting with one, then working my way up. It is like playing a game of reverse bowling; where the object of the game is to *keep* the pins from falling.

"You're doing it! Quit being a drama queen."

I am up to six when we switch to mixed drinks, which Liz mimics with simple water glasses. That is easier because the glasses balance on their own; the challenge is not to let the liquid spill over the side. "I've gotta hand it to you, Liz. This takes talent."

"It's a piece of cake. You're already a pro."

We hear someone come in the back door, but I have my back turned, walking to a table. When I turn around, the same guy who I saw on my first night is standing by the bar. Our gazes lock for just a second, and then he averts his eyes to Liz. "This is my sister, Julia. She's covering for Nelly tonight. I'm just giving her a crash course. This is Colton." Liz addresses me as Colton takes a couple of steps towards me and offers me his hand to shake. His grip is firm, but his hand is soft and warm.

"Nice to meet you, Julia. Sorry if I put you off a few weeks ago. We seldom see Florida plates here." His blue eyes seem impossibly blue. His eyelashes seem even longer. Now that I know his name, I can stop calling him Eyelashes when I think of him…if I'm honest with myself, that is often. When he finishes his sentence, he adds a gentle, sexy giggle.

Liz shoots him a look that I can't decipher. "That's no problem. You weren't off-putting. It would have been if you weren't wearing that shirt with the logo on it."

He glances down at his chest and smiles. "True. Well, anyway, it's nice to meet you."

"Likewise."

The night started off well. It was slow, so Liz and two of the other waitresses took care of most of the patrons. I was mostly responsible for cleaning tables. It wasn't until after ten o'clock, when Colton's brother Wade's band came on, that the place really heated up. "Julia, we need you to take some tables. I've got to cover the dance floor for the next couple of hours, while we're at our peak time. Can you handle it?" Liz asks me.

"Sure, I think I'll be fine."

She points out which tables I'll be looking after, and I go to work. All is going well until some biker chick steps on my toe. The tray, which is full and being carried above my head, keels over on her head, and all hell breaks loose. Biker Bitch must have taken the tray falling on her as a sign of aggression, because the next second, I'm on the ground, and she's on top of me.

The first punch goes to my gut, winding me instantly. The next hit would have gone to my face, but Colton grabs her hand, pulling her up, and locks her arms behind her. One of the other bouncers swiftly removes her from the bar, while Colton helps me up. "You okay?"

I can't answer at first, trying to catch my breath. It has been years since I've been bread-basketed; grade two to be exact, when a fat kid thought I stole his last Joe Louis and rounded me with his chubby fist. "I think so."

Wade's band has silenced, and all eyes are on me. I never felt so embarrassed in my life. If there was a hole in the ground, I'd be crawling into it. Instead, I do the next best thing: once Colton helps me to the ground, I bolt, well, I don't exactly 'bolt' holding one arm over my injured belly, but you get the gist, I run for the first door I can find: behind the bar.

Chapter 6

Maya and Rebel are rubbed down nicely after having a good ride. Rebel, I usually take out, but Maya I leave to the kids. She's a tame beast and used to kids riding her. When I'm not at the bar, I run a riding school, serving mostly children, but some adults come, too. It's not a full-time thing, but it certainly keeps my horses busy, and I figure, what's the point in having a ranch, if I'm not going to make good use of it?

As I stand inside the stable, watering the horses, I see Charles at the doorway. He knocks softly before entering, even though I saw him already.

"Hey, Colton. You had a good set of kids out there today. One of the little boys I've seen here before."

"Jack. He comes every Saturday. Good kid."

"He's a real cute one, ain't he? Reminds me of my grandson."

Charles' family don't come around much since his wife died. I assume they are from her side, not his. Shame either way. The last time I saw little Gavin was about a year ago. "Gavin. I remember. He rode Maya the last time he was here."

"That's right. They said they would bring him back this summer. There's still time."

"He's welcome any time. Hey, you want to give old Maya here a ride some time?"

Charles puts his hands behind his back and walks towards Maya. The brown beast lowers her head so he can pet her. "Fine animal. I had one of my own when I was a young boy."

"You did? Did your family live on a ranch?"

"My Uncle. He kept my horse for me. I spent summers there every year until the horse died. After that I lost interest. My dad wanted me to join the army, so I set off there. Never looked back."

"You served?"

"I did." Charles keeps patting Maya. She whinnies happily receiving all the attention. "Your dad made you go, too, isn't that right?"

"When I was eighteen, I got in with the wrong crowd and did some things I'm not proud of. It wasn't easy for my dad, raising five boys on his own. Wade was only thirteen at the time. Dad gave me two choices and I chose to join the service. Didn't come back for good until I got injured nine years later. That was five years ago."

"Did you get shot?"

"Among other things. I was in combat for most of my time." I don't like talking about my service with anyone else. For some reason, when I discuss the military with Charles, I feel at ease. It's nice to talk to a fellow veteran.

"What was the other choice your dad gave you?"

"Move out. Evidently that thought terrified me more than being up against machine gun fire and shrapnel."

Charles giggles. "You get any good video of those goons from last night?"

I laugh. "Sure, I was going to wait for Wade, but we can watch it again with him when he gets here."

***

In good spirits after sharing a few laughs with Charles and Wade, I arrive at Mingles for work. The moment I get there I know it's going to be an interesting night. The car with the Florida plates is parked in the employee lot.

"Hey, Colton."

"Hey, Bingo. Who's in?" Bingo is carrying some supplies into the bar from the storage garage.

"Liz, I think. Someone else but I didn't see who. I've been out here most of the time. Blake's not here yet."

"You need a hand?"

"No, I'm almost done."

I nod and clap him on the back. "See you in there."

As I walk in, I see Liz standing by the bar, setting glasses full of water, and beer bottles, on to a tray. The mystery woman has her back to me, walking toward the tables, holding a tray filled with beer bottles. While she walks slowly, she doesn't seem to be struggling with balance.

"Hey, Colton." Liz says.

When the mystery woman turns around, Liz introduces her as Julia, her sister. *Aaaahhhhhh.* It kind of shocks me that they are related. There is no resemblance. Liz is pretty, but Julia, my God, she is an angel. We exchange pleasantries and Liz gives me a strange look, but I don't inquire, I'm too busy drinking in the sight of this woman. Her smile can light up the room. She's taller than I imagined. It was hard to tell, since the first time I saw her she was sitting in her car. Even in the cheesy purple Mingles shirt, she is beautiful. Her hair is long and curly, so beautiful and natural. It looks so soft and healthy, with no trace of bleach in it at all. She regards me with respect and not a drop of lust. It's both refreshing and hopeful.

Liz says she's covering for Nelly, and I'm suddenly worried. This beauty is not cut out for waitressing. Inside I want to ask what she really does for a living, because I know it's something special, but I can't bring myself to ask her. I don't want to break the spell.

The first half of the night went well. I found myself looking Julia's way often. Truthfully that is my job, but I usually divide my attention between all the waitresses, not favoring one. She kept her focus and didn't look my way once as she wiped down tables and served when necessary. It wasn't until a biker chick tripped her that trouble came.

I ran so fast over to her, since I'm the closest. The other boys follow behind while Bingo stays at the door and keeps watch over the rest of the crowd. First, the chick sucker punches Julia in the stomach, but I catch her before she hits her face. After helping her up, I was about to offer to take her to get checked out, when she runs for the door by the bar. I look at Liz for direction.

"Go check on her for me." she says, shocking me.

Part of me wants to ask why she doesn't want to check on her sister, but the other part of me is telling that part of me to shut the hell up. "You sure?" And then there is that look again.

Bingo gets the biker chick out of the building and gives a thumbs up. I go to the door behind the bar. Looking through the half window, I see Julia sitting on the table, and I knock softly. The music hasn't started back up yet, so she hears me and looks up. I don't wait for her to give me permission to enter, but when I do, I ask if it's okay to come in.

"Sure, you might as well." Her tone is slightly sarcastic, and her face is red. I'm not sure if it's colored from embarrassment, or if she's about to cry.

"Are you okay?"

She sniffs and wipes at her cheek. Shit. She is crying. "I'm fine." She laughs without a trace of humor. "Here I thought I'd embarrass myself by dumping a tray full of drinks all over the floor, but nooooo...I have to get beat up by a chick that would pass for Easy Rider. Good job."

The room is slightly bigger than a broom closet. It's used for storing empty beer bottles and fresh produce like lemons, limes and olives for mixed drinks. There is a small table Blake uses for preparing the produce, which Julia is sitting on. We had to put a new door with a half window in there after Blake got his nose broken from walking out of the room while someone was coming in.

I take a step closer. "Everyone's already forgotten that it happened. There's no need to be embarrassed. It could have happened to anyone."

"I told Liz I didn't want to do this."

"Then why did you?"

She looks at me and puts her hand in the air, gesturing towards the door. "You have a brother, right?"

"Yeah."

"Do you do stupid things for him?"

Wow.

My silence answers the question better than words.

"Look, I'm fine. I'm always telling Liz to stop being a drama queen, and here I am…being a drama queen." She gives her eyes another wipe with the back of her hand, adjusts her glasses and smooths her hair that she's put in a pony tail before she started working. As she straightens her body upward, she winces.

I take another step towards her. This time I place my hand on her shoulder. "Are you sure you're okay? You don't look so good."

"Probably just a bruise. She didn't break a rib or anything."

As part of my training for the job, I had to take First Aid and CPR. "Do you mind if I check?" I tell her about my training, even though she doesn't hesitate when I offer. She sits up as straight as she can, and I gently check her abdomen from over her shirt for signs of broken ribs. The fact that she only winces when I touch her proves that nothing is broken.

"You're right. She didn't break anything, but I think you should take it easy. You're done for the rest of the night."

Being that close to her is intoxicating. She doesn't ogle me or have any lewd comments when I touch her. Her skin is firm but supple, even through her shirt. A slight scent emanates from her body; soft and fresh. It could have been her shampoo or not; maybe it's natural. It certainly isn't perfume.

"I can go back out and work. It's not a big deal."

"Oh yeah? Lift your arm all the way up." I nod once and fold my arms across my chest.

She gets about three quarters of a way up and stops. I can see the pain in her face, even though she tries to hide it. "You're not doing any more."

"What are you? Some kind of doctor?" she's only slightly irritated. "I promised Liz I would do this, and

I'm doing it."

"How are you going to hold the tray?" I challenge.

"I'll...not hold it all the way up." She shrugs and removes her rump from the table. When her feet land on the floor, she grabs her back and lets out a yelp.

"Okay, that's it. Game's over."

***

I feel terrible that I can't go with her to the hospital. We can survive our peak time with two less waitresses, but certainly not *also* with one less bouncer. But to the hospital I go the moment my shift ends. I didn't even help clean up. Bingo stays late to cover for me. When I arrive at the hospital, Julia has been seen by a doctor and she's in a room in the Emergency department. A nurse directs me to the room, and I knock softly.

"Come in."

Julia is laying on the bed with a gown on her top half, and her pants on her bottom half. Her shoes are off, but her socks are on. Liz sits in the chair next to her. There is nobody else in the semi-private room, so the partition drapes are pulled back. "Hey, Colton. What are you doing here?" Liz asks.

"My shift is over, so I thought I'd come by on my way home and see how everyone's doing."

"I'm fine. I had some x-rays done and I'm just waiting for the results." Julia says. "Thanks for coming by. That was nice of you."

"They gave her a muscle relaxer for her back, so we were just having a little fun."

"No, *you* were having fun. I'm reliving my rotten childhood." Julia feigns exasperation.

"What did the doctor say?" I ask.

"Her ribs aren't broken, just bruised. Her back seems like it's just gone into spasm. It doesn't seem like she's bulged or slipped any discs or anything more serious. She can probably go home and rest and be fine in the morning. She'll just be a little stiff for a couple of days."

"Did I hurt my tongue?" Julia is flippant. "I can speak for myself." Then she addresses me. "I'll be fine. You didn't have to come by."

"You didn't happen to get the name of that biker chick that did this, did you?" Liz asks.

"We generally don't take down customers' personal information, no. But Bingo knows one of the guys that she came with, so we can find out who she is if Julia wants to press charges. We'd have to get the police involved though."

Julia barks out a laugh. "Who the hell's Bingo?"

"Uh oh," Liz giggles. "Those magic pills are starting to work."

I chuckle. "Bingo is the bouncer who watches the doors. The real big guy." I push my hands to my sides, indicating his girth.

"Oh...King Kong!" she laughs.

"King Kong?" I laugh.

"That's the nickname I gave him when I saw you and him that first night that I got here." She puts her hand in front of her mouth, holding back a laugh.

"What?" Liz prompts. "What's so funny now?" she's laughing, too. This is fun.

Julia points at me. "I called him 'Eyelashes'!" she's laughing uncontrollably. It's adorable.

"Well, you do have those girlish eyes, Colton." Liz teases.

Feeling my cheeks heat, I put my head down.

"Ahhh, so cute! I embarrassed you!" Julia's volume is getting higher.

"Shhhh!!" Liz scolds. "You'll get us kicked out!" she looks at me. "Can you stay with her for a minute? I'm going to go see if those results are back. I gotta get her home before she gets us in trouble."

"Sure. Go on ahead. Oh, and I can give you a lift if you need it."

"Great. Thanks. I'll be right back." Liz walks out the door, leaving Julia and I alone.

"So, how are you feeling?"

"Grrrrreeeeaatt!"

I hold back a laugh. "Do you need anything? Like some water? Another blanket?"

She'd let her hair down. It sits on her chest in a pool of brown curls. "No thanks." Her eyes make their way to my left arm. She points at one of my tattoos, a rose, that's poking out from under my shirt. "What's that one?"

"Well...it's a rose." I say, talking to her like she's in Kindergarten.

"It's beautiful."

Not as beautiful as you.

"And that one." she points to the one next to it, a vine, kind of like the one in the children's fable, Jack and the Beanstalk.

I explain the meaning of all my tattoos, until she gets to the one I had done after I finished in the army.

"You were in the army? Did you get hurt?" her face is priceless. She looks so innocent and concerned.

"I did. But I'm okay now."

I'm sitting next to her, in the chair Liz had vacated. With no shame, she lifts my shirt, searching for more tattoos. "Anyone in there?" she laughs behind her hand. "Hey, what's this one?"

My cheeks heat as she finds the small tattoo on my chest. "Who's Pam?"

"Okay, that's enough exploration for now. How about I go see where your sister is?" I don't want to get into that conversation. She wouldn't remember it, but still. What if she did? Her touch and attention are very enjoyable, yes, but at what cost? Nobody else knows about that tattoo and until I can do something about it, nobody else will. I don't want anyone to know about those ghosts. It's bad enough that Wade knows way too much, and he drills into me every chance he has.

Despite all that, for the first time *since* Pam—one of my ghosts—I'm not afraid to let someone in. Having Julia ask me questions and touch me, feels good.

Contact from her fingertips isn't sexual or suggestive. Most women claw their way up my body when they're in the condition she's in. I once had a girl straddle me in the middle of the dance floor when I asked her to leave the premises. It's nice to be treated like a human being rather than like a piece of meat for a change.

I drive the girls home after Julia receives a clean bill of health and a prescription for some pain killers to take only if needed. Julia passes out in the back seat, so I carry her into the house for Liz. When I lay her down on her bed and Liz takes off her shoes, she momentarily awakes. "Colton?"

"Yeah, that's me."

"Where am I?"

"You're at my place." Liz answers. "I'll go get you some ice for your back."

"Can you put it in a margarita?"

Liz chuckles and rolls her eyes as she leaves the room, leaving us alone again.

"Colton?"

"Yeah,"

"Is that tattoo a magic trick? Can you make it say *anyone's* name?"

"What?"

"Come here." She wiggles her index finger towards herself.

I hesitate, but I go in closer, so we're almost nose to nose. "What?" I whisper.

"You really do have long eyelashes."

I smile. "Thanks. So do you."

She sticks her finger in the air and tries in vain to run her finger along my eyelid so she can touch my eyelashes. Instead, she pokes me in the eye. "Ouch." I chuckle, playing along.

"I'm sorry."

"That's okay. How about you go to sleep now?"

"Can I ask you for something first?" Her eyes are half closed, and she speaks like a child.

"Sure."

"Can you kiss me goodnight?"

"Well, I suppose that would be okay." I lean in and kiss her forehead. It's soft and warm, and her hair smells like coconuts. As I break contact and move away, she gently pulls my cheeks toward her and plants a soft kiss on my lips. It's so quick I barely have a chance to kiss her back. She doesn't even open her eyes.

I hear Liz approach and back away. "Hey, Julia? Where do you want this ice? Ribs or back?"

"I think she's out." I say, scratching my head, trying to look as innocent as possible, despite the sudden need pulsing below my belt. I have to get out of here. "You okay here? You got this?"

"Sure, hey, thanks for your help, Colton."

My speech is fast. "No problem, I'll see you tomorrow."

"Okay, but—"

I'm out before I can hear what she's about to say.

Chapter 7

Julia

The house is quiet when I wake up. All the events of the previous night are somewhat of a blur. I remember tripping and falling and going to the hospital, but after that, not much stands out. Feeling better than I imagine I would, I get out of bed and search for Liz. Completely out of it in her bed, I leave Liz to sleep. Nate is asleep, too. My car is not in the driveway and I have a sudden panic, before I remember what happened. Liz left her phone on the charger in the kitchen, and there is a text message waiting. Being the nosey sister I am, I check it. It is the bar owner, Tony, letting Liz know that my car is safe in the lot, and to call him so we can discuss what happened last night in his absence.

He leaves his number in case we need a ride over to pick up my car. I try it, figuring the least that I can do after all the trouble last night, is to deal with my own problems, but there is no answer. "Everything alright?" I hear Liz approach from behind.

I explain the text and phone call.

"I've got everyone's number in my phone." She yawns and looks at her watch, noting that it is after noon. "Try Colton's. He'll be around. He's got riding classes Sunday mornings."

"Riding classes?"

"He lives on a ranch and teaches kids to ride horses."

"And he works in a bar?" I'm flabbergasted.

"That's about Wade, not Colton."

"What do you mean?"

"Never mind. Listen, how are you feeling?"

"I'm fine. My back doesn't even hurt."

"How about your ribs?"

"A little tender but it just feels like I coughed all night." My interest is piqued. "What do you mean about Colton?"

Liz sighs. "Sit down."

"What? What's going on?" I sit down across from my sister and put my hands in front of me on the table. I'm starving, but this seems more important.

"I saw the way Colton looked at you last night. I'm not sure that getting involved with him is a great idea."

I'm confused. "What do you mean? How did he look at me?"

"Like he'd just been struck in the ass by an arrow from Cupid."

My face scrunches. "Get outta here. You're imagining it."

"I don't think so. I've known Colton for a couple of years, and he normally doesn't even look at women. Never gives females the time of day. He's got baggage and I'm not sure that you want to get involved with that."

"But you only know him at work. You don't know anything about his personal life. How do you know he doesn't have a girlfriend? How do you know that that's not why he behaves the way he does?"

"Because I know. That's all I have to say."

"How do you know?"

"Never mind, Julia. Trust me."

"Why are you being so protective? So…reserved about all this?"

"Why do you care so much?"

"I care about why you don't want to tell me."

"For the same reason why you don't want to tell me about your personal life." She folds her arms across her chest. "Seems we all have secrets, don't we?"

Don't pull at that thread, big sister.

"You didn't just come here because Grant left, did you?"

Make up a lie…make up a lie.

"You would have done the same for me." my voice is flat. I try to hide the quiver. If she senses it, she doesn't let on.

"So you left your fiancé, your father, your home, your job…just for me." it is more of a statement than a question, and her tone means she isn't buying it even a little bit.

"Yeah," I say, but with way less conviction than I want.

"Bullshit."

Oh, no...what does she know...what did she find out...

"Why the line of questioning? I came here because I didn't like the way you sounded on the phone in the last couple of weeks before I left. I was worried that you would do something stupid, so I came out here to check on you, and..."

"And what? I'm so much of a basket case that you decided to stay?"

"If you want to put it that way, yes."

"So you gave me your engagement ring, gave up everything with dad; the money, the inheritance, his approval, all for me?"

I nod but I don't look at her.

"I'm not buying it, Julia." She pauses. "So how come you're throwing away practically your whole life for your basket case of a sister?"

Silence.

Then she says something that blows me away. "John is looking for you, you know."

Defeated. She knows.

"I acted like I had no idea where you were, of course, because, like a moron, I thought you had told me everything that happened. But of course, you didn't. He said he caught you cheating on him with some twenty-year-old kid at a bar. Of course, I knew that couldn't be true, because it doesn't sound remotely like you. So, tell me, little sister, why are you running? I'm getting really good at sensing when people are running, since, well, my husband ran out on me too!" she doesn't try to hide the wrath in her voice.

"It's not what you think." I put my hand up defensively. "I didn't cheat on him."

"Okay," she nods, but her tone indicates that she

isn't happy yet. "You show me your hand and I'll show you mine. Tit for tat."

Sitting still I can't look at her. Licking my lips, I shake my head. "Liz, it was bad. I mean, really bad."

She leans forward. Her tone changes from angry to concerned. "Tell me."

"It's the kind of stuff you only read about. I couldn't marry a guy like that. I had to leave and not tell him. It was the only way."

"You took one hell of a risk not telling me about it. What would you have done if I'd told him you were here?"

I stare blindly at the table and shake my head. "Run again."

She draws in a deep breath. "That bad, huh."

"I couldn't tell dad. He would've killed him."

She chuckles, as if he'd deserve it. "Maybe you should."

I shake my head.

"What if dad tells John where you are?"

"He doesn't know. I thought of that. He thinks I'm on vacation with Mary."

"He bought that?"

"I've gone away for the summer before. Not before I met John, of course, but dad doesn't remember that."

"Well, what if he calls John for some reason?"

I shrug. "Then John will take a trip to the tropics in vain."

"And John hasn't been calling you and leaving like a million messages?"

"He's always been weird about that. He rarely leaves me messages. And yeah, he's been calling, but I put him straight to voicemail."

"Have you checked to see what kind of creepy messages he's left?"

I wave my hands in disgust, like when my Granny Abbott used to show me her false teeth. "No, I can't."

"Does Mary know?"

"Yeah, she's the only one who knows.

She...witnessed something, and that's how she found out."

"What did she witness?"

I cover my face. "Oh, God, I don't want to talk about it." Uncovering my face, I reach for her hand. "He never laid a finger on me...it wasn't like that. He's just...really, really...sickly controlling and jealous. Thank God I only work with women, because he probably wouldn't even let me keep my job."

"Jesus Christ." She breathes. "How come you never told me?"

"I wanted to...so...many...times. But it was like 'what can she do about it?'. And, I don't know, I hadn't seen you for a while, and I couldn't tell you over the phone. At first, I thought it was my fault, you know, like, maybe I am being unreasonable, not wanting to call him five times a day. Then, I just thought that he was needy, and he didn't want me to go out with or even talk to my friends. But then...then, it was just sick and twisted. And then I didn't have a chance to tell you, because he was always in my face and checking my phone and stuff."

She squeezes my hand. "And you didn't tell me when you got here, because you figured I had enough troubles of my own."

My silence answers the question.

Drawing in a deep breath, Liz leans further back in her chair. "Oh, little sister...what kind of a mess are we in?"

"We're lost together."

She points at me, as if to say, 'you got that right'.

We hear Nate's footsteps coming from the hallway. "Good morning, sunshine." Liz says, glancing pointedly at her wrist, as if there is a watch there.

The look on his face is puzzling. "What's up, little man?" Liz asks. Calling him that is ironic, considering he towers over her.

"I heard you say that dad left? Is that true?"

...good job, ladies, for keeping your voices down.

46

Chapter 8

Gregory Abbott

Three days after 'Tube Top Tuesday'

The anniversary clock on his credenza reads ten past eight as Gregory writes notes in his business diary from the day's work. His assistant, Myrtle, had been asked to stay back for another half hour. Gregory's office is filled with antique oak furniture, including a wet bar with pot lights. Behind his large desk is a full glass window, floor to ceiling, wall to wall, with a view of a man-made pond and expensive landscaping. Behind that is the golf course that Gregory owns; the first in a string of five upscale golf and country clubs he proudly oversees in the state of Florida.

In his fifties, Gregory is in impeccable physical shape. With a full workout room next to his office, Mr. Abbott works out daily, after his business is done. He is tall and lean, with a full head of whitish dirty blonde hair, and a tan. A signet ring with his initials glints on his right ring finger, complimenting the expensive Cartier watch on his right wrist. The phone on his desk beeps and Myrtle's voice chimes in, announcing that he has a visitor.

"Who is it at this hour?" he is curt.

"John Smallwood, sir."

"Ah, let him in." he says pleasantly.

When John enters the office, Gregory greets him with a smile. "Come in. Sit down, John. So nice to see you."

John is in his early thirties, with short brown hair cut in impossibly perfect lines around his scalp. He is the type who obsessively goes to the barber shop weekly. Bright green eyes are seen behind flashy sunglasses, which he removes and places on Gregory's desk. John is also tall and lean, and wears a starched, pressed, white linen shirt with black dress pants. He looks like he's there to sell Gregory expensive golf paraphernalia. Taking a seat in the dark leather tufted wing chair, he speaks to his future father-in-law. "Sorry to bother you at the office, sir. I did try you at home, but you weren't there."

"You know this business keeps no schedule, John. And it's no bother. What can I do for you?"

"Sir, this may sound rather strange, but I haven't seen Julia in a couple of days."

Gregory's head cranes backward slightly. "That's preposterous. She's gone on vacation with her work friend, Mary."

"That's not possible, sir. I went to Mary's house and she hasn't left yet. Apparently, there was a death in the family, so the trip has been postponed."

The muscles in Gregory's jaw are working. "Well, that's impossible. I've been speaking with Julia. Just yesterday we spoke. Are you sure you went to Mary's house? This is the same Mary that she works with?"

"Yes, sir. I spoke to her boyfriend Chris myself. Mary was out at the funeral home when I was there. Do you have any idea where else she could be?"

A flick of irritation crosses Gregory's face. "Hm, I'm sure you're mistaken. My daughter doesn't lie to me. Well, my *younger* daughter doesn't lie to me. Perhaps this Mary person's boyfriend was drunk or goofing around with you. I understand from Julia that Mary and you don't see eye to eye on a number of matters."

"That's true, sir. Is there any chance that she might be with her sister? In North Carolina?"

Gregory presses his lips together in a feigned smile. "My boy, as I told you, Julia doesn't lie to me. And she certainly would not have gone to visit her sister without telling me."

"But you and Liz don't get along, sir. Maybe she didn't want to upset you."

"John, I may have my differences with my older daughter, but I have never stopped Julia from visiting her sister whenever she wants. She wouldn't keep that from me, there is no reason for her to." He pauses. "Now, is there anything else?"

"No, sir. It's just...she hasn't been answering her phone."

"Did you have a disagreement?"

"Well, yeah," he admits.

John gives him a short smile. "You and Julia will work out your differences, son. She's like her sister and her father: very stubborn. Give it time. She'll come around."

"Yes, sir." John nods and rises from the chair. "Thank you, sir."

"Good evening." Gregory says, but does not get up to see John out. When John leaves, Gregory draws in a deep breath and chuckles. "Kids."

Chapter 9

Colton

The phone rings in the stable just as I'm about to hop on Rebel. He's ready for a ride and I need to blow off some steam that Maya wouldn't stand for. There is an hour left before my first lesson of the day, and I want to take full advantage. Just as I place the saddle on Rebel's back, I hear the twang of the phone from the back panel by the feed area.

"This is Colton."

"Colton? Hi. Sorry to bother you. It's Julia."

There is some muffled yelling going on in the background. "Hi, Julia. Where are you? Is everything okay? I hear people yelling."

"Domestic dispute." She seems to be glossing over the problem, but I don't press. "Listen, I hate to bother you, but I need to pick up my car from Mingles. I tried everyone else at the bar, and nobody is answering. Do you have a little time to spare?"

My ride can wait. There is plenty of time to pick her up at Liz's and drive her over to the bar. "Sure. I can be there in ten minutes."

"Thanks so much. I'll be waiting outside."

Ten minutes later, as promised, she is outside waiting for me. Sitting on the front stoop, she is wearing a pair of blue jeans and a pink 'GAP' t-shirt. Her hair is braided down her back. As she enters the car, she smiles and thanks me again for coming.

"How's the back?"

"Oh, it's fine."

"So who did you piss off?" I tease, referring to the yelling I heard over the phone earlier.

"Oh, it wasn't me. Liz and Nate are fighting. That's why I had to get out of there, and without a car, that's pretty difficult."

"Gotcha." I say as I put the car into gear. I wonder if she remembers anything from last night: the kiss, the tattoos, the cheap feels, etc., but she seems lucid, so I guess not. "Do you like horses?"

"I've never been on one, but I do like them. I'm a huge animal lover."

"Cool. Well, if you're looking for something to do for a couple of hours, you can come and check out my place. I have a riding lesson in a little bit if you want to watch."

"That sounds divine."

We get to the bar, do the car exchange, and I bring her back to the ranch. Her jaw drops as we pull up to the house. "This is your place?" she thumbs at the ranch, as if it is a temple.

"It is."

She stares at it, as though she isn't sure if it is real or not. I chuckle. "Come on. I'll show you inside."

To coax her along, I have to take her hand. It's like she's drinking the place in. The log is still burning on the fire from before I left, so the house smells of maple. Like a moth to a flame, she observes every detail; from the fireplace, to the pictures on the walls, to the oak kitchen and floors, and then I follow her to the back of the house: to the bedrooms and bathroom. One room I reserve as a workout room, then a spare room with a small bed and a desk, and then the master bedroom. Inside my room is a hand-carved oak four poster bed. The dresser and bedside tables are also hand-carved, with raw wood that hasn't been fully sanded. The bark on the outside lends a rustic feel to the room, which is what I wanted...*after* Pam left. We haven't even started on the ranch, and she's blown away.

"God, Colton. I never knew a man could have so much taste."

I don't respond. Half of the taste is leftover from Pam.

"My father's house is fancy, but he had an interior decorator do the work. It doesn't have the natural beauty that this one does."

"You ever lived on your own?"

"No. Not yet." She says as though in a daze. She runs her hand along the exposed bark on the bed, and then sniffs the wood. I have to stifle a laugh. I thought she was going to hug it. Catching a glimpse out of the picture window in my room, she shakes her head. Miles and miles of green spreads far and wide outside the fenced-in ranch area, where Maya and Rebel are grazing. "It takes my breath away."

No, you take my breath away.

"I put the window in here so I could watch the horses. You want to come and meet them?"

Her face lights up. "Are you serious? They're yours?"

I giggle. "I told you I had two horses, silly. Come on, you're going to love them."

Maya walks right over to Julia when she approaches. I open the gate and let her inside. "She's real tame. You can come on in."

Maya's brown head comes down and Julia immediately pets her snout. "Oh, she's a doll. Is she the mom?" she gestures with her chin towards Rebel.

"Yes, Maya is Rebel's mom. He's not quite as tame, but he won't hurt you."

Rebel is brown also, but with a white patch on his belly and nose. He comes over to Julia and gently pelts her on the bottom with his snout. "Now, Rebel, she doesn't have any treats. You be a good boy and I'll get you some."

As if the horse understands, he lifts his snout and waits to be pet. I walk over to the feed area and grab a couple of apples. When I hand Julia one, she gasps. "Oh, I get to feed them?"

"If you want to. Rebel can nip, so keep your hand flat."

She does as she's instructed and he takes the apple gently, making a mess of apple juice and guts as he chomps. Julia doesn't wince or shy away, even though it is gross. "Now Maya can have one too." The mom uses more of her tongue to pick up the fruit, and Julia laughs. "Tickles?"

She nods. "Oh, they're lovely, Colton. I never would have guessed you were...well, a cowboy."

I can't hold back the smile. "I was raised with horses. When I found this place, I couldn't help myself. It was torn up and anyone could have lit a match to it and it would have made an improvement, but I bought it and with help, I turned it into what it is. Come on. I'll show you the stables."

We shut the gate while the horses continue grazing. As we enter the stables, Julia's jaw drops again. "It's like in one of those old-fashioned Western movies." She runs her hand down the oak panels between the pens, and she observes the brass name plates boasting 'Maya' and 'Rebel'. When she looks at the other, spare stables, she asks. "How come you don't have more horses?"

"Well, that gets tricky. It's a lot of work."

"But, why don't you just quit the bar? No offense, but you obviously don't need the money."

"Some things aren't about money, sweetie."

"Oh," she frowns. And I feel terrible, because of the wounded tone. "I work at the bar to keep an eye on Wade."

"I get it. He's been into trouble?"

"Here and there. But it's mostly just to stop him from screwing up his life. I figure if I'm there, he'll be set in the right direction."

"What are you going to do if he ever gets a record deal and has to go on tour? Are you going to follow him around the world?"

Lifting my hand, I place it on her shoulder and give it a squeeze. "You're going to make a great mom some day."

"Nice save." She smirks. "Seriously. What will you do?"

I rub her arm. "How about you worry about your sister, and I'll worry about my brother."

She squints, as though considering her options. "Okay, but we're coming back to this again sometime."

I look forward to it.

It's time to change the subject. "Do you want to ride Maya?"

Her face suddenly falls. "Alone? Now?"

"Sure, why not?"

"I can't ride her by myself. I've never done it before."

"Okay, how about I ride with you? You can ride behind me, just like on a motorcycle."

"Okay, that sounds like fun."

Walking to one of the empty pens, I have an array of different saddles, hanging on iron hooks. Lifting the double saddle, I tell her to follow me while I get Maya saddled up. Placing the saddle on Maya's back, I adjust the straps under her belly. Then I go back and select her favorite reigns. When I put it on Maya, she flicks her head. "Is she okay?" Julia asks.

"She's excited. She loves being ridden. Come on over here and I'll help you up."

Julia walks over and I explain how to climb up onto the back seat. "Just swing your leg over, hang on to the nub, and don't look down."

The girl is a natural. She does it on the first try. I keep my hands close just in case, but it is unnecessary. "Excellent!" I lift myself using the stirrups and high-five her. "That was great. You get an 'A' already and we just started."

"Are we going to go outside the fence here, or just stay inside?"

"Well, whatever you feel comfortable with."

"We can go a little outside, but not too far. You have a class soon, right?"

"We've got some time. It's just a neighbor's kid coming over. He won't mind waiting. He can play with Rebel if we're a few minutes late. He knows what to do."

"How long have you been teaching him?"

I squeeze my legs gently, letting Maya know to move. When she starts, Julia lets out an excited yelp. "I've been teaching him for almost a year now. I haven't been doing it that long."

"What made you start teaching?"

"Well, I love being around kids, and I love horses, so it seemed like a good fit."

"Did Liz tell you that I'm a teacher, too?"

I turn my head towards her as we exit the gate. I bend down to close the latch. "Really? No, she never told me. What do you teach?"

"I've taught fifth grade and up. This year I'll be teaching fifth again, hopefully. If I get the job."

"Well, that's fantastic."

I knew she did something special, and I was right. A teacher...seems...perfect.

"What school?"

She rattles off the school, and I recognize the name. I taught some kids from that school, too. "Is that where Nate goes?"

She giggles as we trot a little faster. Her hands remain on the nub until then, when she tugs at my shirt. "If you feel more comfortable, you can grab on to me. You get better grip. But I'll keep Maya at a gentle trot. We won't go any faster than this."

"Okay. Yeah, Nate goes to this school, too. I'm not sure how he feels about it. He answers everything with a shrug."

"Typical teenager."

She lets out a laugh when I make Maya turn slightly, so we can stay in line with the field. I want to show Julia the whole area but save the wooded spot for another time. That, I don't even show my students. The wooded area is just for me.

The fields are open and freshly cut. I hire help to do that since I usually don't have the time, and I don't have the machinery or interest to do it anyway. It's like a flat bed of green for acres and acres. There was a time when I considered growing vegetables or fruit, but I'm not there yet, and I don't have the mind or the time for it. The wooded area in the back I'd like to build some sort of cabin some day, but for now it's my place to go when I've got to clear my mind, which has been a lot since I bought the place.

"So when do you find out about the job? Classes start up in a couple of weeks."

"Well I only applied last week, and I haven't even had the interview yet, so I'm not sure. Sometimes they hire after the school year has started, too, so I'm not losing hope."

I wonder what she left back at home in Florida, that she didn't mind sacrificing to come here and stay with her sister, but I'm not sure if it's my place to ask. "So you didn't like your job in Florida?"

"I did, but sometimes change is good. So far I like it out here, but we'll see what happens."

Her tone is reserved, so I don't press. It's kind of nice that someone besides me has secrets to keep. Maybe some day we'll share our stories. She keeps her hands planted firmly on the nub, not touching me like I'd offered, but her thighs touch the backs of my legs, and the contact is amazing. We trot with Maya for fifteen more minutes, and then turn around. From afar we can see the teenage boy's hand waving from the pasture.

"Oh, he's here. You want to come watch?" I ask as I squeeze Maya hard, causing her to trot faster.

"Wooo!" Julia yelps, and then laughs in surprise. "Sure, this is fun!"

"Hey, maybe you should be my next student!"

Chapter 10

Julia

In between my legs is a throbbing pain, but it was so worth it. Now I understand what all the fuss is about with riding horses. Never in my life have I felt more liberated or so free. The ride was only half the treat. Colton's house is something to be adored. I've never had an eye for houses, but this one has my attention. It's so welcoming and warm, like a vacation cottage, only better. I felt myself relax the moment I stepped inside.

When Jackson arrived for his lesson, I wasn't sure if it was right for me to stay. But Colton told me to stay on the saddle, and we rode together with Jackson, while he rode Rebel. The kid could saddle him up and get on without any help. It was so much fun. I honestly can't remember ever having so much fun. The horses were playing together while we rode them. I didn't know the animals would do that.

Colton was just fantastic with Jackson. He was great at encouragement, and the boy reacted very well to Colton's instructions. Colton makes a great teacher, and it's clear why he's so good at what he does. It's a real shame that he doesn't do it full time, and with more horses. Maybe some day he will with the right encouragement.

It was only Jackson at the ranch today, no other students were expected. Once Jackson left, Colton asked if I was in a rush to get back to my sister's place.

"Um, not at all. They're probably still fighting."

"Fair enough. Do you know how to marinate steaks?"

"Not really."

"Come on. I'll show you."

Leading me into the kitchen, Colton pulls two thick slices of meat out of the fridge. They aren't in cellophane packages, but in brown butcher's paper. "I get them cut fresh just up the street. Nothing like it." he pulls a bottle of wine from the door of the fridge. "Hand me one of those large plates out of the cupboard down by the stove, please."

The kitchen is galley-style with oak cabinets and glassed-in accent cupboards. A glass overhead vent hangs over the electric, glass-stovetop oven. In the center is an island with a separate miniature sink and gooseneck faucet. The dishwasher is nestled in the island, under the sink, and a butcher's block countertop finishes the island off. To describe the kitchen as large would be an exaggeration; it is small but perfectly proportioned to the practical elements within it.

I hand him a plate as he pulls a pair of tongs out of the non-slam drawer by the fridge and lifts the steaks onto the plates. The bottle of red wine has already been opened once, so he simply unscrews the cap and sticks his thumb in the mouth of the bottle, tilting it just slightly, so the liquid will pour out slowly. His biceps are working with the weight of the bottle, bulging slightly. I try to avert my eyes from staring, but it is difficult, especially with all the tattoos. "You just let a little out at a time. Just enough to cover the meat. You try." He says, handing me the bottle.

Of course, my thumbs aren't as big as his, so I have to put mine in further. The wine pours out a little fast and escaped off the plate onto the black granite counter top. He doesn't seem to flinch, so I keep pouring. "You do the same on the other one while I get the potatoes ready."

"Are you barbecuing?"

He lifts a brow. "What else?"

My knowledge of cooking doesn't usually span beyond a salad or a sandwich. When I was home at my dad's, we had a cook prepare our meals, so I never had a need to learn.

"Well, excuse me, Jamie Oliver."

He chuckles at that. "When you're done there's some steak spice above the stove. I'm just going to go make sure I have enough kindling for the barbecue."

"Kindling? Don't you mean charcoal?"

He winks. "Wait and see."

I find the steak spice, but damned if I can figure out how to open it, let alone pour it. Two minutes later, when he returns, he has a puzzled look on his face, matching mine. "The tab is on the side." He says. "Just sprinkle a little on, like you would salt."

"Okay, I don't want to ruin these steaks. Maybe you should do this." I chuckle, trying in vain not to sound like a moron.

"Nonsense. If you put too much on, we can take it off easily."

I shrug. "Okay."

"Come on out back when you're done. I've gotta cut up some kindling."

Finally getting the tab open, I sprinkle the spice on the meat, and follow Colton out to the back, which I didn't know existed, because it is off the master bedroom. There is an open, cedar porch that holds a covered, two-seater swing, a covered, glass table for six, and a small chiminea. Off to the side of the porch is a wood shed with wood stacked in rows, a workhorse, axe and a woodchip-covered floor. The man does not cease to amaze me. "I had no idea this was even here."

"That's because it's on the other side of the stables. I like it that way, so if I want to entertain, we don't disturb the horses. Some day I'd like to put a pool back here, too, or a hot tub, or both. But for now, this is the piece-de-resistance." He points to a fire pit in the centre of the grass, about ten feet from the porch. It is round, with a metal liner, and a metal, threaded pole in the centre. "I have enough lawn chairs to seat an army on the other side of the wood shed."

"So, where's the barbecue?"

"We're going to use the fire pit. I have a charcoal barbecue, too, but I like to cook steaks on wood. It tastes a hundred times better."

He takes a short, thick plank of wood from one of the

stacks, and sets it on the work horse. The axe, which is jammed, blade side down, in the wooden work horse, he pulls up out of the wood, and in one fell swoop, lets the axe down, splitting the wood into two pieces. I watch him; his toned muscles contracting with the weight of the axe, in awe. In my entire life, I never saw anyone cut wood before. Well...except on television.

He wipes his hand on his jeans and adjusts his white t-shirt as he takes another swipe at the wood. "You can take the wood over and place it in the pit like a teepee or a tent." He puts his hands together as if praying, to demonstrate how to position the wood. "Put those gloves on so you don't get splinters." He points to a pair of gloves sitting on the grass by the pit. I wonder where *his* gloves are. He seems way more at risk of getting splinters doing what he is doing. As I walk over to the pit, I pull the gloves on, and begin placing the kindling into the pit as he told me to.

When he brings over a handful of wood, he looks impressed. "Good job. You like bonfires when you were a kid?"

"We never had one."

He cranes his neck backward in disbelief. "You're serious."

"My dad runs a string of golf and country clubs. He worked during my childhood. There wasn't time for bonfires or camping, and Granny Abbott wouldn't know the first thing about making a fire."

"I take it you don't have a mom?"

"She left when we were young. She went to Puerto Rico and married some Don Juan out there."

"Your dad every remarry?"

"No. He's married to golf and to his job." I raise my hand. "Don't get me wrong. Aside from bonfires, Liz and I were not deprived of much during our childhood. We had every toy imaginable, every piece of clothing we would ever need, and my dad took us away on trips; I've seen a lot of the world."

"But before today you never rode a horse, and you've

never built a bonfire. Two very important parts of being a kid."

I lean my head towards him as if to tell him a secret, and whisper. "You're a boy. Little girls aren't really into those things."

"I suppose you're right. I don't have any sisters."

"And I don't have any brothers. So maybe we're both wrong."

"Could be." He smiles. "I'm going to go grab some newspaper and a book of matches. I'll be right back. You can put some more on top. There's still some wood in the shed."

When he returns two minutes later, we have a perfect tent of kindling ready to be lit. Colton has a full day's newspaper in his hand. He removes a sheet, balls it up like we are going to play a game of catch with it, and then shapes it so he can stuff it in between the slats of the wooden tent inside the pit. "Here, you can help." He hands me two sheets of newsprint and I do the same. We continue until all the slats are stuffed with paper. Then he lights the match and touches it to the bottom of the teepee. Within seconds, there is a flame. The newspaper catches first, then it spreads to the kindling.

"Now I'll split about three or four pieces of wood and place them on top. When the larger wood is burned down to coals, we'll put the grate on, and set the steaks on top. In the meantime, while it's burning, I'll put the potatoes on the charcoal barbecue."

"You mean you can't cook them together?"

He chuckles and shakes his head. "Potatoes take about an hour to cook. The steak'll be kindling by then. We have to cook them separately."

"Oh." It seems like I have a lot to learn.

"Come on. Let's go check the steaks." He takes my hand to help me up. The contact is electric. A warm charge slides up my hands, arms, and goes straight to my chest and belly. I shouldn't be feeling like this. Not after what I've just been through. It is so strong that I nearly trip. Colton places his hand on my back to give me leverage. "You okay there?"

"I'm fine. Just lost my balance a little."

"Did you sneak some of the wine?" he teases.

"No." I chuckle. He doesn't let go of my hand as we walk inside the house. John has never been a hand holder, and I never realized how nice it is. Colton's touch isn't sexual or territorial at all. It's like he wants to keep me safe. The contact is loose enough that I can let go if I want to, but tight enough that our hands won't slide apart.

The steaks are still on the counter. I never thought to put them back in the fridge. "Shoot, should I have put them back in the fridge?"

"No, actually. We want them to rest before we cook them. If they're too cold they'll burn on the grill." He takes the tongs and flips them over. "Do you want to put some wine and seasoning on this side for me while I put the potatoes on?"

"Sure."

"Are you thirsty? My gosh, my manners. I haven't even offered you a drink." He puts his hand on his chest as a gesture of sincerity. It's adorable.

"I'll get us both a glass of water. Sound good?"

"Perfect. There's a filter on the tap."

I pour us two glasses of water, and drink mine down, pouring another for myself. I didn't realize how thirsty I was. After I put the wine and seasoning on the steaks, Colton is back. "Wow, they smell good already and we haven't even started cooking."

"They do, don't they." I draw in a big whiff and grin as I hand him his water.

"Thanks. Hey, you want me to get you home now, so I can eat?" he can't keep a straight face. I play along.

"Well, shouldn't I at least cook it so you can take full advantage?"

Sheepishly he puts his head down, feigning defeat. "Alright, you can cook it, too. But then I'm taking you home."

"You didn't actually think I'd fall for that, did you?"

"You can't blame a man for trying."

Then a thought occurs to me. "How come you have two steaks, anyway? Were you expecting company?"

"I probably would have taken the other one over to my neighbor, Charles. He's an older guy and he lives alone, so I usually make two of everything and share. He's a widower and he watches the ranch for me when I'm not home, so it's the least I can do."

I feel bad. "Oh, well then I don't want to eat Charles' dinner."

"It's okay. He doesn't expect it. For all I know he saw you here and knows that there's no steak for him tonight." He chuckles. "He's a bit of a busybody."

"But won't he go hungry?"

"Don't worry about it. He can fend for himself. He's a tough old bird."

"...okay."

Two hours later we are sitting in front of the fire, sipping wine, with full, satisfied bellies. Colton had set up four tiki lamps on stakes in the yard to illuminate the dark as we chatted over wine and roasted marshmallows. "Oh my gosh, these are delicious! Who would have thought!"

"Oh, you ain't seen nothin' yet. Wait until we have smores."

"I've heard of them. They sound terribly fattening and sugary."

"But scrumptious." Colton says, shoving another marshmallow into his mouth. "You haven't lived until you've had one." The white goo smooshes out of his mouth and all over his shirt. "Oh, geez. You can't take me anywhere. I should go inside and get cleaned up."

"I'll follow you in. I should let Liz know where I am. I'm sure they're done fighting by now."

I follow Colton into the house. There is a console table in the hallway by the bedrooms, where I'd set my purse down earlier. Colton goes into his room and I can hear him open a drawer. The mirror above the console table is a perfect reflection into his bedroom. Although I try not to stare, I watch him pull his shirt over his head. The muscles in his sides contract with his movements, setting my body tingling. His abdominal muscles flex, revealing a perfectly toned belly. Not a scrap of fat lay on his abdomen. I count six, yes, six packs of muscles from his chest to his pant line. Even John never had six pack abs. Colton is a beautiful specimen of a man. Artful tattoos are layered on his chest and arms, perfectly complimenting his skin tone. When he pulls the clean shirt over his head, I silently whimper; I hadn't seen enough. I was just getting to his hips, shaped in a perfect 'V' on each side. His belly button lay flat against his stomach. As he pulls his shirt down, I see him run his hands through his hair, and I can't close my mouth. I haven't found my phone yet, and I can't take my eyes away. It's having a terrible, yet wonderful effect on my body.

I quickly shuffle through my purse, looking for my phone. Finding it just in time, Colton places a hand gently on my back and whispers in my ear, sending delicious shivers down my spine. "Is everything okay? You look like you've just seen a ghost."

Ghost or Greek God?

"Um...no, I'm fine. Just checking messages." My voice is squeaky.

"Is your sister having a cow?"

I look down at my phone, so I can at least have an honest response. There are two text messages and two voice messages. One of each from John and Mary.

...oh boy, the party's starting.

Chapter 11

Mary

We were supposed to go to Barbados; me, my mom and my Aunt Agnes, three weeks ago, just after our escapade at *'Proceed with Caution'*, but unfortunately, my mom's other sister, Florence, passed away suddenly. I wasn't terribly close with Florence, but my mom was, so we had to postpone our trip for a few weeks while she settled her affairs. God bless cancellation insurance. The morning that we were getting ready to leave, mom and Agnes were meeting me at the airport.

Barbados was not my first choice, but I sucked it up since my mom was paying for the trip. If I had my way we'd be going to Barbados in the winter. Florida was hot enough in the summer, but my mom got a really cheap getaway package at some 'I-didn't-want-this-sucky-ass-trip-for-three-in-the-middle-of-summer-when-it's-already-hotter-than-hell' online travel site, so I decided I didn't have anything to lose. She all but begged me to go, since Agnes was about as fun as watching a washing machine in its spin cycle. Actually, the washing machine would get my vote for who was funner.

There was only three weeks left until school started up again, which left two weeks for me to burn off any remaining anxiety from the previous school year. Chris, my boyfriend, is driving me nuts with things to do like gardening, organizing closets, and cleaning the house, so I figure I'd rather fry my ass off in Barbados with my mom and my 'oh-wow-was-that-a-deerfly-or-a-house-fly?-let's-go-find-out' Aunt.

Chris is more than happy to help me pack my things and drive me to the airport. He is on his way to another fishing trip, anyway, and it's on the way. The nice thing about going to a hotter place from a hot place, is that you can pack lightly. My suitcase doesn't even weigh enough to keep the door from closing, when we try to use it as a door stop so Chris can unload some crap he bought from the hardware store. "Jesus, you're not bringing your ten tons of makeup with you?"

"Love, I'm going to melt by ten in the morning, why would I bother with makeup?"

Chris scoffs. "Well, that's a first."

"So keep your paws off my mascara while I'm gone."

Kissing my forehead, he chuckles. "I'm going to miss you and your big mouth."

"And I'll miss...parts of you." Chris is a gentle giant. Tall, but plump, lovable, and his sense of humor can break even the toughest tension. He even made my mom laugh the day that my aunt died. That takes talent.

He lets that one go. "Did you remember your passport and your medical insurance papers?"

"Yes."

We go through a list of things before heading into the car. There is a white BMW parked on the other side of the street, one house down. I just glance at it, and the car turns around, driving past us. The driver does not look up. Recognition hits me like a sack of potatoes. "Shit, that's John!"

"What the hell is he doing here? Oh....shit...Wait a minute, I forgot to tell you, he came by the day that you went to the funeral parlor with your mom."

"What???!!!"

"Shit, I'm sorry, babe. With all the confusion I totally forgot to tell you until just now."

I bite my lip to stop a stream of expletives from escaping my mouth. "What did he say?"

"He was looking for Julia, of course, and you."

"What did you tell him?"

"I told him the truth: that there was a death in your family, and you were looking after it."

I look at him directly, trying not to burn right through him with my glare. "What did you tell him about Julia?"

"I told him that I didn't know where Julia was. Isn't

that what I was supposed to say?"

"Not exactly." I'm cold and curt, and I can't help it. The one thing that I said before I left that day, and he couldn't get it right. "I told you if he ever calls or shows up here, that Julia and I are in Barbados . Not that I'm in Barbados, or that the trip's been postponed. Dammit, Chris! Now he's on the prowl and it's all your fault!"

"Why did you want me to lie, anyway? Doesn't he have a right to know where his girlfriend is?"

"She's his fiancé," I correct. "And don't you remember what I told you about this loser?"

He pauses. "I've only met him a couple of times, Mary. I remember Julia coming over and talking about him, but you girls are always talking in some kind of female code, I don't understand half of it."

"The guy's a possessive, territorial stalker. She fled to North Carolina, to her sister's house, to get away from the guy. If he came around looking for her then, he's certainly losing his marbles over this, and he's for sure spoken with her dad. I deduce what the next step is. "He's probably heading straight for North Carolina now." I pull my phone out of my purse. "Let's get going to the airport. I have to warn Julia. I'll call her on the way."

Chapter 12

Colton

Julia is a natural on a horse. It tickled me to the core. I couldn't wait to get her on Maya alone. Maya is great with first-timers. She would have the time of her life. If I could be the one responsible for that kind of bliss in a person's life, I'd be truly honored. Her ear-to-ear smile while she rode behind me was something to behold. The feelings that I had while she was so close to me were exquisite. It had been a long time since I felt anything like that. Her soft breasts would press up against me, causing me to lose focus. For a moment, I imagined what it would be like to feel them pressed up against my chest, not on my back, and suddenly I had to divert my focus, and instead think of Wade's chest, so I wouldn't hurt myself. We were on a horse, after all.

Her laugh, her gentle sarcasm, the way she looks at me, it's like magic. But am I ready to feel the things that I'm feeling? Is it too soon? There is something about Julia that has me thinking it is too soon for her, too. The hesitation, the pauses during sentences, the vague eye contact with certain topics, are all indicators that this girl has a past. Perhaps she's troubled? The thought of that sweet girl having any kind of man trouble is beyond me. Who wouldn't want to give her everything she wants? Who would ever want to mistreat her?

I suppose I felt a lot of the same things with Pam, though, and look what happened. Maybe I'm feeling this way because it's been so long since I've been with a woman. But even the girls at the bar and the moms that bring their kids over for riding lessons, they're all different people, and none of them make me feel the way that Julia does. Am I up for another relationship? Is she? Probably no on both counts. It's good that I haven't put any moves on her, because I'd likely crash and burn from failure. I get the feeling that she'd wither like a week old rose if I touched her. I'm glad I enjoyed that little kiss she gave me before she passed out at the hospital. That little tidbit of memory has kept me going ever since. And it'll probably keep me going for a while.

She's a good sport, too. She didn't have to stick around and cook dinner with me. But she did, and from what I could tell, she enjoyed it a lot. I've never seen a woman dive into a steak like she did. Not even Pam. Pam was a vegetarian. It sucked. Julia isn't afraid of biting into a juicy slab of meat and devouring it with grace.

As we sat in front of the fire, chatting and eating marshmallows, it was so simple, yet so much fun. I was this close to telling her my story, but I'm not sure that she's ready to hear it yet. I'm not sure I'm ready to tell it. We don't know each other enough yet to open those gates. Hopefully soon we will be, but for now, I'll just enjoy what I can of her and let the rest fall into place.

When I changed my shirt, I came back out, and she had a strange look on her face.

"Is everything okay?"

"Yeah, I just...I should go. Liz isn't answering her phone and she doesn't know where I am. I don't want her to worry."

An obvious lie because if she wasn't answering her phone, then why is this a problem? If Liz wasn't reaching out to her, she clearly wasn't worrying about her. But I didn't argue. Something is up and she isn't ready to tell me. "Okay, no problem. I'll take you home. Just let me go douse the fire in the back."

When I come back a minute later, she is standing by the door. "You're sure everything is okay? You look strange."

"I'm...fine. I just need to get home."

I hesitate. "Okay."

She doesn't say two words to me on the way to Liz's place.

"You're not feeling unwell or anything, are you? The steak and the marshmallows didn't make you sick, did they?"

"No, no I'm fine. Really." She says unconvincingly.

I feel helpless, but a little frustrated, too. If I didn't want to know what was going on, why would I ask? As much as I didn't want to admit it, I cared about this girl. The last thing I want to do is watch her suffer through something alone, when she can have my support. "Listen, Julia. Whatever troubles you have, maybe even just to have an ear might be helpful. I'm sure it's something I can handle hearing." *Oh God, should I tell her? No, now isn't the time.* "If you want to tell me what's wrong, I'm here. But there is no pressure."

Her chest rises and falls as she draws in a deep breath, considering my offer. "Colton, you're a great guy, really. And I appreciate you wanting to help. But this situation needs to be dealt with by me. I made my bed. I have to lie in it. There are already too many people involved as it is, and it seems to have made the situation worse. I don't want anyone else getting hurt. Besides, there truly is nothing you can do to help."

We pull up to Liz's house. I put the car into park and nod. "Okay, fair enough. But if that does change, and there is something I can do, please let me know, okay?"

"Sure. Thanks." She opens the door. "And thanks so much for dinner. It was lovely and fun." A weak smile creeps across her face.

If it hadn't been for whatever problems came from her messages, we might have had dessert, too.

Chapter 13

Gregory

After a long, hard day full of financial and operations meetings the previous day, Gregory felt he'd earned his right to have an early round of golf before the start of business. His CFO Dan, and his CEO Drew, are more than happy to join him. The Florida sun beats lightly on the course that early in the morning. Gregory places his tan Tilly hat on his head and hops into his golf cart to go meet his friends on the course.

Dan resembles Clark Griswold with his tall, slender body and thinning brown hair. "Good morning, old man." Drew says, pulling his cream leather golf gloves on. "Don't you think you've had enough failure for one week, after all those meetings yesterday?"

Gregory smiles, clapping his old friend on the back. "Still biting the hand that feeds you, aren't you, old boy."

"You couldn't fire me. I know way too many of your lies. And look, here's one now." He comments as Drew pulls up in a cart, driven by a younger man with the company uniform on and his name embroidered on the right breast pocket.

"Stop talking shit about me." Drew says as he disembarks and tips his hat to the driver. "Thanks, Tim. Appreciate it." Drew reaches in and takes his golf bag out of the back before Tim pulls away.

They tee up and begin playing a long round of golf. "I haven't seen Julia around in a few weeks. Isn't she still on summer break?" Drew asks.

"She's in Barbados with a friend from work." Gregory answers as he lines up his shot with a nine iron.

He swings as Dan speaks. "Barbados? Geez, she'll be like jerky."

Watching his ball fly in the air, Gregory shrugs. "Kids. What do they know? They see these deals online and run for it. Some of the things they can sell you on the internet are ludicrous."

"True enough." Drew agrees.

"My Julia, though, she's got an eye for it. Got a head on her shoulders, too."

"When's she getting married?" Dan asks. "I haven't seen an invitation yet."

"And don't hold your breath." Gregory says, feigning a warning tone. "Kids these days they get engaged one week, and they get married the next or wait five years. Who knows." He adds. "They fight one week and the next they love each other again. I can't keep track. As long as I don't get a grandbaby out of wedlock, I could care less when they finally tie the knot."

"John go away with her?" Drew asks.

"No." Gregory is flat. "They're having some sort of quarrel, so she left without him."

"Good girl." Drew is impressed. "I think that John boy is a bit much for her if you ask me."

"I didn't ask you." Gregory growls.

"He's a little high-and-mighty for her, I think."

"She's got herself a good man. Better than that one my other daughter's with."

"Liz? How's she doing?"

"Far as I know, okay."

Dan intervenes. "You still don't talk to her, huh."

"Not as long as she's with that loser, I won't."

"What about your grandson?"

"We speak on the phone sometimes. I send him cards and things. He's a good kid."

"Wasn't he here last summer with Julia?" Dan asks.

"Yeah, he was supposed to come down this summer on his own, but he changed his mind."

"Oh?"

Gregory waves. "He's thirteen. More into sitting in his room playing on his phone than he is into hanging out with his old grampa at a golf course. He'll come for Christmas. He'll want the good gifts."

Drew chuckles and then Gregory's cell phone begins to ring from his back pocket. He grumbles as he pulls it out. "Can't get a moment's peace, huh, old man." Drew teases.

"Great. Speak of the devil." Gregory answers curtly. "Gregory Abbott."

It is John. "Mr. Abbott, sir, sorry to bother you."

Gregory rolls his eyes. "What can I do for you, John. I'm right in the middle of a golf game."

"I apologize, sir, but I thought this was important. Um, Julia is definitely not with Mary in Barbados, sir. I just saw Mary in the car with her boyfriend, leaving her house. And Julia still has not answered any of my calls."

Pinching the bridge of his nose, Gregory draws in a deep breath, trying to calm his temper. "John, I'm getting tired of this."

"I know, sir, I know. I'm sorry. I just wanted to tell you that." John sounds like he's tattling on her, which irritates Gregory to no end.

"Fine, John. You've told me. Now, I'd like to get back to my game. Good day." He ends the call.

Drew laughs. "So has your shining future son-in-law finally lost his shine?"

Gregory shakes his head. "I don't like it one bit. Julia never lies to me, ever. She always promised me that if she ever did lie to me that it would be for a really good reason." He directs his phone pointedly in the air, as if John is right there with him. "I have a feeling my daughter is hiding from this buffoon, and something tells me I shouldn't blame her for it one bit. For a boy who's so concerned about his fiancé, he was more interested in ratting on her to score points with me than he was about her well-being." He lowers his phone and pauses for emphasis. "As if I'd take his side over my Julia's. The boy is an idiot."

Dan asks. "So, what are you going to do?"

He sighs and pulls his hat off his head, running a hand through his thick hair. "Something I should have done a long time ago."

Chapter 14

Julia

I don't want Colton to think less of me by telling him about my engagement, or rather, broken engagement, to John. The last thing he needs to know is all the drama. Colton seems like the type of drama-free guy that enjoys the simpler things in life. Not some needy, problematic woman who can't fight her way out of a wet paper bag.

Liz is watching television when I walk in the door. She cranes her head back from the couch. "Hey, stranger. What's going on? I thought maybe you'd headed back to Florida." She chuckles good-naturedly. There is a half-eaten bowl of popcorn on the coffee table and an empty beer bottle. It is her one day off all week, and she enjoys it.

"I was at Colton's. He took me to get my car, and I stayed while he did a riding lesson. I figured you two needed your privacy to work through things. How did it go with Nate?"

She blows a piece of hair away from her forehead. "He was upset at me for not telling him the truth. He knows his dad's gone and he's probably not coming back. He cried. I cried. We were both a weeping mess. He's mostly upset because Grant didn't tell him anything: where he was going or why. The worst part is he hasn't bothered to call, and Nate tried calling him, but it went to voicemail. That was hours ago. I told him not to have much hope that he'd call back."

I flop down on the couch and pick up the bowl of popcorn, searching for kernels that are covered in butter. There aren't any, so I put the bowl back on the table. "You won't believe the night I've had."

Liz lifts a brow. "What did you and Colton do?"

I wave. "Nothing like that. I mean I got two messages. That's why I hurried back."

She sits up straighter. "I didn't figure you'd do anything with him. That's the last thing either of you need is another freaking relationship."

There is that elusive comment about Colton and past relationship problems again. I let it go; there are more important things to discuss. "John knows I'm not with Mary."

Her eyes widen. "Oh, shit."

"Yeah, her trip was postponed, and he was there when she left for the airport this morning. Chris said he'd been there the morning after I left, looking for me. But that's not the scary part."

"What?"

"John left me a message, too."

"What did he say?"

"It was creepy. It was as if we were still together and I've just gone out for the day. He was all 'Miss you, babe. I'll see you later.'".

"See you later??? What does that mean? Is he coming here, or has he just lost his marbles? Jesus, maybe the psycho is on his way here right now!"

"I think he's lost it, Liz." I rub my arms, suddenly feeling chilled. "What do I do?"

"You didn't call him back, did you?"

"God, no!"

"I didn't think you were stupid enough to do that. Do you think he'll come here? He knows where I live, right?"

"Well, of course he does." I pause, biting my lip. "I'm scared."

"Maybe you were better off at Colton's house."

I sigh. "I don't know if that's a good idea."

"Think about it, Julia. If you're here and he shows up, there's going to be trouble. At least if you're not here, he'll be thrown off and maybe he'll leave...for good." Her lips form a tight smile. "Christ, we've got one freak who flies the coop without notice, and another we can't get rid of. There's no happy medium here, Jules."

"Jekyll and Hyde." I add. "But what if he does show up? What will *you* do?"

"Just tell him you're not here and laugh in his face

for making the trip in vain."

"The man is psychotic, Liz. Don't encourage him."

Liz rolls her eyes. "Well, of course, I know that. I'm just teasing. I *will* tell him that you're not here." She pauses. "But if he called you this morning, he could already be here. I'd split now if I were you. Go back over to Colton's. I'm sure he won't mind."

Sighing, I sink down further into the couch. "I really don't want anyone else knowing about this. Especially Colton."

Her brow rises again. "Why, *especially* Colton?"

"Because he's so not your average cocky, testosteroney kind of guy. He's sweet, patient, kind, and smart. He won't appreciate this crap." I bite my lip again. "Plus, I left in kind of a panic. He's not stupid. He knows something's up. It's not like I can just show up on his doorstep and say 'hey, I thought I'd come back and finish what we started, don't sweat it, I'm just bipolar, that's why I flipped out earlier'. That *so* will not go over well."

"I think you're over-thinking this, Julia." Liz states. "Just tell him you need a place to crash for the night because me and Nate are still at it."

"So lie?"

She sighs and shakes her head. "Sometimes you have to do what you have to do."

There is a knock at the door. "Shit. Go hide in the bedroom."

"What's the point? My car's in the driveway."

Liz rises and peeks out the front window. "There's a limo on the street."

"What?!!" I follow her to the door. John is a rich guy, but why would he drive a limo to my sister's house? Unless he's *really* lost his marbles.

Liz opens the door and both of our jaws drop.

Chapter 15

Colton

It pains me to see Julia in such a panic. Clearly there is something going on in her personal life, but it isn't my place to know what that is. I'm one to talk; I have secrets, too, and I'm hell bent on keeping it that way. Wade and my brothers are the only ones who truly know what goes on in my life. That's the way it'll stay if I have my way about it.

After dropping Julia off at her sister's place, exhaustion hits me like a ton of bricks. Sleep doesn't often come so easily, but tonight I am feeling it. Frustrating, the moment I close my eyes, my mind starts. Suddenly, I'm back in Afghanistan, standing behind enemy lines with my commanding officer, Donald, shouting unheard orders to my brigade. The gunfire is like cannons going off in the distance. We're trapped inside a trench, just a quarter of a mile from Afghan troops, who are firing at us like it's their last dying wish to annihilate us...all of us.

Knee deep in mud and sludge, my boots are soaked to the skin, and my bones ache with cold and exhaustion. I've been shot in the arm. Just a superficial wound, but it's still aching from the tight wrapping. The blood hasn't even soaked through the dressing. By morning it will be warmer, and we'll be past this danger zone, but for now we are fighting through the darkness, the hunger, and the pain, to get to our next post.

All I can think about is getting home to Pam. The girl I loved at the time more than anything else. She'd written to me from home, and I received her letter from my last post. Her words are kept tight, safely against my chest, not in my backpack, which can easily be lost if we have to run. The envelope crinkles each time I take a step, which is a comfort to me. I know I have something to go home to. I know Pam is waiting for me to come home on my next leave. We will start a family this time; it has been more than four years since we married. I'd taken Pam all over the world when I was on leave. That was the plan; we would travel, see the world, and then settle down and start a family.

Growing up with four brothers and no mother was tough. Dad was tough as nails; he had to be. I get that. When I was seventeen and a snot-nosed little punk, my dad warned me to bring up my grades and clean up my act, or he'd send me to the military. After my eighteenth birthday, when I had barely graduated high school, I thought it would be fun to take my dad's car out after hours, even though I had my own vehicle, on a joyride with some of my buddies. He got the call in the middle of the night, from the police station, after I'd smashed into a hydro pole. The next week I was shipped off to the army.

Admittedly, being in the army turned me into the man I am today; there's nothing like nine years of combat to make you see reality and appreciate the simple things in life. After Pam and I got married, she begged me to quit the military, but it was all I knew. That and horses. The fourth year of our marriage was a year I'll never forget.

***

Four years ago

I can see her from behind the glass at the arrivals gate. My body aches to touch her, to hold her, to kiss her. It had been one of the longest missions I'd been assigned to; lasting more than eight months. I'd taken only one other leave five months ago. Five months without my wife was a long time. This is my favorite part of being in the military: coming home. It's always best when you have someone to come home to besides your four brothers and an indifferent father. At first, she doesn't see me. Her back is turned, but I would know any part of her from a mile away. Long blonde hair snakes down her back, almost touching her rear end. She's let it grow since we met; it was my idea: I love long hair.

We'd married quickly; on one of my leaves. I fell hard and fast for her from the first moment I saw her when we sat together on a plane on the way home from Afghanistan. She was on a connecting flight after having to shorten a trip with her church to get home to her ailing mother. We talked the whole ride and by the time we landed home in North Carolina, we'd made plans to have dinner. The rest is history. We married fast and every trip home was like the first.

Her body is perfect; long and lean, and all mine. As she turns around and sees me coming down the escalator, her face lights up like a Christmas tree. I don't wait for the stairs to move me, my feet start. Tearing down the escalator, I squeeze by four different people, who give me a sour look, but I don't care. It's like my feet are on fire and I can't just stand there. Dressed in my camouflage uniform, I stick out like a bright pink flamingo in a room full of elephants. A few people clap, displaying their gratitude for my service to the country. I don't stop to bow. I run as fast as I can to Pam, who is running through the glass doors to get to me. I can see her eyes redden as she draws closer, tears begging to be shed. Wetness pricks the backs of my eyes, too, as she's inches away from me. Leaping into my arms, Pam wraps herself around me, straddling me as I hold her tight to me. We are both a mess of tears as we stand in the center of the airport arrivals gate, listening to the din of clapping and whistling from onlookers.

Every time I arrive home it's like this, ever since I met Pam. We spend the next few minutes wrapped in each other's embrace, until neither of our arms can hold any longer. I let her down and we kiss several times as she slides down my body and reaches the glossy, polished floor in the airport.

"God, I missed you." She breathes, looking into my eyes, brushing my cheeks with her fingers.

"You have no idea." I say, chuckling with happiness.

We get my one lonely bag from the baggage claim, standing, waiting hand-in-hand watching everyone's bags plop from the hopper in the back, onto the rotating baggage holder. Every ten seconds we look at each other and kiss again. When we finally reach her car, I throw my bag in the back and steal another kiss as we get into the car.

"How long are you home for this time?" Pam asks hopefully, as she puts the key in the ignition.

"A couple of weeks."

Grasping my hand in hers, we head home. Our little bungalow is our pride and joy. Every time I come home, she's done something more to improve it. When we got married, we combined our savings and the small amount we made from the wedding and bought the little fixer-upper. It was Pam's mission to make the house look as fancy as a magazine, and it showed. This time she's done the bedroom. Before I left, the beige carpeting was tattered, pulled up in some spots by the worn baseboards, the white and dirty wallpaper was also torn in spots. A picture window that had lost its seals years ago stood opaque with grime and humidity over the years. What I see when I walk in is something to behold.

Wooden blinds frame the beautiful, new window, boasting a cushioned seat. The dark, mahogany floor gleams with newness, warming the chocolate brown painted walls and cream bead board where the chipped chair rail used to be. She even bought a sleigh bed and two matching cream night stands to match. "Wow." Is all I can say.

"You like it?"

"I love it. How long did this take you to do?"

Pam shrugs and pulls off her shirt, revealing a fancy bra underneath. With hooded eyes I look at this beautiful woman who is mine. "God, I missed you." I say. My body ached for her every night I was away.

"I missed you too, baby." She pulls her jeans off and stands in a matching pink bra and panties.

If I were ever to die, this is the vision I would want to see right before death. Her creamy skin appears soft and warm, begging to be touched. Modest cleavage teases the corners of her bra. The triangle of lace before the crest of her womanly area allows a tiny breath of hair to poke out. She's had a pedicure as well, so her toes match her undergarments. Pam always makes a meal out of our first time when I arrive home. I love that about her.

I last a second later before I take a step towards her and tear off her bra and panties. She makes quick work of removing my uniform. Through practiced hands, she has me naked in twenty seconds. We plunge onto the bed as though diving into water after a drought. Then I slowly climb on top and place both my hands on either side of her face. "I love you so much, baby."

"I love you to the moon and back." She says. A tear falls down her cheek and I kiss the spot where it lands, trailing kisses down her neck as she moans, calling my name as though in a dream. Pert breasts stare up at me with rounded nipples and suppleness that I can't resist. Taking her breast in my mouth, I suck gently, forcing her to push her back up from the bed, into me. Her nipple instantly hardens as I tease it with my tongue. Painted nails pull at my hair, directing me to the other breast, feeling left out.

"God, Colton. I can't wait. Get a condom. I want you in me right now." Her voice quivers with need.

My eyes open. "Do we need a condom, baby? I thought we were going to start trying." After years of birth control, I figured old habits die hard.

"Oh, baby, not now." She opens her eyes; a twinge of irritation sweeps over them. "You won't last."

Duration had never been a problem before. "It'll be fine. We can always do it again if you're worried. We've got all night. And...um...we can be inventive." I wiggle my eyebrows, knowing how much she loves the feeling of me in her mouth.

"Colton, please. I can't wait. Just get a condom." Her voice and the expression on her face are strange, but I let it go. We can talk about it later. All I want is to be with her. After months without her, she can have anything she wants as long as we get to make love...a lot.

The next morning, and six condoms later, we lay in bed all tangled in the new pink silk sheets, both of us spent and sore from making love all night, I stroke the skin between her breasts with my fingers. "How come you wanted to use condoms? I figured after the first, we would just go without."

Licking her lips, Pam inhales deeply. "Colton, I've been thinking about it, and I'm not ready to have kids yet."

Closing my eyes tightly, I take my hand off her. "You've been saying that since we got married, Pam. What is it? Why aren't you ready yet?"

I try like hell to keep the edge out of my tone, but I can't help it. Pam knows I want to have a big family. We could have one or two children and buy a bigger house; that was the plan. That had always been the plan. With the bedroom done now, all that is left is the two spare rooms and a little landscaping outside, which is half done anyway. Did she want to move to a bigger house first? Did she want to do more travelling? Was there something I didn't know about? Did something happen while I was gone?

"Because, Colton. With you being away all the time, I just don't know if having kids is a great idea. I don't want to raise them alone."

"But I've only got two more years left on this post." I'd planned on retiring from combat after this mission was complete. It had two years left. "So, you're saying you want to wait until I retire before starting a family?" That isn't terribly unreasonable. I just wish if that were true, that she would have been more honest with me. I get it.

Raising kids alone isn't easy; my dad did it, so I can attest.

"Maybe." The uncertainty in her tone is unsettling.

I turn so I'm facing her. "What do you mean...maybe?"

"Well, when you're done, then what are you going to do?"

"What does my career have to do with us having kids?"

She guffaws. "Uh, lots, Colton. How are we going to raise kids if you're not making enough money to support them?"

I sit up. "What are you talking about? We have plenty of money. That's never been a problem. You know I want to open up a horse ranch some day, and—"

"Yeah, *some* day." She spits. "Seems like a pipe dream to me, Colton. We don't have that kind of money. Not unless your dad forks some over."

"Whooaaa...." I lift a hand. "My dad's money is my dad's money. It's got nothing to do with me."

"Yeah," she kicks at a bundle of sheets at the bottom of the bed.

I ignore her tantrum. "You know I also have my degree. That's part of the reason I joined the military."

"And what are you going to do with it, Colton? Are you going to design North Carolina's next airplane?"

"You know who my dad is."

"I know very well who your dad is. But he doesn't even *talk* to you, Colton!"

Cutting the air with my hand, I find my voice. "I never asked for anything from him, and that won't ever change. You know I've been paving the way for when I'm finished in combat, and I know it will be fine. I'd never suggest placing any burden on you. I promised I would finish in combat soon and I will. After that, I'll still be part of the military, but in the aerodynamics division, and *not* in Afghanistan."

"I don't want to fight anymore!" she shouts. "I...I don't think I'm cut out for this anymore." Pam rises, pulling the sheets with her, so she is properly covered. As if after the last twelve hours of us being naked together, now she feels modest. "I can't do this for another two years, Colton."

"Well, we can wait and have a baby after that, if it means that much to you."

She rakes a hand through her disheveled hair and sighs. "No, this. I mean, I can't do this anymore. I can't wait any longer."

"For what? You just finished saying that you didn't want to have a baby. What else are you waiting for?"

While she doesn't answer, I can see right through her. The remodeling, the new sheets, the pedicure, manicure, the credit card bills she'd written to me about. I finally knew what she'd been waiting for this whole damn time.

Chapter 16

Julia

My expression is a combination of surprise and worry. "Is everything okay? What are you doing here? How did you get here?" Liz looks like she's swallowed a frog. Silent at first, as though thinking of appropriate words to say to the father she hadn't seen in thirteen years and just showed up at her doorstep without notice. Dad is carrying a bag in each hand; one much bigger than the other. He's wearing a blank expression and divides his glance between both me and Liz.

"I flew here, of course." Dad has a private jet that he uses to travel from the different courses he has outside Florida.

"Well, come in, dad." That is all that Liz can think of to say. "Can I take your bags?"

"They're actually your sister's." he says, glossing over the other two questions I asked.

"Mine?" I say, taking the bags and placing them in the hallway.

"Come sit." Liz says. "Is everything okay?"

Dad looks around the house and seems pleased. "The place looks nice. Where's my grandson?"

"Thanks. He's out with friends. If I'd known you were coming, I would have told him to stay back. He would have loved to see you."

"That's okay, dear. I'll see him later."

Liz and dad sit on the couch, while I take the end chair. "Do you want some tea or something, dad?"

"Not right now. Maybe later." He has somewhat of a singsong tone, indicating that he's happy.

"Where is...um...Grant?" Dad's pasted on smile is transparent.

Liz doesn't dance around the answer. "He's not here."

With that, dad turns to me. "I thought you were in Barbados with Mary."

"Dad, something tells me that you know more than you're letting on. You wouldn't be sitting here, otherwise." I say bluntly.

He draws in a deep breath and presses his back into the couch, folding his arms across his chest. "Well, I received a visit from John a couple of weeks ago."

"What did he want?"

He chuckles. "He was looking for you." He says it as if he is humored by the fact that I seem to be hiding from my fiancé.

"I bet. What did you say to him?"

"Exactly what I knew; that you were gone away with Mary."

"Thanks for that. What else did you say?"

"Very little." Dad is direct. "I don't get involved. If you needed me, I know you would have called."

Liz intercepts cautiously. "So why did you come here?"

"Because I received a call from him this morning."

"So did I." I admit.

He looks at me with the same speculative eyes he had when he asked me if I was sure I wanted to go away for University. "Is there something that you need to tell me?"

Dad and I have always communicated almost telepathically. It's like we can read each other's minds. He knows there is something going on besides a lover's quarrel, and I know that he knows that, too. But for me to go into detail is unnecessary and it will only upset him. "You know there is. But I'm a big girl and I can fight my own battles."

His glance goes down to my left hand, absent the ring on my left ring finger. "Is the engagement off?"

"That's putting it mildly." Liz's tone is derogatory. Like dad has set me up to marry the devil himself.

"Hm," Dad pauses for thought. "Well. It seems like I've read wrong again." With the word 'again', his voice raises an octave.

"What do you mean?" I ask.

He rises, walking over to the front window. "Thirteen years ago, I thought your Grant was...well, that's neither here nor there now...and now it seems I've read John wrong. I thought he was a decent young man with clear goals and a good heart."

Liz walks over to dad and takes his arm. She gives it a squeeze and he turns to her with glassy eyes. Her voice is soft when she says. "No, Dad, you were right about Grant. He's gone. He left me and Nate. That's one reason why Julia's here."

Dad's head cocks sideways with compassion. He pulls his arms around her, kissing her head. "I'm so sorry, love. I...I know it's hard."

Feeling left out, I go over and wrap myself around both of them.

Dad is a lot of things, but he's also a huge sap when it comes down to it. From the way he is weeping with Liz, it's pretty obvious that he's been wanting to reconcile with her for a while. It's a revelation, and it's the happiest moment in my life since I got my teacher's license...well, that and since someone started posting sexy, poignant memes of Matthew McConaughey on Facebook.

"Let's go and make some tea, okay?" Dad says, finally breaking free. "I'm feeling a little parched."

"Sure, Dad." Liz wipes her eyes with the back of her hand. "What kind do you like?"

While they discuss and prepare the tea, I take my bags to my room.

"So, how long are you going to stay with your sister, Julia?" Dad asks as I rejoin them in the kitchen.

"I applied for a teaching position at Nate's school. I hope that's okay with you."

Dad waves and frowns. "You're welcome to stay as long as you like. Do you have room for her, Liz?"

"She's staying in the old laundry room. Did you know that she snores?"

Ignoring the comment, Dad continues. "There's space on one of the courses out here if you like, Liz."

On every golf course dad owns, there are houses. Some are small cottages, but others are larger, and some are mansions. Always the one to help, dad offers me my own house, even the guest house, but I always decline. Until I was married, I'd live with dad, and then the plan was for John and I to buy our own house with our own money.

"No, dad, thanks, but I'll stay with Liz." I have more than one reason to stay put. Now that John and I are through, I have to come up with my own funds to buy a house, but I also don't want to live alone. Staying with Liz until this whole situation settles doesn't seem like a bad idea. "I'm better off here."

The look dad gives me is telling. "Do you need me to file a complaint against John? Do you need me to get you protection from him?"

As much as I don't want to upset dad, I also don't want to lie to him, either. "Not at this point, dad. It's too early to tell."

"Fair enough." Liz fills the mugs she put on the table. Dad nods his thanks. "You let me know."

"I will. I promise."

Sitting at the table, Liz takes a sip of her tea. "How long are you staying, dad?"

He winks at her. "As long as I want."

"It gets cold here in the winter, dad. Your blood might thin out." I joke.

"How about you tell me how this job turns out, when you get it." Dad reasons. I notice he doesn't say 'if you get it' and my heart swells. He lifts his mug and taps it on my mug, and then on Liz's. "Home is where my girls are."

As we sit and play a game of cards, enjoying catching up with each other, I realize how my life has changed in the last few weeks. Some for the good, some for the bad. The rest remains to be seen. Dad seems so happy and comfortable to be here, and I'm glad that this piece of the puzzle of my life has finally come together. We sit at the kitchen table until dad calls his limo to take him to the hotel he's reserved for the night. Liz offers to sleep on the couch so he can sleep in her room, but he doesn't want to impose. As we stand at the door, saying our goodbyes to dad, I smile.

None of us see the headlights that suddenly turn off up the street.

Chapter 17

Colton

When I feel like this, that is when I go to the woods. Deep inside the wooded area beyond the pasture, I cleared a path large enough to one day build a cabin. It is quiet, and nobody else except my brothers know where it is. So, if I want to be alone, that's exactly where I go. There is a small pond where I sometimes fish or swim, and a great spot for a fire, where there is an open area, clear of trees. On nights when it is a full moon, that area is completely illuminated.

The horses always let me know if anyone comes around. Sometimes I ride Maya over to the small area, too. I never bring a phone with me, and I always carry a flashlight. I built a brick fireplace in the ground by the water and I leave a metal bucket so I can douse the flames when I'm done. There are four chairs available, in case my brothers come, but only one is ever left out.

After the Pam flashback, I'm angry for two reasons: because I let that happen then, and because I let it get under my skin now...again. That woman got under my skin even two years after she left me. If Wade knew I was out here thinking about her again, he'd hang my balls by the fire. Since day one, Wade never liked Pam. He said something about her was fake. He called it, and he's never let me live it down since.

I brought some marshmallows leftover from dinner with Julia. After forging for a twig with my flashlight, I cook the gooey treat and pop it into my mouth, remembering how much fun I had earlier with her. Regretting not bringing a beer, I'm almost tempted to turn back and get one, when I hear Maya whinny from the stables. The air is chilly with a late summer breeze. There is a half moon in the sky, illuminating the area slightly. As I rise, I hear her whinny again, and I quickly douse the fire with the bucket at the ready on the side. At a quick pace, I jog back to the house, where

I hear Maya whinny a third time.

Coming around to the front, there is a lone man standing at my door. He's tall, wearing a three-piece suit. It looks navy blue, but it could be black in the dark. His car is parked behind mine, a bit too close for my liking. I've never seen him before, and he speaks with a British accent. "Hi, there. Sorry to bother you." He offers me his hand to shake. "Wendel James."

"Colton." I say, not offering him my surname. Since being in the military, I make it a habit not to share my last name until I know a person well enough. I decide when that is.

"This is a beautiful ranch you've got here, if you don't mind me saying so."

"Thank you. What can I do for you?" I can't help the terse tone in my voice. I'm not a fan of strangers, especially ones that show up unannounced, late at night.

"Sure, sure. I'm a property investor." He hands me a card and I open the door slightly, so I can turn on the porch light. After observing that it is, in fact, a business card with his name on it, with some company name I've never heard of, I look at him expectantly.

"And what do you want from me?"

"I was driving through North Carolina, looking for properties to invest in. There have been a few, but this," he holds out his hand, indicating my ranch, "this is out of this world." He compliments.

"Thank you. It's not for sale." I'm about to turn around and bid him goodnight, when he asks me to hold on.

"Please, sir. I don't often find such quaint pieces of land, this is rare. Can I trouble you to take a look?"

"I don't think so." My tone is cold. "As I said, it's not for sale."

"What do you plan on doing with it? I heard your horses...how many do you have?"

"Two."

"Are you going to get more? Does the stable

accommodate for more?"

"Sir, really, I have no intention of selling this property. You're wasting your time...and mine." I turn around and go back into the house, before he has a chance to say anything else.

"Thank you, kindly, sir." He says, as he walks away. "Have a good evening."

Just before I'm about to shut the storm door, I watch him pull away. The car had been parked so close to my car I couldn't see his license plate.

Then I see it....

...it is a Florida plate. I look at the address on the business card; it says Florida. Rushing into the house, I grab my tablet out of one of the kitchen drawers and fire it up. Typing in the name of the company, I see that it does exist. Scrolling through the staff names, I don't see his, but I do see a twenty-four-hour number to call for any investment advice. Dialing the number, I follow the instructions and enter his name into the phone. His name does not come up. Figuring that maybe he's new, I dial zero for an operator.

A woman picks up a moment later, relaying the name of the investment company, and her own. "What can I do to help you?"

"Hi there. Can you connect me with Wendel James please?"

I hear another call come in from her end.

"Can you hold for a moment, please?"

"Sure."

I listen to elevator music for about five seconds, when she comes back on. "Sir? Can you repeat the name please? Did you say 'Wendel James'?" when she says the name, her voice raises an octave, as if unsure.

"Yes, that's correct."

"Sir, I'm afraid there is no Wendel James here."

"Are you sure? Maybe he's new or something?"

"No, I'm afraid not, sir. This is a very small office, and I've been here for five years. Never have I heard of a Wendel James."

I thank her and click off, as my mind begins reeling.

....and then it hits me.

....*Julia.*

Chapter 18

Julia

Dad offers one last time for me to stay with him at the hotel, but I decline. The hotel is no more than a five minute drive away. If things get ugly, dad won't be far. Plus, it's late, and dad is accustomed to early nights and mornings. His favorite expression is 'the early bird catches the worm', and he lives by that. If I know him well enough, he has morning meetings lined up, taking full advantage of being in North Carolina.

Liz is sitting on the couch, fighting sleep. "Go to bed, girl. I'm not far behind you." I say to her. Nate had called while dad was here, asking to sleep over at his friend's house. Dad and Nate made plans to have lunch together tomorrow.

She yawns. "You would never know that I work until sometimes three o'clock in the morning. I can't keep my eyes open past eleven on the nights that I'm home."

"That's because it catches up to you. Don't worry, it won't be long before you start school, and then hopefully you'll have a career where you won't have to burn the midnight oil anymore."

"Yeah, speaking of which, I should hear by Monday if I got accepted into the Culinary Arts program."

"That's awesome! I should hear hopefully next week about this job at the school."

"Cool. Hey, listen, not that I don't think it's a great idea, but I signed up for driving classes. I love the idea of you teaching me to drive, but I think this might be better for both of us. This way I get a discount on my insurance rate, too."

"True. But I can still take you out and show you a few things here and there if you want."

Liz yawns again. "I gotta get to bed. See you in the morning, sis."

"See yah."

I put the kettle on for a cup of chamomile tea. Since

moving out here, sleep does not come easily. The drapes and blinds are closed, and the doors are locked, and my car is in the garage, but I still feel the hairs on the back of my neck stand up whenever I hear a car drive down the street. I've been ignoring my phone; too afraid to check it. When the kettle boils, I make the tea and sit down to watch some reruns of 'Friends', which is always foolproof for helping me take my mind off things. It's one of my favourites: the one with two birthday parties. This is the one where Rachel's parents, who are in the middle of a nasty divorce, both show up to her birthday party, and the gang has to come up with inventive ways to keep them apart for the night. My favorite line is when they have a close call and Chandler jumps over the couch, shouting "Quick! What would Jack and Chrissy do?!" That line always makes me laugh out loud, and I bark out a soft one, conscious that Liz is sleeping, and that's when I hear it: the soft knock at the door.

At first my heart pounds. I freeze and think that there is a slight chance the visitor will go away, thinking that there is nobody home or that we are sleeping. *What if it's dad?* That is a remote possibility. Rising, I go to the door and look through the peephole. This is not helpful. In the dark I can see nothing but a shadow. "Julia? It's Colton."

I let out the breath I'm holding and open the door. "Colton, what are you doing here?" I whisper.

He looks around. "Oh, is Liz asleep?"

I nod. "Is everything okay? What are you doing here?" I ask again.

"Do you want to go for a drive? I need to talk to you."

I scrunch my face. "Now?"

"Yeah. Grab your purse and lock up." He looks around the house as I grab my purse and lock the door.

He walks to the passenger side door and opens it for me, then he walks over to the driver's side and slides into the seat. "Sorry for coming by so late. I hope I didn't scare you."

"You kind of did, but that's okay." I watch him put the car into reverse and drive onto the street. "So, what do you want to talk about?" I have no idea what's going on. This is very weird. Maybe it has something to do with how I left things earlier? He has balls the size of dump trucks if he's coming out this late to dig deeper into my personal life, especially when I told him I wasn't ready to share it yet.

He reaches into the center console and pulls out what looks like a business card. "Do you recognize this name?"

I look at it. He reaches up and turns on the interior light, so I can see it clearly. "No, I've never heard of this person. Why?"

He turns off the light. "That's what I was hoping you'd say."

"Who is he? What does he have to do with me?"

"I hope nothing. He *is* from Florida though. He showed up at my doorstep a little while ago, saying that he was interested in my ranch. I thought it was odd that he came so late to do business. But he didn't press so I let it go. My gut told me something was up, so I checked him out. The guy doesn't exist at this investment place. The card is bogus. I thought maybe he was connected to you, since you were acting kind of funny earlier."

Wow, this is far-fetched. Colton is assuming that since the guy is from Florida that he has something to do with me? "Um, no. Like I said, I never heard of the guy."

"Not like an old boyfriend or anything, huh." Colton's tone is casual but with a pinch of suspicion.

"No." I don't want to get into details with Colton...yet.

Colton seems to be driving back to his place, but I keep quiet. It doesn't really matter where we go, the hairs on the back of my neck aren't standing up anymore.

"Were you in a relationship back in Florida?"

"I don't see how any of this is related, but yes."

"Did the guy speak with a British accent?"

I bark out a tiny laugh. "No." But after seeing the perplexed look on his face, I feel bad. "Sorry."

"That's okay. Hey, I don't mean to freak you out or anything. And I'm sorry if I am."

His face is sullen. Now I feel *really* bad. I wish I can help him figure out what's going on, but I'm not sure how. "What did he look like?"

"He was tall and thin...built, like he worked out regularly. He was wearing a blue three-piece-suit. Well-dressed. Definitely a business-type."

John is well built and dresses well, but then so do all of his friends, family and co-workers in his father's business. There is only one other way to tell. "What kind of car did he drive?"

"A white BMW. Two doors. Kind of souped-up. Tinted windows."

My stomach does a flip-flop as my hand goes to my throat.

"You okay?"

Shit. That's John. He's here. He's looking for me. He must have been following me for a couple of days if he knows where Colton lives.

As we pull up to his ranch, I blurt. "Oh, God, Colton, turn the car around. I can't go to your place. He knows I'll be there." My speech is fast and frantic.

"Who?" he places his hand on mine. "Hey, it's okay. Who is this guy?"

He puts his car into park and squeezes my hand. "What's going on?"

A ball forms in my throat. I almost can't speak. "Oh, God, Colton, I'm so sorry I brought this to you. I had no idea that it would escalate this bad."

"What? What...tell me. What's going on? Who is this guy?"

I look around, feeling my heart flutter in my chest. Tears begin streaming down my face. *Is he here? Can he see me? Is he watching us?*

"No, no, you can't touch me. He might see." I say,

batting his hand away as if it were a bee trying to sting me.

"Who? Is he...like an old boyfriend or something?"

I wipe the tears from my eyes. "No, he's my fiancé. Or my ex-fiance. I left him in Florida. I had to. It was just...so...awful."

Colton takes his hand from me and nervously scratches his nose. "Did he beat you?"

"No, no, it was much worse than that. He's psychotic. And I did something really bad to upset him."

"What...you left him, right?"

"Yeah, but before that. I did something really stupid and then I left. Now he's so pissed off. He followed me here. He must have been here for days, weeks. I'm so sorry. I'm so so sorry I brought this to you."

Colton pinches the bridge of his nose and places his hands on the steering wheel. "Okay, we need to get you in the house and pour you a stiff drink."

"No, no. He'll know I'm here."

"So?"

"So, he might come after you."

He scoffs. "Sweetheart, I'm not afraid. If anyone comes around here the horses let me know."

"No, you don't understand. He's psychotic, Colton. If he's gone to these lengths; printing out phoney business cards, wearing disguises, talking in a fake accent, he's desperate. I don't know what he'll do to me...or to you."

He places his hand on mine. "Julia, sweetie. Look at me." he lifts my chin with his hand. "Look at me." he divides his glance between both of my eyes. "There's nothing to be afraid of. I fought in the military for ten years. Some weenie loser who's hunting down a defenceless girl I could probably eat for breakfast...if Rebel doesn't get him first."

The car door opens, and Colton slides out. I freeze in my seat. I want to argue, to tell him to take me home, but I'm so confused. I don't know what's safe anymore. The fear is making me hysterical. Next thing I know,

Colton has opened my door and taken my hand. "Come on. Let's go get you a glass of scotch."

Ten minutes later I'm sitting on Colton's couch, drinking what I'll now call 'truth serum', which is exactly what this smooth, brown liquid makes me do. Colton has no idea what he's getting into.

...neither do I.

Chapter 19

Colton

Whoever this asshole is he'll pay for what he's done. I'm a believer in karma, and Lord, this guy is in for one hell of a ride. I've never seen a girl flip out so bad over a guy. He's got one hell of a hold on her, that's for sure. I bet his balls are the size of raisins. No male should ever treat a woman like that if he's got any balls at all. That's a cardinal rule: never intimidate a woman, ever, whether physically or emotionally. Not allowed in my books. No exceptions. Though, Julia doesn't strike me as the kind of girl who would let a guy walk all over her. With an air of independence and confidence, she seems like she can hold her own. If it weren't for the loser showing up on my doorstep, she would never have told me about him. She wants to take care of herself. I admire that about her.

One thing she can't handle, is alcohol. After making her down a highball of scotch, she's finally settled down enough to chat. Through glassy eyes, she watches me pull out a bowl of chips, hoping to soak up whatever overage of booze is sitting in her stomach. As I sit on the opposite side of the couch from her, we share a bag of barbecue chips.

"I don't see you as a guy who eats chips, Colton."

"They're not for me. I have them for the kids I teach. We sometimes have snacks afterwards if the parents aren't due to come pick them up for a while."

"So, if you were in the military, how come you aren't anymore?" she stuffs a handful of chips in her mouth and waits for my answer. Her long, curly brown hair is in a messy bun at the back of her head. Tendrils of curls have fallen from the bun and are playfully bouncing at the sides of her head. It's all I can do not to go over to her and brush the hair from her face.

"Well, that's kind of a long story."

A clever expression sweeps across her face, as if she's

come up with an idea. "Tell you what. You answer a complicated question for me, and I'll do the same for you. Deal?"

What harm could come of this? She's no threat to me, and I get the distinct impression that anything I tell her, will stay between us. We both have personal leverage, so neither of us is going to blab about the other. "Alright. Um, I was in the military for ten years, and I decided after my last mission, that I'd had enough for now."

"You think you'll ever go back?"

"Maybe. But not to combat."

"Where?"

"I have a degree in Aerodynamics through the military. I'd go back to pursue that."

"So, you mean you'd build airplanes and jets and things?"

"For the military, yes, not for commercial use." I clear my throat. "Okay, it's way past my turn." I watch her sit up straighter. I'd given her a glass of water to wash down the scotch, and she takes a sip. "Why did you agree to marry this 'John' guy? Didn't you have any indication that he was trouble?"

"Before John, I'd never been in a relationship. His intimidation tactics, his controlling ways, nobody ever saw them except me, and I thought it was normal. It was my friend Mary who opened my eyes. Her boyfriend worships her, and so did the guy before him." she sits back, sinking further into the couch, and gets comfortable.

"Go ahead." I say, pushing my hand in front of me, inviting her to take a turn asking a question.

"You're enjoying this, aren't you?"

"Not especially, but if this is the way to get to the heart of the matter, then so be it."

"Have you ever been engaged?"

I swallow. Oh, boy, I'd almost rather talk about being in the military than talk about this. But I go with it. She's just shared about her past relationship, and I agreed to play this game. "Yes."

"Did you—"

"Nope," I tease. "You asked your question."

"Okay, I'll add a rule here: no yes or no answers. You *must* elaborate."

Chewing my lip, I relent. "Fine. Yes, I was engaged, and I married her. We were married for four years."

She folds her arms across her chest, waiting for me to take my turn. This game is kind of fun. It's like the quicker you answer to the satisfaction of your opponent, the quicker you get to ask a question, and have it answered to your satisfaction. Quid quo pro.

"What made you decide to come out here and stay with your sister?"

"To get as far away from that prick as I could. Also, I didn't want my dad knowing about it, and my sister's husband just traipsed out the door the week before I came, so I figured all the more reason to be here." She pauses for a second. "Why did your marriage fail?"

My cheeks are heated. This is uncharted territory. Only me, Wade, and Pam know the true story. "Lots of reasons. We wanted different things."

The look on her face says that isn't enough. She taps her finger on her arms defiantly.

"Okay, I wanted kids, she didn't."

"And you didn't discuss this beforehand?" she blurts, her eyes dancing.

Licking my lips, I then smile. "Yeah, we did. There was a plan and everything." I scratch the tip of my nose. "As you know," I gesture toward her, "plans don't always work out." I lift from the couch slightly. "How come you didn't want your dad to know you had to leave your fiancé?"

"Because my dad is the one who set us up. It would break his heart. And he had a plan, too." She smirks, "But as you know, plans don't always work out." She doesn't even pause. "So, she lied to you, or did you lie to her?"

I chuckle, and then draw in a deep breath. "Oh,

shoot. This is getting way too deep for a Sunday night."

"Tell you what. You answer my question and then I'll answer one more of yours. Then we'll call it quits."

Considering the deal, I think of the perfect final question, and then I answer simply. "She lied to me. She said she wanted kids from the beginning, and then she lied to me for four years. Then she left me."

"Wow." She shakes her head. "Cold."

I lean across the couch, looking poignantly at her. "You mentioned you did something stupid before you left, to piss him off. What did you do?"

She smiles a deviant smile, as if she's a bit proud of what she did. "Mary took me and some girls from work out to this bar. John was away on business, so he didn't know I was out, otherwise I'd never be allowed to go. Anyway, it was 'Tube Top Tuesday' at this bar, so we were all in tube tops. The girls straightened my hair and put makeup on me, so I looked...well, better than I look tonight." She chuckles, pulling a loose curl behind her ear. "This guy was dancing with me and being decent, not groping me or anything. Suddenly John shows up...pissed! He grabs hold of this guy and before John can hit him, I ploughed John in the face so hard I knocked him on the floor. His lip was bleeding and everything."

My eyes bulge. "Wow." I nod, impressed. "See, I don't think you're really that scared of him."

She gives me a 'seriously?' look. "I was drunk, Colton. You know? Liquid courage?"

"Still. The fact that you were able to stand up to him, drunk or not, says something." I sit with my elbows on my knees. "If I've learned anything from my years as a bouncer, it's that it doesn't matter how big a guy is, you strike him in the right spot, he'll be down for the count before he can blink."

"Maybe for a guy, Colton, but that was a one-off. If it hadn't been for the crowd of people surrounding us, John probably would have taken me down."

"Nah, he's a coward. Going after a woman? With the

right moves, you could totally take him."

"You saw the size of him, Colton! He'd cream me!"

She's relaxed enough. It's time. "Stand up."

Chapter 20

Julia

Wow. I just shared more about my life with Colton than I've shared with anyone for as long as I can remember. Maybe it's the scotch or the stupid vulnerability, but I just told him about John, something I promised I wouldn't share with anyone other than Mary and my sister. Jesus, Colton was *married?* That's insane. Well, not really *insane*, as much as mind blowing. I mean, he's smart, sexy, extremely good-looking, and he seems to be the deep but simple-yet-complicated kind of guy who keeps his distance. Is he only interested in what went on with John so he can find out where he is and kick his ass? I know Colton is pissed that he came around the ranch and is faking his identity, so maybe Colton is just being territorial? Who can blame him? This ranch is gorgeous, and he's worked hard for it.

Now he has me standing in the middle of his living room, while he moves furniture around. For what, I have no idea, but whatever. The scotch is wearing off, and I'm tired as hell, but I'm so curious as to what he's up to that I just stand here with my mouth half open.

"Take your socks off." Colton says as he does the same.

"Why?"

He winks at me. "That's an order."

I play along and take my socks off. But not without giving them the sniff test first.

Colton does a double-take. "Did you just…smell your socks?"

"Well…yeah. Haven't you ever done that before?"

He chuckles. "I guess not."

"When you're at a guy's house and he tells you to remove your socks…you check first. That's just a rule I have."

"And?" he says, pulling the coffee table out a little

further from the couch.

"And what?"

"Well, did they smell?"

My face is red as a tomato. I can't look at him. I answer, staring at the ceiling, feigning stubbornness. "No."

"Good. Are you ready?" he stands next to me with his thumbs hanging from the loops of his jeans. There is a clear circle in the centre of the living room. He's even moved the area rug that was under the coffee table. His couch is pressed up against the wall with the window, leaving a healthy amount of space for doing a workout, or performing a dance, safely.

"What are we doing?"

"Okay, grab me from behind, like you're going to steal my hat or something. I'll act like I don't expect it."

I laugh. "Are you serious? What are you doing this for?"

"I'm dead serious. Now, you already had the guts to deck this John guy, right?"

Shrugging, I answer yes.

"So, you've got what it takes inside to defend yourself." He pounds himself on the chest for emphasis. "Now, all you need is the moves to know what to do next. If he ever came after you."

"And you're going to teach me? Are you serious?"

"Well, why not? You're not going to let some weasel push you around, are you?"

"No."

"Alright then. Tackle me from behind and I'll show you what I'd do."

Colton takes a few steps towards the window. Thankfully the drapes are drawn. I walk up behind him and take a handful of his hair in my hand. Instantly, he grabs my arm from behind, blindly, and takes my wrist, turning it so my body has no choice but to follow. He gently takes my head in his other hand as he turns around, and he leads me slowly, straight to the floor. "There. Now, that's one thing you do if someone comes after you from behind. You wanna try?"

We are face-to-face on the floor for a second. I didn't realize how blue his eyes are. They almost glow in the dark. His eyelashes still go on for miles. Slightly winded, he speaks in a hushed tone, which is as sexy as hell. It's like pillow talk, and for a second, I imagine being face-to-face with him, just like this, in bed. Shaking my head, I pull myself out of my reverie. "Sure. But I'm not as strong as you. How will this ever work?"

He helps me to my feet. "Julia, when I first joined the military, I was seventeen. I was a skinny little runt and so uncoordinated I would trip over my own damn feet. You learn quickly during combat that size doesn't matter. It's moves and speed."

"Okay. Let's go."

"Walk just like I did, and I'm going to grab your hair. I'll lead you on what to do."

He repeats what I did a minute ago, and then instructs me on how to grab, turn at precisely the right angle, and pull him down to the ground. "Oh my God! I did it!" I squeal.

"Now, you just have to practice. And the key is to be ready. Always be ready for an attack. Be mindful of what's going on around you at all times. Know where exits are and where someone can hide, so you save yourself from being vulnerable." He smiles. "Come on. I'll show you a few more."

The next one he shows me is something he called 'Peeling a Banana'. When he says this, I scrunch my face. "What the hell?"

"I'll show you. Face me and grab my arm."

I do what he says, and he pulls my hand away with the opposite arm, bending my finger back so I'm forced to the floor. "Holy shit, Colton! This is awesome! Show me how to do that!"

"This is the easiest one. I learned it from a guy who is a black belt in karate."

A thought occurs to me. "Hey, do you use a lot of this at Mingles?"

He nods emphatically. "A lot. You didn't see anything the night you worked, because it was a quiet until you left. You missed a couple of good ones, though."

"Do you have to punch guys out sometimes, though?"

He shrugs. "I try not to, but yes, especially if they have a weapon that sneaks under the metal detector."

We take a break. He pulls the couch back to where it belongs, and I slide the carpet over. We both take one end of the coffee table and put it back in front of the couch. "I'll teach you how to do all these and more, and help you practice if you want."

"That's awfully nice of you, Colton." I study his face. He's looking through a small space of drape that had opened when we moved the couch back. "Why do you want to help me so much? What's in it for you?"

"I don't know. I guess peace-keeping is in my blood. That's one of the reasons why I joined the service, and that's why I work at Mingles."

"What about Wade?"

"What *about* Wade?"

"Well, did he get beat up a lot? Is that why you work there, too?"

"It's more of a babysitting thing than it is about being his bodyguard."

I drain my glass of water that Colton had given me earlier. "Does he get into trouble?"

Colton rises and goes to the refrigerator, taking my empty glass with him. I can hear him refilling my water. When he returns, he has a glass for himself, too. "It's more about him making bad decisions. He's my little brother. It's my job to keep him in line."

"Do you have any older brothers?"

"Yep. Three. Jack, Garrett, and Dalton. Me and Wade are the youngest."

"Wow, five boys?"

"Yeah. Wade was a surprise, though. That I know for a fact."

"How do you know?"

"Well, it ain't rocket science when there's only a one-year difference between each of us, except there's five years between Wade and I." he chuckles. "Wade definitely was unplanned."

"Your mom was busy."

"Wouldn't know. She left dad when Wade was a baby. Though I think I've mentioned that to you before. Your parents are split, too, right?"

"Yeah."

We stay silent for a moment. "I should get you home." Colton says. "It's so late." He looks at his watch. I look at mine. It's almost two o'clock in the morning.

"Colton?"

"Yeah?"

"Can I stay the night?"

Chapter 21

Colton

Jesus. She wants to stay the night? I think my heart just stopped. Thank God I wasn't taking a sip of water, because it would have flown out my nose. Touching her, being so close to her, talking about personal things, all that...was too much. Her staying the night, sleeping under the same roof as me...oh...God. She said she felt safer here, and it's all my fault. I should've just followed the guy out of town and pounded him the moment he pulled over for gas or to take a leak. Am I ready to have a woman sleep in my house? God, the thought is just too delicious. I can't. I'm not ready. It's too soon. Just hours ago, I was laying in bed, thinking about Pam again. And now, here I am with Julia. Mentoring her, getting to know her and letting her get to know me. What for? What can it lead to? No good, that's what.

She can't stay. She just...can't. It's one thing to help a female in distress, but another thing entirely to get personally involved with her. But so what if she sleeps on my couch? Well, for one thing, I'll see what she looks like in the morning, and I don't think I can handle that. That long, lustrous brown hair all pooled around her as if she were a cherub. One hell of a sexy cherub, that is. She'll probably sleep in just her t-shirt, or worse, in my jogging pants and t-shirt. Oh God, I have to adjust my belt just thinking about it. What if she calls for me in the night? Like if she has a bad dream or something? I'll see her, I'll never be able to get that image out of my head. Just like I can't get Pam's imagine out of my head. But maybe that's what I need. To get Pam out of my head and get Julia in. Jesus. I'm so confused. Wade would be having a field day right now if he knew.

But she looks at me so innocently. No woman has ever looked at me like that before. Completely vulnerable and placing her safety in my hands. She looks exhausted; like she hasn't slept in days. Maybe she hasn't. Maybe this ass crack has made it so she can't stop thinking about what his next move is. My fist clenches at the thought. She wants to learn how to defend herself, and she was being completely serious about it, too. I'm happy to teach her. It's such a valuable lesson in life, and one that not everybody bothers to learn.

When she looks up at me for an answer, I can tell she silently wants me to say no. Because she doesn't want to impose. She feels like she's caused enough bother, but she's torn between causing more bother and being terrified. I can tell she's fighting tears because she has that redness rimming her eyelids like before, in the car, when she first told me about this scumbag.

"You can sleep in my bed. I'll take the couch." I finally say. "I've been meaning to put another bed in here but haven't gotten around to it. When my brothers come around, they usually stay in a hotel anyway; they can't stand the smell of the horses." I'm babbling, further embarrassing myself. "I have t-shirts and sweat pants in the first two drawers; you're welcome to wear any of it. Just let me grab what I'll need, and I'll make up the couch out here for me."

"Thanks, Colton. I really appreciate it."

I tell her there's an extra toothbrush under the sink and she runs into the bathroom to use it. While I rifle through my drawers, finding my t-shirt and sweat pants, the smallest pair, and place it on the corner of my bed for her. As I grab my shorts and t-shirt, I walk out to the linen closet, and grab my bedding to make up the couch. In minutes, I hear her pad into my room and grab the clothes from the bed. When I hear the bathroom door close again, I know she's in there changing. Oh Lord…give me strength. My heart is doing flip-flops inside my chest, thinking there's a naked woman in my bathroom. I picture her brushing her soft, brown hair and pulling my t-shirt over her naked breasts, and I have to stop myself. I'm never going to get any sleep tonight. Not a prayer. Yeah, cold showers and horror movies are what's in store for me until sunrise.

Five minutes later she walks into the living room, as I'm laying there, wrapped up in the blankets, watching some Friends rerun. "Goodnight, Colton." She says in my white t-shirt and blue sweat pants. "Thanks again, for everything."

"Don't sweat it. Sleep well." I say, saluting her from the couch. I try to make like I'm indifferent, but really, I'm trying to hide the tent under the sheets. She's not wearing a bra under the shirt, and the outline of her pert nipples is showing just enough to see. Not that I was looking, but I could tell from the corner of my eye.

About an hour later, Netflix asks me if I was still there, watching Friends. As it pauses, I hear a weird sound coming from my bedroom. It's a muffled noise, soft sniffling. As I approach the bedroom, I realize that Julia has left the door open, something I always did when I was a kid and had a bad dream or felt unsafe. The floors are nailed down well, so my footsteps are soft. The sound comes again as I'm a few feet from the door. "Julia? Are you okay?"

"I'm fine." The 'n' in 'fine' sounds like a 'd', so it sounds like she said 'I'm find'. Then I realize...she's crying. "Hey, what's wrong?" I whisper, taking a step inside, forgetting about the hour-long hard-on I had.

"Nothing really."

Switching on the bedside lamp, I sit on the side of the bed. "Don't lie to me. Come on, you can tell me." I rub her back gently, since it's facing me, and I don't know what else to do. I don't dare go crawl in beside her from the other side.

"Colton, you really don't want to know."

"Then why did I ask?"

"Because I woke you up with my blubbering." She scoffs. "Thank God Liz snores like a pig and never hears a thing at night."

Jesus, she does this often?

My heart sinks. "Hey. Hey, turn over."

"I don't want to. I look awful." She puts the covers over her head. "My eyes and nose are swollen and red. I've got snot hanging out of my nose, and my lips are chapped. You don't want to see me."

"I'll expect you to wash my bedding in the morning."

"Don't worry. I will." She sobs, as another flood of tears comes.

"Hey, hey. It was a joke. Come here." I pull the covers off her head and push on her shoulder, gently forcing her to go onto her back. She's right, her face is beet red and swollen, like she's come down with a horrible case of the flu. But it's the pain in her face, that comes from her heart, that is truly what doesn't sit well with me. "Are you still feeling scared?"

"No." she sobs. I go to pull a tissue out of the box I usually have on the bedside table, but notice it's gone. Next thing I know, she's lifting it out from under the covers and helping herself to one. Dabbing her eyes and blowing her nose, I rub her arm while she tries to compose herself. Her skin is so soft it makes me ache. "I feel bad."

"You feel bad? Why?"

"Because I'm a mess. I'm this helpless, needy mess. The very person I didn't want to be. And...well, never mind."

Leaning over her, so I'm closer to her face, I push my lips together. I slide my arm down so it cradles her body. "You're not any of those things. What you are is a brave girl who has had a rough time with a real jerk, and you've made the best out of it. You left the first opportunity you had, and now you're doing all you can to move on." I pause, watching her let that statement sink in. "What was the 'never mind' part?"

"I don't want to talk about it."

"Well why not? We've talked about everything else tonight."

"It's not appropriate."

My face scrunches. "Okay." Did something

embarrassing happen, like did she get her period? Did she have an accident?

"Do I need to wash the bedclothes *now*?"

"No, nothing like that." She wipes her face again. The redness is starting to fade as she calms.

"Well, what then?"

She licks her lips, buying time to think. I can tell she wants to choose her words carefully. "I get the feeling that things between you and Pam are still in the air." She pauses. "I wouldn't want to make her think I'm coming between the two of you."

God, is it that obvious? Did my past feelings for Pam really show that much?

"No, sweetie. Things between Pam and I are over. She left over two years ago and never looked back."

"I get that. But…" she trails off.

"But what?"

Then she says four words that I've never been asked before, and they hit me like a clap of thunder.

"Are you over her?"

Staring at this gorgeous, courageous, intelligent woman laying in my bed, I ask myself, if Pam were here right now, who would I choose?

Stroking her cheek, I look deep into her eyes and answer truthfully. "For a long time, yes. I just never knew it until you asked."

Chapter 22

Wade

My head pounds from that last shot of tequila I had last night, or maybe it was the last four shots...who knows. A warm body lies next to me, chest rising and falling, spent from hours of drunken sex after hooking up at a bar last night. The ladies tend to follow me to other clubs, not just when I play at Mingles, which is my regular gig. Thankfully my big brother Colton took the night off from being my bodyguard, so I had my pick of any of the hot chicks clawing their way into my life last night. I chose the brunette, both Colton and I have a thing for brunettes. It's never been a problem, though, big brother stays away from chicks since Pam fucked him up royally.

Mine was smoking hot, way hotter than any other one I've had before. She had legs up to her neck and tits that wouldn't stop...real ones, too. I can tell. I've seen enough of them. This chick howled and grunted and begged me for more all night. It's the rock star thing, see? I mean, I'm not a rock star, but chicks like to see it like I'm one. They treat me like I am, no matter where I go. Once my guitar comes out of the case, and my voice plays over the microphone, they're creaming their jeans waiting for me to finish my set. It's the life.

I don't even remember this chick's name who's in my bed. There's nothing of any value at my place, so I never have a problem leaving them in the morning. Fact, I prefer it that way. Last thing I need is some woman pining over me. I like to get in and get out. Never had a problem with that. Hell, I don't even cook them breakfast in the morning or anything. If I'm lucky, sometimes they hit the road before I even open my eyes. Rolling out of bed, I walk to the bathroom, naked. She doesn't stir, thank God. After relieving myself I hop into the shower. I'm supposed to go over to Colton's place this morning and help him with a few things around the ranch.

Just as I'm finishing up, I hear the shower door open, and my guest appears. Mascara is smudged all over her eyes, since she was too drunk to wash her face after I fucked the life out of her last night. "Morning." She says to me in a gravelly voice, like she's smoked half a pack of Marlboros last night. "Mind if I shower? I've gotta be at work in a half an hour."

"Err...sure. I'm done now anyway." I say, briskly grabbing a towel and wrapping it around myself. Before I finish dressing, she's already done, making me wonder if she washed everything. Suddenly, I feel like I need to take another shower. She walks out of the bathroom, surprisingly fresh, pulls her dress over her head and stuffs her feet into her heels. With a swift kiss on the cheek, she's gone, without even a 'see ya later, babe'. Just the way I like it.

When I reach Colton's place, I go and say hi to the horses first. Maya's chomping on a stick of hay, while Rebel is grazing in the pasture. Colton must have left them out last night, because the stable door is wide open. He does that if it's a mild night and the wind is low, like it was yesterday. "Hey, guys." I say, patting Maya on the flank. "Did your daddy feed you breakfast yet?"

Maya flicks her ears, indicating that she's happy, but I see no feed in the trough. "I'll go see what your daddy's up to." I tell her, but not before scratching Rebel on the snout. Using my key, I open Colton's door and find my way inside. Removing my shoes, I listen for the shower. Nothing. *The lazy fuck must still be asleep.* Turning on the coffee maker, I check to see if he's got any bacon and eggs in the fridge. Bingo! I set the food on the counter so I can prepare it after I wake the fucker up, and I head over to his room.

Colton never closes his bedroom door, so I just walk in.

Whoooaaa!!!

"Oh, shit. Colton, sorry. I didn't know you had

company."

Colton is laying on the left side of the bed, on top of the covers. His head is on the pillow, one hand is under the pillow, while the other hand is draping the body of his guest on the other side. His guest is under the covers, tucked tight like a burrito. First Colton shouts out, then his guest squeals, sitting up straight.

"Jesus Christ, Wade! What the hell are you doing here?"

"Oh, fuck! I'm sorry, bro! I had no idea!" My hands are in the air as if I was being held at gunpoint. Until I realize who the guest is. "Whooaaa...hey...Julia, is it?" I snicker, giving her a once-over. Her t-shirt is just transparent enough that I can see her nipples underneath. Instant fucking boner! I can't take my eyes off her chest until she realizes that's where I'm looking, and she covers up. Colton looks like he's going to skin me alive. His icy glare says, 'back off!', which is why I keep my hands in the air. "Sorry, man. If I'd known you two were..." I clear my throat, "Well, if I'd known, I would have knocked first." I say, even though the bedroom door is open.

"It's not what you think, Wade." Colton says, saving Julia's honor. "We didn't sleep together."

I chuckle. "Well you're in bed, and...*she's* in your bed. Sure looks like you slept together to me."

"Alright, asshole. We *slept* in the bed together. But nothing beyond that happened."

Turning my back, I shake my head. "Alright...if you say so...sure ain't what it looks like to me."

"Just what in the hell are you doing here at eight o'clock on a Monday morning anyway?" he calls after me. I turn back around to him.

"Did you forget? You asked me to come over and give you a hand here. It was Saturday that you asked me, I think."

Colton rolls his eyes. "Jesus, I said *next* Monday. The fundraiser isn't until *next* Saturday. We've still got nearly two weeks to prepare for it."

Fisting my hand into a ball, I look up at the ceiling and hit my forehead with my hand. "Shit, seriously, sorry big brother. My mistake. You know I don't know one day from the next."

"That's alright."

I look at Julia, who is mortified. Her knees are bent up to her chin, and she's hugging herself. She looks like shit, aside from her hair hanging out nice all over the bed, like Colton had fucked it out of the tidy ponytail she had it in when I saw her the first time. "You're Liz's sister, aren't you? The one who got creamed by that biker bitch at the club Saturday night?"

Julia gives me an eye roll. Colton sighs. "Not helping, man."

"Sorry. Anyway, did Liz give you the boot? That why you needed somewhere to crash?"

"I liked it better when you thought your brother and I had sex." She says, unimpressed.

Colton makes a snorting noise. "No, she didn't get kicked out. It's none of your business why she's here."

Raising a hand again, I take it down a notch. "Okay, okay. You're right, it's none of my business. This has all been just a misunderstanding."

"And you're not going to blab to anyone that she was here, right?" Colton's tone is firm.

Taking my index finger and thumb, I drag them across my closed mouth. "My lips are sealed, my brother. Hey, you guys hungry? I'm starving."

Glancing at Julia, Colton asks her if she's hungry. "I could eat." She says. "Can I use your shower first?"

"Sure." Colton glares at me. "I'll meet you in the kitchen, Wade." He says through gritted teeth.

I hear him get her clean towels and two minutes later, he's in the kitchen with me. As nonchalant as possible, Colton begins pulling the frying pan out of the cabinet, and breaking the eggs into the pan, while I set three mugs on the counter for coffee. I keep looking at him expectantly, but he's hell bent on ignoring me.

After flipping the eggs over once, his nostrils flare as he widens his eyes at me. "What?" he all but shouts.

"What's the deal? She stayed overnight but you didn't bang her?"

"Quite a concept for you to understand, I know."

I ignore the slight. "Is she like...frigid? I've heard of that. Some chicks are like guys...can't get it up."

"You're sick."

"What the fuck's going on, man? You haven't had a chick in bed since Pam, and now you have a chance, and...nothing?"

"Would you keep your voice down? She didn't come over for sex, she came over for..."

"What?" I'm dying.

"I can't tell you." I can tell it pains him to say that. There's nothing we don't know about each other. I know all his secrets. He knows all mine.

"Oh, I get it." my voice is low. "She's got like...issues." I shudder.

"*She* doesn't have issues. It's...fuck! I can't tell you!"

"Fine."

We're both silent as the plates get filled with eggs, bacon, and hash browns. I fill the mugs with coffee and place them on the table. "So, what is it with you and chicks, man? Always gotta get one with issues?"

"She's not...it's not..." his face is reddened with anger. "I can't fucking tell you!"

Julia walks into the room then. "You might as well tell him, Colton. He's probably going to find out anyway." There's a pissy edge to her tone.

"No, hey, it's okay, Julia. I respect your privacy." I try to save face.

"Yeah, he doesn't need to know. It's okay." Colton says, pulling a chair out for her at the table. Her hair is wet and straight and spans all the way to her ass. She has no makeup on, but her face is still okay-looking without it. Her bra is back on, which makes me sad.

Colton serves her a plate full of food and she begins eating it like it's her last meal. Big brother keeps watching her as we eat. "You need anything else?" he asks her, but she shakes her head no.

Suddenly, when her plate is almost empty, she blurts. "Wade, you ever see a guy with a white BMW, souped up, cruising around town?"

I think Colton's eyes are going to burst out of his head. "Souped up?" I have good experience with cars, seeing as I drive a good one myself.

"Yeah, like, tinted windows, two doors, lowered, Florida plates?" she adds.

"Hm. Skirts?"

"Yep."

"I'm not like a hundred percent sure, but I did see a sweet white BMW last night on my way home. But I was a little distracted, so I didn't really look that hard." When I say 'distracted' I wink.

"Distracted?" she asks.

Colton places a hand on her arm. "Believe me, you don't want to know. It's some lewd story, guaranteed."

"So, in other words, you were getting a blow job by some chick you met at a bar, right?" Julia says bluntly, surprising us both.

"Err...well...yeah," I chuckle. *I like this girl.*

"So, you think you saw this car, but you couldn't swear to it." she repeats.

"Sure."

"Do me a favor and keep your eye out for it. If you see it, pull over and kick the shit out of him for me, okay?"

Holy shit.

Colton's jaw drops.

"Tell all your friends. Tell everyone you know. In fact, Colton," she looks at my big brother, and he closes his mouth. "I should tell the police, shouldn't I? Especially after last night. You still have the bogus business card, right?"

"Whoa, whoa, what?" I raise my hand.

They both ignore me.

"Yeah, I do. Are you sure you want to do that?"

"Of course. This guy is an imposter. He should be reported."

"Hold the phone, here. What's going on?" I interrupt.

Julia looks at me and tosses a lock of hair that had fallen on her chest, over her shoulder. "The reason I slept here last night is because my ex-fiance, who is a lunatic, has followed me here from Florida. He was looking for me last night here and showed up at Colton's door with a fake business card, posing as some property investor."

"What?" I squeak.

Okay, this chick is Cuckoo for Cocoa Puffs! Colton, you sure know how to pick 'em!

"I was too scared to go back to Liz's last night, so I stayed here."

"It's true, Wade." Colton grabs a card from the counter and shows it to me. "See? The guy is a fraud. He doesn't exist at this company. I checked it out."

"Then you should report it for sure. Give the cops his license plate number and call it a day."

"Well, if he's gone to the trouble of getting fake business cards done up, then there's no telling what else he'll do to disguise himself. He's got money; he can switch cars."

Colton is suddenly interested. "What does he do for a living. For real, I mean."

"Him and his brother run a specialty car shop with his dad. They distribute obscure yet extremely expensive and hard to find car parts. His dad also sells his cars at those Barrett Jackson car auctions."

"So, he'll have no problem switching cars." I add.

"Exactly." She says.

"So, what are you going to do? Assuming you report him to police?" I ask.

"I don't know. I mean, he's not violent, but he's a psychopath. Staying out of his way would be best."

"She can't be left alone." Colton says. "Not until the cops find him."

"Why doesn't she come to the club with us tonight?

Blake won't mind if she hangs out there. She can wipe down tables and stuff."

"I'm not sure if that's such a good idea after what happened the other night." Julia says.

"Ah, come on, you were more embarrassed than anything, right?" I argue. "Your back's fine, isn't it?"

"Yeah," she mutters.

"Listen, babe, it's up to you." I put two hands in the air. Colton shoots me a look, probably because I called her 'babe'.

"I think it's a good idea, Julia." Colton says.

"Alright, fine." She relents.

"So," I say, feeling brave. "How come you didn't just sleep on the couch, Colton?"

Chapter 23

Colton

When I answer her question, 'are you over her?', I feel it fitting to ask another question of my own. After she wipes her eyes again, she consents. "Why did you agree to marry the first guy you had a relationship with? Was it just because your dad hooked you up with him?" My tone is not condescending; more like I'm asking her to level with me.

"It's not as simple as it sounds, Colton. My dad and I are very close, and because up until today, he and my sister didn't talk for thirteen years, and my mom left and remarried years ago, so I'm all he really has left, aside from business associates. I didn't want to let him down. Dad means everything to me, and he thought he knew what was best for me."

"I bet he feels like a turd now...wait, does he know?"

"Yeah, he found out. The loser called him looking for me. Dad's in town now."

"He sounds like an honorable man."

She smiles warmly. "He is. Aside from Liz, he's my best friend. He would do anything for me, and I would do anything for him."

"Poor guy. How was he to know?"

Julia shrugs and her eyes begin to get heavy. Watching her wind down I yawn. It's contagious. "You think you're okay to go to sleep now?"

She wiggles further into the sheets and sighs contentedly. "Just stay a little while longer. Just until I fall asleep."

It's endearing that she's so child-like. I climb over the bed and lay on the pillow beside her. "You want me to turn the light off?"

"Hm." She answers, opening her eyes halfway.

Her eyes close and after a few minutes, I'm scared to move, to startle her, so I stay. I don't even bother to turn off the lamp. I had no idea Wade would be here in the morning.

What an asshole when he showed up. The hungry look he gave her, checking out her breasts, made me want to plough him. If he wasn't my brother, I would have. It looked bad; us sleeping in my bed together. Thank God I had the sense to stay on top of the sheets. I didn't trust myself to go under them. Knowing her warm, soft body was laying there, I might not have been able to stop myself. It has been way too long since I've been with a woman.

The idea of having her at Mingles tonight isn't the worst idea. It just means that my attention will be divided between her and Wade. Although Wade I watch for different reasons. Knowing him, he hooked up last night when he wasn't under my watchful eye, so tonight he might be a little tamer with the ladies, among other things. As long as both are safe, Julia can hang out at the club every night until the dirt bag is caught or gone for good.

After Wade left, we called the police. They came by and took a statement and a description of what John looks like. Julia provided them with a recent picture and his contact information. They said the only thing that could be done at this point is to pick him up for questioning. Unless he does something out of the boundaries of the law, they can't arrest him. So far all he's done is impersonate another person, which isn't illegal. They said they'd keep an eye out for him, though, in case there is any trouble, but there would be no arrest at this time. All the more reason to keep Julia close.

Maybe even get closer to her...

***

Bingo and Blake are already at Mingles when I arrive. I don't see Wade's truck anywhere, and none of his band members' vehicles are there, either.

"Colton!" Blake calls when he sees me. "Give me a hand with this shipment of hooch, will ya?"

"Yeah, sure. I'll be right there."

We both scooch down, picking up the box of alcohol that had just been delivered. "I'd ask Bingo to give me a hand again, but he already gives me grief about helping with the chairs." Blake chuckles. "I swear he's worried he'll break a nail."

"Naw, he just doesn't like manual labor. He's happiest standing by the door."

"He's a damn paper weight." Blake smirks, unimpressed.

"What do you think...will it be busy tonight?"

We place the box on top of the bar, and I help Blake pull the bottles out of the box one by one, setting them on the counter. Blake then begins unscrewing the caps and replacing them with metal valves he pulls from a towel he'd laid down, so the valves can dry after being in the dishwasher.

"Nah, it's hard to say. Mondays can go either way. You know how it is." he hesitates. "Why do you ask?"

"Liz talked to you about her sister, Julia, right?"

"Yeah, damn shame that. Of course, I told her she could bring her by whenever she wanted. Liz's a good girl, I imagine her sister is, too." He winks and holds up a bottle. "So long as she don't sue me for getting shoved the other night, we'll be fine."

"I'm certain she won't."

"She ain't hard on the eyes, neither, eh? Wouldn't hurt to have another pretty face 'round here. Course, she's young enough to be my daughter." He chuckles, and then something catches his eye on my face.

"What?"

"Well I ain't seen that look in a while. Maybe never."

"What are you talking about?"

Blake is about my height, but wiry. He points a finger at me and closes one eye. "That. That look. The one that says 'keep your hands off, she's mine'. Never seen that look on ya before. It suits ya."

"I don't know what you're talking about, Blake. There's no look on my face other than from the reaction to your cheap cologne."

"Haha, yeah, we'll go with that."

The front door opens, and Julia and Liz walk in.

"There's another look I ain't never seen on your face." Blake murmurs under his breath. The bottles have valves on them, and the damp towel lays on the stainless-steel bar.

"Shut up, old man." I chuckle, picking the used towel up and throwing it on his chest, good-naturedly.

Chapter 24

Julia

Sleeping in Colton's bed last night was...great. Never thought I'd say that about another man again, but it was definitely a pleasant experience. In fact, until his brother Wade walked in and scared the dickens out of me, I was having the best sleep I'd had in a long time. I felt bad for Colton. Brothers, I've heard, can be a real pain in the ass when it comes to embarrassing situations. Hopefully Wade will let it go and not razz Colton about it for too long.

It was fun learning self defence with Colton. I can see why he makes a great bouncer at the club. He knows how to handle himself. Granted, I'm a girl, and we were just practicing, but he knew exactly how to show me what to do in the event of an attack. He didn't have to show me, but he wanted to. Colton's a sweet guy and cares a lot about people. That's pretty obvious from the way he helped me out, and from the sounds of it he looks after his neighbor a lot, too, plus his life revolves around his little brother Wade, and he talks a lot about his other brothers. He has a big heart, and cares about keeping people safe.

Going to Mingles tonight isn't exactly what I had in mind, but it's better than staying at home alone, watching every second, waiting to see if John comes around. For all I know, he went back to Florida the second he saw Colton. From the sounds of it, Colton told him where to go in not so many words. If he's smart, he'll heed the advice. Then again, John is crazy, there's no doubt about it. So I guess it's best to prepare for the worst.

Liz loaned me another shirt and a pair of pants to wear so I blend in tonight. Here's hoping things go better than my last experience at Mingles. At least I know a few moves now, so if someone tries to get in my way, I'll be better prepared. As we sit at the kitchen table, Liz helps me with eye makeup, as we get ready to leave. Dad had taken Nate out for lunch and instructed me to keep my car in the garage, out of sight for now. He would send over his limo to take us wherever we needed to go. Whenever. God bless Dad.

Nate walks by the table, munching a sandwich as big as his head. "Didn't you just have dinner? And didn't grampa take you out for a huge lunch?" Liz asks.

"I'm hungry."

"Jesus. I'm glad I get good tips. You would starve."

"No, I wouldn't. I'd just go over to Pete's house."

Pete is his best friend. Nate is always over there if he's not at home.

"Does Pete's mom have trouble keeping her fridge full?"

"Don't know. He just brings me food when he gets some."

She slaps him playfully on the rear end. "Did you have fun catching up with grampa?"

"Yeah," his voice cracks with pubescent charm. "He's cool. He's gonna take me golfing tomorrow morning."

"You sure you can manage getting out of bed before the crack of dawn?" I ask.

"Sure." He shrugs. "I get free food."

"Get outta here." Liz says, giving him a shove as she giggles. Then she turns back to me, when she hears Nate's bedroom door close. "So, tell me the truth this time. You just slept in his bed...there was no hanky-panky going on?"

"Why is that so hard to believe? Do I *look* like I'm easy? Do I *act* like I'm easy?"

"No."

"And does Colton?"

She gapes at me. "Of course not! Jesus, I'm surprised he doesn't have a sign on his door that says, 'No Women Allowed'."

"I told you what happened with his ex-wife."

"Yeah, I figured something like that happened. I'm surprised he told you though."

"I told him enough, too. It was only fair."

Leaning back, Liz inspects my face. "Perfect. Want me to French braid your hair?"

Lifting a brow, I say flatly. "We already talked about this. No."

An hour later, we're dropped off by dad's limo driver at the front doors of Mingles. Bingo is standing at the door, giving it a scrub with a cloth bar towel and a bottle of some industrial strength cleaner. I call him King Kong. He doesn't seem to mind. "Wade and the band aren't here yet, but Blake and Colton are. Go on in."

Liz shoots me a look. "What?" I ask.

"Nothing." She speaks in a higher, teasing tone.

Colton is helping Blake pull all the chairs down off the tables. The floor is freshly cleaned. With all the lights on, the bar looks strange, almost industrial; like we're entering a warehouse.

"Hey, ladies. How's it going?" Blake asks, giving us both a wink.

"We're good." Liz calls so her voice can carry to where they are at the other end of the room. "Where do you want us to start? Over here?" Liz points to the grouping of chairs that are still on top of the tables.

"Nah, just grab a couple of polishing cloths and give these tables a wipe. They've been cleaned but not polished yet."

Colton walks over to the bar and picks up a set of polishing cloths from the box Blake had placed on the counter earlier. He tosses one to each of us. "Did you get to take a nap?" Colton addresses me. He has a rag hanging out of his back pocket. For whatever reason, it looks sexy. His purple Mingles shirt is strained at his biceps as he tosses the towels to us. A memory of waking up next to him last night, as his arm was draped over me, comes into my head. I shake it off quickly.

"For a while, you?"

"I crashed the whole afternoon on the couch."

"Thanks for breakfast, by the way."

"Don't thank me, thank Wade. He's the one who made it." We are interrupted by a bang on the back door. "Speak of the devil."

Wade walks in, carrying his guitar case. "Hey, big brother." He shoots me a look that says we shared something intimate and embarrassing earlier, that he is sure to lord over me for a while. "Hey, Julia. Nice...shirt."

"Wade." I say in greeting, pursing my lips together, unimpressed.

An hour later the bar opens for business. Wade is playing a few mid-range tunes; soft rock. One of the other waitresses, Michelle, gets up and sings a catchy duet with him. Blake comes over and watches. "You girls can take a break and do a little dancing if you want. There ain't nobody here yet, anyway." He says to me, Liz and Cheryl, the fourth waitress. It's just past ten o'clock, and there are only five other patrons sitting in the back; five older ladies, one looks like she's been crying.

"What the hell, sis...you feel like dancing?" Liz says to me, twirling her towel above her head like it's a lasso.

"Sure," I say, mirroring what she's doing. "Woooo!" We start dancing, and Wade pumps it up a notch, interacting with us.

"Hey, ladies, which one of you wants to hear us sing a sexier tune together? Think Michelle here can handle it?"

We both answer with a loud whistle. In the corner of my eye, I see Colton come over and stand next to us. He has his arms draped over his chest, tucked into each other, and he loosens them, letting his arms hang by his sides. Wade catches sight of him. "Ooo, what about you, big brother? You wanna hear a sexier tune, or a slooooow one? Any requests? I do covers, too!"

Blake has one in mind. "How about 'Take This Job and Shove It'?"

Wade shakes his head. "Listen, Grampa, something that isn't as old as you!"

Bingo lets in a pack of about ten people; girls. One is wearing a banner across her body that says, 'Bride to Be'. Behind them is another group; a mix of people. They all look to have arrived together.

"Since when do chicks have a bachelorette party on a Monday night?" Blake says to us.

"Check to see if our 'Bride to Be' drinks anything...could be a shotgun wedding and she's expecting." Liz says, pointing to her temple.

"Ah," Blake is impressed.

Wade heeds the onslaught of guests and starts playing. Michelle goes back to her post, on the other side of the bar, and I go over and clear the table for the five ladies who had arrived earlier. Taking their orders, I walk over to the bar and set the tray down, removing the empty beer bottles. Behind me, Colton comes over and places his hand on the small of my back. "I let Bingo know about our potential guest, hope you don't mind."

His touch startles me at first, but then the warmth of it relaxes me. "Sure, I figured that was the plan. What will he do if John does show up?"

"We'll have a little chat with him and politely ask him to leave." Colton says, pushing a lock of hair off my face. The touching I can get used to. Those bright blue eyes seem to warm when he speaks to me.

"What if he doesn't?"

Colton smiles. "We have protocols in place for guests like that. Not to worry." Rubbing my back gently, he then gives me a friendly pat, and walks towards the entrance. I watch him walk at a slow, measured pace. He has the perfect back under that shirt; his muscles are just enough, and they look squeezable for soft embraces and tight for grabbing hold of in a moment of passion. For a second, I picture my hands draped by his shoulder blades, pulling him closer to me from under him.

Eyes widening, I shake myself from my reverie as Blake asks me a second time what I want to order. I hadn't heard him the first time. After pulling the scratch pad out of my apron, I give him the order. When I look back at Colton as I wait for the order, his gaze is directly on me. Arms crossed over his chest and tucked into his underarms, he looks as sexy as hell. A small tattoo pokes out from under his shirt on his left bicep. His hair is curling with the humidity looming in the air. Soft curls behind his ears, almost reaching his shoulders, begging to be touched. *What is wrong with me?*

Blake pokes me on the shoulder. "Hey, Dazed and Confused. Your order is up."

"Sorry." I blush, walking away with the tray. I can feel Colton's gaze watching me as I walk back over to the table and deliver the drinks.

"Looks like our 'Bride to Be' *is* knocked up after all. I should have made a bet." Liz brags as she comes over to me on her way to the bar. "Six weeks pregnant and heading to DisneyWorld for the wedding and honeymoon."

"Wow, that's ambitious."

"I'll say. All I got was a Pastor and dinner for ten at Pizza Hut."

"I remember."

"This place isn't so bad, is it? I mean, Wade's pretty cool with the music, and there isn't too much trouble here, right? I think I might hang on to this job part-time, even if I do get accepted into college."

"*If?* Don't worry, Liz, you will get accepted. And yeah, it's not a bad idea to work part-time. That's what I did."

Wade begins playing a slow ballad. Despite the even number of males and females in the bar, nobody is on the dance floor. "Shit, what does he do when he clears the place like that?" I ask Liz.

"He either changes gears back to faster stuff if he can, or we grab a guy and make for the dance floor if nobody's causing any trouble. Quick! Go grab Colton and I'll make for Dan over there by the washrooms."

Dan is another bouncer; he looks like his eyes are glazing over, since the bar is so quiet.

"Are you crazy? I'm not dancing with Colton!" I hiss, trying to keep my voice down.

"Why not, you slept in his bed, didn't you?"

I look at Wade and he widens his eyes at me, and then cocks his head towards his older brother. His expression says, 'Please rescue me'. Colton catches the look and at the same time, we look at each other. Once more, I look at Wade and he gives me the same eyes again. I consider running for the washroom, but it's too late, Colton is already making his way over to me. Liz has Dan's shirt by the hem and is dragging him to the floor.

"Care to help my little brother out?" he asks. He offered me a thin smile, but his eyes are dancing with delight.

"S...sure."

Taking my hand in his, Colton leads me to the dance floor. He softly brushes his hand over my side as he lets go of my hand. Fumbling, I can't tell if he wants to do this high-school-style, with both my hands around his neck, or grown-up-style, with one hand around his neck, and one hand on his chest. When he takes my hand in his, I realize we aren't in high school. He senses my nerves and smiles. "It's okay, we only do this until the dance floor fills up. I usually don't get picked to dance; Blake normally does the honors, but my little brother's getting back at me."

The warmth of his hand caresses the small of my back as he gently rubs with his thumb, sending delicious shivers up my spine. His other hand, muscled and able, embraces my hand in his like a protective cocoon. My head gently leans towards his neck, where I catch his scent; woody and musky, just the perfect blend of man and clean. I can feel my pulse quicken with the closeness to him.

"For what?" I ask. "Is he mad at you for something?"

"Believe, me, you don't want to pull at that thread,

sweetie." He chuckles softly. "You know my brother has a lewd streak in him."

"Really." I say knowingly.

"He doesn't always like my advice."

"Ah. I guess girls are different. Liz and I almost always see eye-to-eye."

"Probably because there's such a small gap in age."

The music is slow and soft, and Colton holds the rhythm with his hips. I can feel him moving my body with his hand, guiding me with the music. Every few seconds he slides his thumb down my hand or rubs the small of my back with the other hand. It takes everything in my power not to rake my fingers through the hair at the back of his neck. It's sitting softly on my hand, begging to be touched. Finally, I can't *not* touch it. He lets out a soft gasp when I snake my fingers across the nape of his neck. The sound sets my heart pounding, and I'm suddenly aware that he can feel it against his chest.

Part of me wants the dance floor to fill so I can flee, the other part of me wants to grasp all his hair and bite his neck, suck it until I leave one of those big red hickies, branding him as mine. The skin looks so soft, and I can see a large vein pulsing, responding to my touch. This is all so foreign to me it's scary. The very bulk of his arms tightens around me, as though he can lift me without effort, and I picture him forcing me against the wall while kissing me hungrily. I have to clear my throat to stop the intensity of my fantasy.

When the song is coming to a close, Colton gazes at me with those sexy blue, intense eyes, and says. "Well, thanks for the dance."

Speechless, I simply nod.

Chapter 25

Colton

My little brother is a punk; always has been and always will be. He'll do just about anything to get a rise out of me, and he sure did. Of course, it wasn't the fact that I had to dance with Julia that annoyed me, it's the fact that the girl is vulnerable, and doesn't need to be pressured into anything, and what Wade pulled tonight, put pressure on her. He *never* plays a slow tune when the dance floor thins out. *Ever*. He did it tonight just to get my blood boiling. He knew I'd have to dance with her, and he picked the right moment to do it.

Alright, I'll admit dancing with her was phenomenal. With her body pressed up against mine I lost all sense of everything. Her body fit perfectly in mine, and don't think I didn't notice that straight off the hop. When that happens, I know there's going to be trouble. The poor girl was nervous as a teenager, dancing for the first time with a boy, and I felt badly for her. I tried to be as gentle and as platonic as possible, but *man*, she's like a magnet. When she touched the back of my neck, I thought that was the end of it all; that every physical defence I had was done. It took everything in my power not to kiss her right there.

When the song was over, she scurried away from me like a scared rabbit. That woman...does things to me. I keep picturing her sleeping next to me, her soft, glowing skin, shimmering in the moonlight. Her perfect mouth, plump and supple, just waiting to be kissed. That smile, that voice. I wanted to go after her and make sure that she was okay, but something stopped me. *Maybe she doesn't feel for me the way I feel for her? Stupid...she's probably completely turned off men for good after the loser she was engaged to.*

"Colton!" Blake shouts. "Bingo needs you by the door. Says he needs to take a leak."

"Be right there." I answer, making my way to the

front door. When I arrive, Bingo has a lineup of about ten people waiting to get in.

"Thanks, man. Be two minutes."

"Take your time." I say, scanning the guests for those who need to be carded. Mondays we don't charge a cover, so I'm letting them in, one by one, past the metal detector. One guy sets it off; he'd forgotten he had metal studs on his belt. Once he takes it off, he gets in on the first try.

"Hi, Colton." A female voice says. It's the brown-toothed girl from a couple of nights ago. The one who was talking with Cheetah. "Fancy seeing you out here." She purrs.

"Just covering for Bingo. Have you got I.D.?" I ask, even though she's probably in her fifties. I ask just to piss her off. I don't like her or her friend.

"Flatterer." She says, evidently taking my request as flirtation.

"Your friend Cheetah with you tonight?" I ask, filling the void of silence while she searches her purse for her driver's license.

"He ain't no friend of mine." she answers, handing me the card with her name on it. I study it quickly, even though it's unnecessary.

"Head on in." I say, just as Bingo reappears.

"Blake needs you in the back. Another damn delivery came after hours."

Unimpressed, I shake my head. "Alright. Call me if you need anything."

"Thanks, man."

Blake is already pulling beer boxes off the back of the truck when I arrive. "There's just a few here, Colton. Apparently, the guy short-shipped earlier in the week. It's not a big deal, just a pain in the ass."

"That's no problem, Blake. You head back in behind the bar and I'll take care of this."

Nodding once, Blake disappears. A set of headlights catches my eye in the distance. There is a car sitting in the rear parking lot. When he sees me, he turns around and heads back towards the front. I can't see the license plate in the dark, nor can I tell the color of the car. It definitely isn't a white BMW; maybe a maroon or dark red Charger; something bigger than a sedan. "He been here a while?" I ask the delivery driver.

"Couple minutes. No more than that."

He's probably looking for a place to smoke pot or something. I don't pay more attention, but I put it in my mind to let Bingo know when I go back in. After I sign the delivery slip, I bring the beer in and put it in the storage room, slamming right into Julia on my way in.

"Shit! Sorry, sweetie...are you okay?" I blurt, putting the beer box on the floor. Julia is holding a pile of trays in her hand. She must have been in the storage room getting more while I was out getting the beer. "Sorry, you've gotta turn on the light when you come in here, or nobody'll see you."

"I'm okay. Sorry, I was just coming in for a second to get more trays from the top of this box here. Blake asked me to. The crowd is starting to grow out there."

She's holding a set of square trays; the wrong ones. Blake must have forgotten he'd pulled the round ones out earlier to wash. But I can't think to tell her that, because the glint in her eyes in the darkness is playing with my mind. "Sweetie, those are the wrong ones."

Looking down, Julia is confused. I take the trays from her and place them back on top of the boxes. "Oh," she breathes. The look in her eyes is dark, like she's counting the fleck in my eyes or something.

"You okay?" I whisper, sliding a hand down her face. Taking a step closer to her, I close the gap between us. Her back is against the storage room wall, and there are only a few feet of space between us and the door. With the light off, it's like we're the only two people that exist, and nobody can see us. The scent of coconuts from her hair is wafting up my nose. The softness of her face makes me crave touching her all over. Remembering how she touched me on the dance floor, and how I nearly lost it, I can't hold back with her inches from me.

When she nods, I cup either side of her face with my hands, and hungrily kiss her lips, like it's the last kiss I'll ever have in my life. At first, she doesn't kiss me back, she lets out a small cry, but doesn't push me away. Instead, she opens her mouth, and takes me in. Our tongues dance to the gentle, yet needy rhythm of the kiss. My teeth find her lips and I bite her gently. She breathes heavily, and finds my tongue, sucking it greedily. Below the belt, my cock twitches with need. If it wasn't for us being stuck together in a five-foot-deep broom closet, I'd take her right here and now.

Suddenly, we hear a crash, and the door opens quickly. "Colt—" It's Dan, breathless. I break away from Julia quickly and swear under my breath. "Shit! Colton, we've got trouble out front." He speaks quickly, like a bomb is about to go off.

"Be right there." Both our chests heave as he closes the door. I lean my forehead against hers. "I'm so sorry about that. I don't know what I was thinking."

She doesn't respond, but she tries to catch her breath by licking her lips.

"I'm really sorry." I repeat. "It won't happen again." I run out the door, leaving her there breathless.

Chapter 26

John

I knew she was mine from the moment I saw her. All her brown hair in tangles, green eyes, and an endearing smile that grabbed my heart instantly. Julia is perfect for me, and I'm perfect for her, in every conceivable way. My father, the avid golfer, met her father on the course one day, exchanged notes on business, and became instant associates. As soon as Julia walked in on a business meeting between the three of us, I knew my life would never be the same.

Two years later, we were engaged. It was my plan to marry right away, but my father can't make up his mind on where to place me permanently. Hence, the wedding had to be put on hold. It frustrates me to no end, but there is nothing I can do if I want to stay in my dad's good graces. He's a hard ass and doesn't bend the rules for anyone. Julia has been very patient, but there have been backlashes. Case in point: frequent business trips pull me away from my girl. As often as I can take her with me, I do, but my dad forbids me from taking her on all of them.

The one time I leave her alone, that *thing* she calls a friend…*Mary*, took her out to some disgusting, degrading, meat market club, dressing her half naked in clothes unfit for a vagrant. She let her dance with some pervert who looked young enough to be in high school; grinding and touching what's mine. Oh, I found out about it. I have my ways. I know everywhere she is all the time, whether she knows it or not. That's my right. Protecting what's mine. Sure, I tried to hit him, this juvenile who copped feels on my girl, but Julia was so drunk, she didn't know what she was doing.

She's angry at me now, for embarrassing her. She went to visit her sister in North Carolina, only she lied to me and told me she went away with that *thing* Mary she calls a friend. I know why she lied. It was the anger. We'll kiss and make up when I talk to her. This cat and mouse game is getting annoying. Especially since she's hanging around with some Neanderthal her sister introduced her to at that armpit of a pub she works at. I can take him. I know it because I staked him out at his house. Sure, he's all muscle and he's got that look in his eye, the eye of the tiger, but I can take him. There is no doubt about it. I'll pick my moment and go in for the kill.

Sure, he's got money, probably more than me, but he can't give her what I can. I've got it all: money, a huge cock, contacts that would put his to shame, and a father who gives me everything that I want, as long as I give him what he wants in return. Plus, when my dad retires, all that's his is mine. He told me as much. I stand to be one stinking rich son of a bitch when he makes his mind up. Julia has no problem waiting. She's just a schoolteacher, making a pittance for putting up with all those brats. But when we marry, she'll stop doing that. We haven't discussed all the plans yet, but she'll be happy to wait on me hand and foot, preparing our huge house for guests and business meetings. She loves to entertain; way more than she loves the brats.

Gregory Abbott is a fool. He was smart to do business with my dad, but as far as his daughters are concerned, the man might as well have his head buried in the sand. Liz, the stupid whore, got herself knocked up when she was too young to drink at her own wedding and married some loser who couldn't rub two pennies together, and foolishly, she had his kid. Not shocking, after thirteen years of being caught up in a peddler's life, he flees, leaving no return address. I love Julia way too much to ever do that. Hell, I'd follow her to the ends of the earth and back. Nothing would get in the way of keeping what's mine. Gregory thought Julia was away with Mary, but I knew better. He's here in North Carolina with them both; who's laughing now?

Julia spent the night with the Neanderthal last night, but I know my girl wouldn't do anything foolish. She loves me more than life itself and she'll forgive me. If I can keep that Mary thing away from her, she'll come to her senses. My girl could never stay away from me for this long. She's at the sleazy club with her sister and the Neanderthal tonight. I've been waiting outside for her. I know when she sees me, she'll come running. The Neanderthal called the cops on me for sniffing around his house, so I had to change cars. I'll do anything to get my girl back. She'll see that.

As I sit in the back parking lot, I see the Neanderthal come out back to pick up a delivery. My fist balls up instantly, but I keep my temper at bay. It's too early and I have to pick my moment carefully. Julia doesn't like to see my temper, but I'll bare my teeth at that Neanderthal if he puts his filthy paws on my girl. I'll crush his skull with the baseball bat I keep in my car. Or slice his throat with the knife I have in the glove compartment. He won't know what hit him. He'll be too worried about his hair; he's a pretty boy. I'll fix it so his face is fucked up like Sylvester Stallone in the Rocky movies.

Some stupid fucker parks beside me while I wait in the front. He checks out my wheels and I figure he looks dumb enough to do a favor for a hundred bucks. His car is a beat up Ford Escape with rusted rims and sidewalls. He's got another, even stupider looking, guy sitting next to him. They murmur something to each other before getting out of the car. I roll down my window and look at them. The parking lot is well lit. I can see that the driver is missing a tooth. He's wearing a cap that says 'Cheetah' on it.

"Hey, nice wheels. Where'd you get the sick color? I've been looking at a paint job like that. This is my work car. I bring it here because I don't want the good one to get stolen from this place."

"I co-own a specialty car parts company."

They both look at each other and high-five like two fags. "No shit, eh?" the stupid one sticks out his hand. "Hey, I'm Cheetah. That ain't my real name but nobody knows the difference."

I shake his hand and he introduces his friend who has a forgettable name. I'd forgotten it before we finished shaking hands, interrupting him with my request. "Hey, you feel like making an easy hundred?"

They open their mouths and stick their tongues out, holding their baby finger and thumbs in the air. If they didn't stop doing that, I'm going to have to forget the whole thing and punch the shit out of them both. "All you have to do is go up to the bouncer; the big guy in the front, not any of them inside, and ask if Julia Abbott is in there tonight."

"Well, shit, how the hell're they gonna know that?"

"Don't worry; they'll know. She's related to one of the waitresses."

"Ooohhhh, we know the waitresses there." Cheetah makes a disgusting whistling noise. "That's half the reason we go every night. I've had so much titty from this place."

"I'll bet."

Cheetah gets his back up. "Well, hey, I ain't doing a thing until I see the cash first."

I reach into my back pocket and pull out my wallet. "Here's fifty. You get the other fifty when you do what I asked. If you don't do what I ask…" I reach over to the passenger seat and pat the baseball bat.

"Hey, there ain't no need to threaten me, man. We're all friends here." Cheetah says.

"Fuck, let's go." His friend says, grabbing the fifty. "I wanna go get a pint of beer."

Watching the two dickless assholes walk up to the front, I smile. If word gets out to Julia that I'm here, she'll come running. If she doesn't, I have another, more perfect plan.

Chapter 27

Julia

Whatever just happened, I want more of it. At first, I wanted to slap him, for ravishing me like that in a broom closet. But then, I let myself melt into him. Never in my life have I been kissed like *that* before. *That* wasn't a kiss. It was a full body 'come-to-me-baby' lip tease that extended from my mouth to my toes. If that was a preview of what he's like in bed...*mercy*. Legs like jelly, lips swollen and throbbing...other things throbbing, too, my panties were soaked from ten seconds of Colton's touch. What came over him, I have no idea. I just went in to get a stack of trays, and I left feeling like I'd been through a hurricane...hurricane *sexy*.

Then he apologized? What the hell for? And he said it wouldn't happen again? Good Lord...I hope it does. Not in my wildest fantasies have I ever been ravaged so deliciously, begging for more. Colton *is* my wet dream. A dream I never knew I could have, or experience in the flesh. Flesh...hot, sweaty flesh...man, I'm getting ahead of myself. Okay, need a cold shower. Or another five minutes with Colton. Maybe it wouldn't even take that long.

Colton is one of those guys you dream about. Gentle but hungry, sexy as hell but he doesn't know it. That man hasn't got a conceited bone in his body. Wait...*bone*. Yeah, I could feel his girth on my belly. Raw, ready, there's no telling what might've happened if Dan hadn't walked in and interrupted us. Doing it in a broom closet seems cheap, but no, this was, and would have been...*closet ecstasy*. Worth the rumors and looks.

But then Dan comes in and ruins my only moment of lust since...ever. Colton runs out of there like he's trying to catch a purse snatcher. I follow him out a few seconds later, after I adjust my shirt and catch my breath. When I get closer to the front door, I see Colton forcing a guy against the wall. This guy looks like he lives in a trailer park; he's wearing a hat that says 'Cheetah', but it falls off the moment Colton takes him by the scruff of his shirt. I can tell Colton has his knee pressed up against the guy's balls, so he's pinned and can't move. Colton's shirt is strained with the flexing of his muscles. It turns me on even further, making me feel kind of guilty for the response at such a time.

"Tell me, you son of a bitch!" Colton seethes, pushing his body further into trailer park boy.

"I...I don't know him, I swear! He paid me a hundred bucks to ask!"

Bingo has opened the other side of the door, and is letting people in through there, while Colton grills this guy for information.

"Who? What did he look like?" Colton's nose is pressed up against his. "Tall? Dark hair? What? Tell me or I'll shove my knees so far up your balls, you'll have to go in after them!"

"Yeah," Cheetah pants, wincing. "He's got dark hair."

"What kind of car was he driving, asshole!"

"A sweet lookin' Charger. Who the hell's Julia, anyway?"

"None of your fucking business." Colton says, letting him go. He takes off into the parking lot at lightning speed.

"Ma'am, you need to stay inside." Bingo says to me.

"What? Why?"

"Colton's orders."

"Okay."

Watching Colton run through the parking lot, Cheetah turns to me. Winking, he licks his lips, like he's about to take a bite out of a Porterhouse steak. He looks me up and down like I am one. "You must be Julia. He your boyfriend? The guy who wanted to know if you was in here?"

"I don't see how that's any of your business." I say, suddenly feeling the need to take a shower.

"Oh, it's you alright." Cheetah is pleased that he's

figured something out by himself.

I remain silent, distracted by Colton's absence. He isn't visible in the parking lot anymore. Part of me is nervous that John and Colton, if John is, in fact, here, would get into a fight. Colton could handle himself, but with John's temper and jealousy, there is no telling what he might do.

Liz walks up to me. "Hey, what's going on? The tables in there are going nuts; this is the first chance I had to come check it out."

"I'll tell you later," I mutter, not wishing for Cheetah to hear our conversation. He's still leering at me, waiting for me to talk to him, as if I owe him.

"Oh, this little chickie here has some score to settle with some guy out in the parking lot. Paid me fifty bucks to ask if she was here." Cheetah brags, lifting his fifty dollar bill.

Liz's eyes widen at me. "Shit, is he here? Now?"

"I don't know. Colton went running out into the parking lot to find him."

"Oh, he's here alright." Cheetah interrupts. "He still owes me the other fifty. I ain't leaving until I get it."

"Shut up, Cheetah." Bingo says, growing tired of hearing him. The incoming crowd on the other door has thinned. "I'll kick your ass."

"You will not. You'll get fired. It's against the rules."

This spurs Cheetah on. "Ah-ha! See, I'm right, aren't I?"

"I won't get fired if I kick your ass." Liz states firmly. "And don't think I won't, either. I've got a thirteen year old boy who'd kiss your ass, too."

Seconds later, a red Charger drives too slowly out of the parking lot. The tinted window on the driver's side slides down. I see the chillingly calm look on my ex-fiance's face. He stops for a moment, glances at me, as if I should say something, and he drives away grinning.

"What the hell did he want?" Liz says.

I don't answer. Cheetah tears off after him, screaming that he wants his money.

When Colton appears, he says five words that both thrill and terrify me at the same time. "You're staying with me tonight."

Chapter 28

Colton

That skinny, spoiled, daddy's boy, son-of-a-bitch is not going to act like he owns Julia. Not if I can help it. The smug look on his face, I'd like to wipe it off...with my fist. Mount a couple of his teeth on my dashboard, and mount his ass in my stable. As I walk over to his souped-up faggot-mobile, I have to stop myself from just whacking him one, right after I kick a couple of dents into his side panels. He sees me approach and giggles to himself, like just the sight of me is funny. Cream puff. This loser is too much of a pretty-boy to throw a punch; probably afraid he'll ruin his manicure.

"What'd you go and call the cops on me for?" he laughs.

"Listen, chuckles. You don't know who I am, but I sure as hell know who you are. Stay away from Julia; she wants nothing to do with you. Didn't her leaving the *state* give you any clues? Or are you just too stupid to read between the lines?"

"Ah, come on. We're friends here, aren't we? I just want to talk to her." his patronizing tone makes me want to crush his skull into the windshield.

"Is that why you're following her around? Stalking her like some desperate, pathetic freak?"

"I'm just making sure she's okay." His tone is way too smooth. "Hey, tell me, is she as good a fuck for you?"

Lips curled into a snarl, I can feel my fingernails digging into the inside of my palms, as my fists ball up. My voice is a low growl. "You watch your mouth, asshole."

"Hey, I'm just asking." He lifts his hands in mock defence. "Say, hey, do me a favor and give that skinny little runt and his friend this?" he asks, handing me two fifties. "They did me a little favor and I owe them."

I say nothing, but my chest heaves up and down.

"I asked them to find out if my girl was inside the

bar. And she was."

"She won't come out to see you. You wasted your time."

"Ah, I didn't want her to come out and see me." he looks me straight in the eye. "This is the reaction I was looking for." He sticks his hand out to me for a shake, but I don't move. "Nice to meet you, Colton. I'll be seeing you around."

"You stay away from her." I warn; eyes slit into a seething glare.

He winks at me and puts his car into drive. I watch him pull out of the parking spot, and he gives me a single wave through the side view mirror. I stood there, feeling my pulse race faster than when I rode Rebel for the first time. He'll never get that close to Julia again. This guy is sick, delusional, and psychopathic. How he won that sweet girl over is beyond me. His charm is more transparent than a fishbowl. She must love her father to the moon and back to have agreed to marry this guy. No wonder she fled. No wonder she's scared. This guy is bad news. I just need to figure out some way to get rid of him...permanently.

***

When we pull up to the house, she has a forlorn look on her face as I turn the engine off. "Hey," I say, taking her chin in my hand. "You okay?"

"Yeah," she says, but her eyes say that no, she's not okay. It looks like she's just been told bad news.

"Look, you don't have to stay here. You can go stay with your dad. You mentioned that he's in town. If you're not comfortable here, I'm fine with that. I'll take you straight over to your dad."

"It's not that."

"You want to tell me what's wrong?" I ask gently. "I'm all ears."

"I'm just...." She sighs. "I'm afraid."

"Well, of course you are. Anyone would be."

"No, it's not what you think."

I giggle softly. "Then what?"

She offers me a tight smile. "I can't tell you. Not yet."

Nodding once, I take her hand in mine. "You're not ready. I'm okay with that. No pressure here."

Exiting the car, I walk over to her side and grab her overnight bag from the back seat. When I open the passenger side door, I take her hand in mine. For a split second, the memory of our passionate kiss tonight shoots through my head. Eyes to her lips, I have to stifle the urge to steal another kiss. But I'd made a promise to her. I told her it wouldn't happen again. What I did earlier was nothing short of taking advantage. Why she didn't slap me I'll never know. Why she's decided to stay the night with me despite what happened in the closet, I'll never figure out, either. In the dark, it's hard to tell what her eyes are saying, but her body language says that she's scared and nervous. I would be too, with a jackass like that following me around.

As we get inside the house, Julia looks around, as if through fresh eyes. "You want some tea, or do you just want to get some sleep?" I ask, feeling the tension in the air. "You can take the bed. No arguments."

"No, I'm fine." Her expression changes. "You aren't expecting any visitors in the morning, are you?" a ghost of a smile appears on her lips.

I return a tiny smile. "Sorry about that. That's my fault. I've never given Wade any boundaries. I suppose I never needed them."

"Not even when you were married?"

"Ah, that was never a problem. Wade and Pam never got along. He didn't make any trips over here. We got together outside of the house." I clear my throat. "Well, I'll just grab some things out of the bedroom, and you can hit the hay if you want."

"Colton?"

She stops me in my tracks, "Yeah?"

Her face takes on a child-like expression. Like a young girl asking if she can have cookies before bed. "I don't mind if you sleep in the bed again...with me." It isn't a sexual thing, that I can tell. It's as though we just finished watching a horror movie. Problem is, I'll have to stuff the ice packs from my freezer inside my boxers to make it through the night.

"Err...sure. I'll stay on my side if you stay on yours." I say playfully, feeling my thighs ache already.

"Okay."

"You go ahead and take the bathroom first." I offer, while I make my way to the kitchen, to look at pictures of when Maya gave birth to Rebel, hoping that will turn off any steamy thoughts I have lurking around inside my brain.

It's going to be a long night.

Chapter 29

Gregory

Having just turned off his bedside lamp, Gregory hears his cell phone ring from the next room. The suite he is staying in is as large as a small cottage, complete with an eat-in kitchen and a full bathroom with a hot tub and sauna. This suite is usually reserved for special guests, but Gregory's team let him know the previous day that it was vacant. The bedroom and kitchen have dark mahogany flooring throughout, with a marble bathroom floor. The wing chair by the four-poster bed has a small, oak console table in front of it, where Gregory keeps his laptop computer.

Rising, Mr. Abbott takes his robe from the top of the wing chair and throws it over his shoulders before exiting the bedroom via the grand oak door. His phone shrills one last time before he picks it up and barks into it.

"Mr. Abbott, so sorry to wake you." John says.

"This better be good." Gregory does not hide the note of warning in his voice.

"Sir, I know that you're aware that your daughter is in North Carolina with her sister. As are you."

"I don't see how this is any of your business, young man. I'll thank you for letting me get some rest." About to hang up on John, Gregory hears John giggle teasingly. "What is this nonsense, boy? The nerve of you calling and wasting my time at such an hour!"

"Oh, I'm not wasting your time, sir."

"Just what is the meaning of this!" Gregory demands.

"Did you know your little girl is shacking up with some hot-headed cowboy?"

"I don't know what you're talking about, fool! She's with her sister! You just said so yourself!"

"Try calling her right now. I dare you." John teases.

"Don't be ridiculous." Gregory seethes. "What are you trying to pull, young man? What kind of game is it you're trying to play?"

"No games, Mr. Abbott. I know what I saw."

"What you *saw?*" Gregory pauses in disbelief. "You mean you're here? Following my Julia around like some animal?" he chuckles without a trace of mirth. "It's no wonder my daughter couldn't wait to get away from you. You're a vile, vile boy. You stay away from my daughters...both of them...and my grandson."

"Oh, Mr. Abbott, bad choice." John's voice is smooth as silk. "I think I'll keep my eye on her. Someone has to."

"John, you'll leave town immediately, and get back to your father if you know what's good for you." Gregory warns. "I can take care of my daughter. You just mind your own business. If she is making friends with another boy, I'll get to the bottom of it. My daughter is honorable, and I'm sure that she has good reasons why she is doing what she is doing. If she is, in fact, doing what you claim she is. Perhaps she's afraid of you, and she's staying with this other boy for protection from you." His voice is gruff.

"Oh, I think it's more than that, Mr. Abbott. If that were the case, why wouldn't she just stay with you? She knows you're here in town."

"Well, Julia doesn't like to trouble me. Bless her. It's too bad you didn't learn more from my daughter. I'm sure your father would be very displeased knowing what you're up to."

John squirms, changing the subject. "If you're not going to do anything about this, then I will. Julia is engaged to me, she belongs to me, not to some two-bit horse farmer who spends his nights fighting in a bar. I'll get her back, all right. She'll come back to me when she sees what kind of low-life he is."

"You'll do no such thing. The engagement is off, John. Like it or not you'll never see Julia again. You'd be smart to keep your distance from her, or you'll have me to deal with." With that, Gregory hangs up.

Staring at the phone, John bites his lower lip in

anger. "That's what he thinks."

Chapter 30

Julia

The shower is running as I lay in Colton's bed, listening to him humming softly to some ballad I can't decipher. I'm nervous about sleeping here, but at the same time I feel comforted. Colton is too much of a gentleman to let anything happen, he said so himself. But if I'm honest, part of me can't forget about that passionate kiss in the closet. His body against mine in that hungry yet gentle way was enough to imprint in my memory forever. The inside of my thighs are warm just thinking about it. Wrapped in his blankets, I hear the water turn off, and I picture him standing naked, toweling off his wet skin. Beads of water dripping down his back, collecting on his forehead, glistening under the light. *Are you kidding me? Maybe I need a cold shower!*

When he enters the bedroom, he's wearing only a towel around his waist. His hair is dripping down his back, just like I imagined. "Sorry, forgot to grab my pyjamas," he smiles sheepishly, "not used to wearing any." *Oh great, that makes it better.*

I hear the water in the sink running as he brushes his teeth. I've already brushed mine and changed into my pyjamas, and I almost want to make a similar comment, that perhaps I should borrow his shirt and shorts again, as I don't have anything *appropriate* to wear in his company, but I don't. Even though my 'Mary' jar is telling me I should. Three minutes later he emerges, smelling as fresh as a daisy, driving my senses wild. "Do you read before you go to sleep? I've got some books in the nightstand if you want to look." He offers, pulling a book out of the nightstand. It's a title and author I don't recognize, but the cover screams thriller.

"I usually read textbooks before bed. Brush up on my skills for work. Or I run through my lesson plan for the next day." I say, lifting myself so I'm leaning on the pillows. I'd been stuffed in the bed like a burrito before he came back into the room. "I kinda miss that. It'll be nice when I hear about the job."

"You'll get it." he says with a finality that makes me smile. "So, you plan on staying here for sure? You don't miss Florida at all? Not your friends or anything?" he asks as he sits up on the bed, propping himself on the pillows, so our positions are mirrored.

"Florida isn't far. Besides, I can go back anytime, or my friends can visit. I'm glad to be closer to my sister at any rate. I've missed her for all these years. It's almost like everything happens for a reason."

"And you think your dad will be okay with you staying here long term?"

I wave. "He's fine. If he misses us that much, he can stay here. He has enough business all over he can move wherever he wants." I pat him on the shoulder. "What about you? Do you miss your other brothers?"

"They visit a lot. They'll be here this weekend for the fundraiser. They don't live far, either. Wade and I are closest anyhow."

"What about your parents? Where do they live?"

He places his book on the nightstand, as if he didn't intend to read it. "My mother left us years ago, and my father died a few years ago." He sees my expression change and raises his hand. "I wasn't ever that close to him, and I hadn't seen him in a long time."

"Oh," I can tell by the lack of eye contact that this is a sensitive topic. "Sorry, we can talk about something else, or nothing at all, if you'd rather just go to sleep."

He purses his lips together and looks at me. "I just haven't talked about it in a while is all. Not a lot to tell. My dad hated me and shipped me off to the military when I was a teenager. My other brothers got less punishment and did way worse." He lets out a light guffaw, tipping his neck back, "Shit, my one brother stole from him once. Got a slap on the wrist."

"I know what you mean. My father banished my sister from the family for getting pregnant. When she eloped that was the end of it for her for good. Took thirteen years before he would speak to her again."

"When I got hurt overseas, my dad didn't give a damn. If it weren't for Wade, I probably wouldn't be here."

"Really? He was that bad?"

"Really." Colton looks at me and nods once. "Dad was so pissed at Wade he took him out of the will. Now Wade doesn't get any of dad's money until he's married or turns thirty, whichever comes first."

"Wow. That's cold." I look at him. "And what about you? Was your dad rich? Did he leave you any money?" I lift a hand. "Never mind. That's not my business. Sorry."

"No, that's okay." His hand grazes my arm, sending shivers down my spine. "Yeah, my dad owned an airline. Two of my brothers still run it, and I have some....connections with it that I'd like to pursue some day, but, err...surprisingly, yeah, he left me some. Lord knows why."

"Maybe he didn't hate you after all."

Colton shrugs. "Don't make a bit of difference now, he's gone."

"What is it that you want to pursue with your dad's airline?"

He licks his lips and sighs. "When I was married, my ex-wife didn't want me to continue with the military, even though I had my degree in aerodynamics. I'd like to go back some day and build aircraft for the military."

"Would you have to go back on the front lines?"

"No, no, nothing like that. I was discharged from that on account of this." He's wearing a pair of black boxer shorts and a tattered Mingles t-shirt. Lifting his shirt, he reveals a large scar, about four inches long that extends from his left pectoral muscle down to his rib cage. A faint stitch pattern outlines it. There are various tattoos surrounding it, some cut off, suggesting that the tattoos came before the wound. I can't help the look of shock on my face.

"My God! Did you get shot?" My hand instinctively inches toward the scar, and I look up at Colton, as if asking for permission to touch it.

"Three times. If it had been close range, I would have been blown away. By the look of me I was." He brings my hand to his skin and lets me touch it. The skin is soft and smooth but has a rubbery texture, and the stitching feels like it's an effect done for Halloween. "Took me six months to recover. Nearly died just of blood loss. Wade took care of me when I was well enough to come home."

My jaw drops. "Where was your wife?"

"She couldn't handle it. And believe me I don't blame her. I was a mess and the bandages had to be changed a lot. For the first couple of months I couldn't do anything without help. Back in the hospital several times for infection and other complications. I'm lucky to be alive."

"Did she leave you then?"

"Naw, we were together and apart a couple of times, and then she stayed with her parents for a while. When she came back the last time, we were okay. I took her traveling when I felt better. Thought that would help bring us closer but it didn't. She left me long before I got hurt, I think, when I look back and I'm truthful with myself. Anyway, she didn't want me to go back to the military, combat or not, so I gave it up."

"When she left, how come you didn't go back to it?"

He puts his shirt down and smooths it over his stomach. "I guess part of me thought she might come back."

I look at him. "Do you think she will?"

His hand grazes my cheek. "No." he looks over at the clock on his bedside table. "It's late. We should get some sleep."

But I'm not tired. "So what's this fundraiser about?" I ask, changing the subject.

"Oh, that." He clears his throat. "For the last three years since this place was built, I hold a fundraiser to raise money for mental illness. Rebel and Maya get ridden all day and we have bouncy castles, hayrides, face painting, a barbecue, a couple of local business come and display their stuff, too, like a kids' dojo, a dance studio, and there's usually a magic show, and of course, Wade and his band are there, too."

"Wow, sounds awesome. Is it a good turnout?"

"For sure. Last year it raised over twenty thousand dollars. And I match the donations dollar for dollar."

I place my hand on his forearm. "Colton, that's wonderful. That's so gracious. I'm humbled. How can I help?"

"There's lots of stuff you can do. We need someone to sell tickets for all the attractions, we always need help on the barbecue. And you can always volunteer to be dunked in the dunk tank." He winks.

"Whatever I can do I'll be there."

"That's great. Liz always comes too. In fact, all the bar staff are there."

We hear his phone ringing from the living room. "I'll be right back." Colton says, sliding off the bed. His shirt is still up a little, and I can see a 'v' from his hips down to his pelvis. It's so sexy, I can't help but stare. I hear him talking on his phone. It sounds like he's talking to Wade. He comes back in the room, saying something about not being able to talk about something right now. His gaze crosses over to me for a second, and then he says he has to go and hangs up.

"Everything okay?"

"Wade." He shakes his head. "Such a nosey little shit. He knows you're here. I hope that's okay."

"Well, at least this way there won't be any interruptions." I say, not meaning for it to sound presumptuous, but it comes out that way and my cheeks heat.

Colton licks his lips and draws in a deep breath, stretching his muscular arms over his head, almost in exasperation.

"What's wrong? I didn't mean to insinuate anything."

I hesitate. "I...I just meant that we won't have any explaining to do like this morning."

He lifts a hand. "It's not that."

"Then what?" I ask, sensing that he's having second thoughts about our arrangement. "If this is a bad idea, I don't mind going back to Liz's." I say, even though it was his idea for me to stay in the first place. He's standing five feet away from me, looking like he can't decide if he should proceed back to his side of the bed, or flee. "Colton, it's fine. I can go." I say in a soft, comforting tone as I rise out of the bed.

He stops me with his hands. He places one on each of my hips. The t-shirt and shorts that I'm wearing are crumpled, but he finds that sensitive spot on my sides that sets my heart thumping. "No, it's fine. Please. I was just worried that Wade would be a pain in the ass and spread the word that you and I slept together again...and not in the innocent way that it's happened, either."

"Colton, I get the feeling your little brother isn't as much of a pain in the ass as you make him out to be." I tip my head to the side, watching his gaze divide between each of my eyes. "He didn't say anything at the bar tonight, and he didn't taunt you on the phone just now."

"I didn't give him the chance." He states, hands still on my sides. My thighs are damp and warm from his touch.

There is a silence. Colton's gaze inches down to my lips, but then he clears his throat and removes his hands from my body. This makes me sad. I was enjoying the contact. It was sexy but comforting. He walks away from me and sits on the edge of the bed. His elbows find his knees and he rakes his hands through his hair. "Colton?"

"Yeah."

"Are you okay?"

"I'm fine, sweetie. You worry too much." He says, rising. His hair is drying, and it's flopped down on his forehead. I instinctively pull a piece up and drape it over his forehead, raking my hand through his hair. *Are you crazy? Don't do that!* His eyes close for a moment. When they open again, his pupils are wide; I can barely see any blue in his eyes. His beautifully long eyelashes sway against his cheeks as he gives a swoon-worthy glance at my lips. *Oh my God, he's going to kiss me again....!*

"Julia," he whispers, "I promised you I wouldn't...kiss you...again."

There is a pause. My voice is barely audible. "What if I kiss you?"

He presses his forehead against mine and closes his eyes, as though just that slight contact is unfathomable. His hands find that spot on either side of my hips again, and he gently massages with his thumbs. "What are you doing to me?" he breathes.

The same thing you're doing to me.

Chapter 31

Colton

I could have killed Wade for calling when he did. That kid will pay for the interruption. We were just about settled for the night when he called. Now Julia's all worried about things she shouldn't be worried about. When she offers to go home, it's all I can do to not touch her or comfort her. It's an odd feeling, but it's like she belongs here, with me. I barely know this beautiful woman; I've known her only a short time, yet I feel like she should stay here with me. I'm so torn; my mind is telling me to heed my promise to her that I won't take advantage of her again, like I did earlier. She has enough problems and is probably turned completely off men. I should feel the same about women after Pam. But somehow, when I'm with Julia, I don't have the same reservations I usually do around females. Julia is different.

When she says she wants to kiss me, I just about faint. I'm afraid I'll lose control the instant her lips touch mine. Being so close to her is doing...things to me. Things she probably can feel with her body pressed up to mine. "Julia," I whisper, "I'm not sure if that's a good idea."

Her forehead is still against mine and we're swaying slightly, as if there is a soft ballad playing in the bedroom. "Why not?" she says to me. "I want to kiss you, and I know you want to kiss me."

Oh God...

"I do. So much." I kiss her forehead. "But if I kiss you...in my bedroom...alone...." I trail off, my voice is still a whisper.

"Then you're just as afraid as I am." She says.

"You're afraid of losing control?" I ask.

"No." she licks her lips. "Colton, I've never..."

"Lost control? Yeah, it's more of a guy thing." I chuckle softly, still swaying and leaning my forehead against hers. My hardness is pressed up against her, pulsing every time she breathes in and her soft breasts press up to my chest.

"No." she smiles. "I've never had sex before."

My eyes widen. "You're not serious." I take a step back and look at her. "That's impossible...look at you."

Shaking her head no, she purses her lips. "I'm a daddy's girl, Colton. And daddy always told me to save myself for marriage." She lifts her hands in the air, as if defeated. "I'm not married yet. And I can tell you that John hated it that we couldn't have sex until we got married."

"Jesus." I say, running a hand through my hair. No wonder the guy is nuts. Being with her all the time, and not being able to be *with* her? That would drive me nuts, too. "You never did...no, never mind." I say, not wishing to know about her past with John.

"We did things, yes." She says sheepishly. "Does this freak you out? The fact that I'm...inexperienced?"

"No, no. Why wasn't John in more of a rush to get married then?"

She scrunches her face. "Do you really want to pull at that thread?"

"Was he cheating on you?"

"Probably." She admits. "Truth is, I never really cared."

"Wow." I lick my lips. She watches. Her eyes remain at my lips.

Her voice is low again. "Do you still want to kiss me?" she asks.

Does a bear shit in the woods?

"Since the moment I first saw you."

Her gaze is intense. Slowly, she pulls her arms up on my shoulders, closing the gap between us. She breathes deeply, and her breasts are right against my chest, making me instantly hard again. Snaking my hands around her waist, I pull her close. All I can hear is my heart pounding in my ears as she slowly inches her face towards mine. Her touch is slow and gentle at first, and I let her softly kiss my lips, as I respond in kind, reminding myself to relax and stay in control.

When she pulls away, I tilt my head and envelop her lips with mine. A dull groan comes from her throat, making my hardness twitch. Then she dips her tongue in my mouth, finding my tongue. The soft, sweetness of her flesh makes my cock like steel. With my hands, I press her body closer to mine, paying special attention just above her rear. She breaks contact and turns her head in the opposite direction, finding my tongue again. Her hands gently rake through my hair and the back of my neck. Her hands are so soft, and I can't help thinking about what they'd feel like against my cock, rubbing it in a rhythmic motion up and down.

I want to touch her all over, but I'm letting her steer this boat. She's inexperienced and I don't want to push her. As much as I want to push her on the bed and climb on top of her, I wait for her cue. For someone so inexperienced, she has an expert touch. She breaks contact from my lips and finds the sensitive spot on my neck. With just enough suction to drive me wild, she licks and sucks at my neck. The groan that escapes my throat spurs her on. Her hand comes away from the back of my neck and finds its way to my cock. Behind the shorts, she gently squeezes with delicious pressure.

"Easy, easy, baby." I breathe, trying to stay in control. "Hey," I gently pull her away, rubbing her back. "Don't you want to...keep your promise to your dad? I mean, you didn't come all this way for nothing, did you?" I kiss her softly, for reassurance.

Her eyes slide to my lips. "I don't want to wait any longer, Colton. I've never wanted anyone as much as I want you...right now."

"But...I don't want you to regret anything." I kiss her neck chastely, making a smacking sound. "We can do lots of things to have fun without actually having sex."

"I've done all that, Colton." She says, not trying to hide the disappointment in her voice.

Exhaling, I pull her ass towards me, so she can feel

my hardness. "Not with me, you haven't."

She closes her eyes, taking in my dick, that's pushing right up against the apex of her thighs.

"God, Colton. I want you now."

"Didn't your daddy tell you not to let your hormones run your life?" I say, half-teasing, as I pull my shirt off. Playfully, I push her on the bed. The look on her face is priceless. Her nipples are sticking up from under her shirt. I nip them with my lips, making her squirm. She lifts her arms to pull her shirt off. "No, not yet." I say, teasing her flesh with my lips over my teeth, lifting and lowering her nipples, the pressure just enough from behind her shirt. Lifting her ass, her chest rises, begging for more contact. Reaching down, I pull her shorts off, and take in the sight of her beautiful flesh.

Automatically, she lifts her knees and separates them, exposing herself to me fully. "God, you're so beautiful." I say, cupping her face with my hands, before lowering myself. Setting my hands on her waist, I kiss her belly and nip at her belly button. She writhes under me, her back is arched. Kissing the inside of her thighs, I tease her, nipping and sucking at her skin. When her breathing hitches, I slowly take in the flesh between her legs, pulling gently, separating her folds. Her moan spurs me on and I take her fully in my mouth, sucking her flesh. My tongue bathes her swollen clit. Using the tip of my tongue, I batter her most sensitive area, making her cry out.

My cock twitches watching the scene before me, as the most beautiful woman in the world lays down at my mercy. The sounds coming from her tell me she's on the verge already. My name is repeated time and again, like music to my ears. Reaching up, I place my hands under her shirt, gently squeezing her perked nipples. This woman is so responsive to my touch, it's a turn on itself. I'd love to plunge inside her with my cock, but it's not time yet. Her hips move rhythmically, telling me the speed she wants, and I do as she commands. A large gasp comes from her, and I know she's going to come any second. Her pelvis is tipped upward, and her feet are cemented into the bed as she cries out my name one last time before her flesh begins to spasm. I watch her hands grasp the sheets. "Colton, I'm coming!" she gasps, as if I need to be told.

It's the sexiest thing I've ever seen. This goddess is having an orgasm on my bed, courtesy of me. The only thing sexier would be if she was coming all over my cock, and I'm inside her. It lasts and lasts, as I continue to lick her pulsing flesh, until she finally begs me to stop. Her hand reaches down to my face as she cups my cheeks. "God, you're so good at that." She whispers, satiated. Her eyes are half closed as she comes down from utter ecstasy.

"The King," I joke, chuckling softly. I give her thigh a gentle kiss and rub her leg as I inch my way up her body and lean over her.

Then she asks me a question I don't expect.

Chapter 32

Julia

"And what can we do for you?" I ask salaciously, after having the best orgasm of my life. John could never stay down there long enough to finish me off. Colton accomplished it in no time. There is no comparison. It was mind-blowing. My legs are like jelly, and I'm dying to see what Colton looks like under those shorts. His six-pack abs are telling enough, and I see it poking out from under his shorts. John had a cocktail weenie, but it looks like Colton is an Adonis. Based on what he's done to me in the last ten minutes, I'd say he's capable of accomplishing a whole lot more.

His weight is delicious on me, and I can feel his hardness pressing on the spot he's just quenched. But I want more. I want him inside me. I'm not afraid anymore. I'm ready. Colton is so sweet to worry about my principles, but if I'm honest with myself, I think that those were set in place by my dad when I was a teenager, and I just kept them when I was with John, because the idea of being with him never felt right from the start.

"I love your face." Colton says, touching my cheeks with feather-like softness. "You look so...satisfied." He smiles.

"That's because I am." I sigh, reaching for his penis. He lifts slightly, knowing where I'm going. "Now, what can we do about this?" Under the waistband of his shorts, I reach for him, wrapping my hand around him. He's huge, and he can tell by my face that I'm pleasantly surprised. He lets out a sexy sigh as I pump his flesh teasingly with my hand.

"This is nice." He says, as if what I'm doing right now is enough. Pressing his forehead against mine, he takes in the contact, breathing deeply.

"I want more," I say, kissing him on the mouth.

"Well, what do you want?" he says, his breath

hitching as I continue to pump him.

"You know what I want." I answer, bringing his penis closer to me, gesturing clearly what I want.

"Well, sweetie," he chuckles softly, as if defeated. "I'm not sure if that's what is right, and I'm having a hard time making the right choices with your hand doing…things to me."

"Oh, it's right, Colton." I say smoothly.

"It may be, but to be truthful, I don't have any condoms." He admits as his eyes close and a soft moan comes from his throat.

"Oh," I say, kissing him again. Lifting my hand to my mouth, I wet it with my tongue as he watches, half-curious, half completely turned on with the sexy way I do it. When I place my hand back on his penis, his mouth makes an 'O' as he gasps. Gently pushing him onto his back, I climb to his side as he lies there at my mercy. Half of me wants to take him in my mouth, but I can't yet; that was John's favorite and I try to push that thought out of my head quickly. Instead, I wet my other hand and rhythmically pump with one, while keeping them both moist.

Colton grunts as his hips buck. There is nothing sexier than a man completely in the throes of passion. One of his hands is on my naked rear, massaging it and grabbing it, the other is grasping at the sheets. His penis is as hard as steel and there is a bead of moisture on the tip. As his breathing becomes ragged, he says, "I'm. Close. Oh, Lord," which spurs me on. Wetting my hand a final time, I pump faster as his breathing hitches and he calls out my name. When he comes, I watch his seed shoot out of him in long spurts, but the sounds he makes are even sexier. There is a lot of "mmm, ooohhhhh," as he releases.

When he's silent, he looks at me and smiles, stroking my rear. "That was phenomenal," he comments. Grabbing his shirt from the bed, I place it on his belly so he can wipe himself. Seconds later I'm lying on his chest as he pulls the blankets over us. "I like the thing you did with your hand…when you licked it. That was hot." He mutters. His tone is still laced with sex.

"I'll keep that in mind." I say, lifting to kiss him. He cups my face with his free hand and kisses me deeply. The look he gives me makes my heart melt. "I hope you're not disappointed."

"Disappointed? That we didn't have sex?"

"Well, yeah." He answers, still cupping my face. "I just…I don't want you to make the wrong choices."

"Colton, since I met you all I've done is make the right choices." I say honestly. "You seem to bring that out in me."

"I think you're smarter than you give yourself credit for." He strokes the side of my cheek. "Not a lot of women have the kind of integrity that you do. I don't want to be the one to change that."

My heart swells. We spend the rest of the night in each other's arms. In the morning, I get an unexpected phone call.

***

Colton is in the kitchen preparing breakfast while I'm in the shower. As I replay last night in my head, it makes my thighs heat, but it also makes me glow. That man has more respect for me than anyone. I all but begged him to have sex with me, and he didn't. He wouldn't. The fact that he didn't have condoms was moot. He could have easily gone to get some; there are plenty of twenty-four hour drugstores in town. He doesn't want me to sleep with him because he's afraid I'll regret giving up my stance to remain a virgin until marriage.

But are those principles still important to me? With John, it was like a game. It was like his prize for marrying me, whether he deserved it or not. At first, it was the excitement of waiting; the anticipation of our wedding night, and how it would be so much more special if I lost my virginity then. As our relationship became marred with his possessiveness and control issues, I think it was more that I was withholding sex from him because of how he treated me, convincing myself that when we were married, things would change because I would be his, and he wouldn't have to worry about the same things as before we were married. Then when things got really bad, I just lost interest entirely.

As far as my father is concerned, yes, he always encouraged Liz and I to wait until marriage, but after Liz's pregnancy with Nate, I think it downplayed the whole celibacy thing. I think he realized how unrealistic and old-fashioned the idea of withholding from pre-marital sex was. But I still used it with John for convenience. And I still held on to it to save my father's honor. Do I think my dad would be hurt if I had premarital sex? Maybe. But I'm twenty-seven years old, let's be real here.

With Colton, it's deeper than sex. When I'm with him, I feel...different. I feel like he looks at me and sees more than a night of passion. If he just saw something physical with me, he would have put the moves on me long ago. He would never have apologized for kissing me in the closet. And he certainly would not have thought twice about doing it again. I made the first move last night...not him. I called the shots, and he was happy to let me. If I wanted to walk away, he would not have stopped me, other than for my own safety.

As I towel off, I hear my phone ringing from my purse on the bathroom counter. "Mary! Oh my God, girl! Are you back?" I squeal.

"I am!" she says.

"How was Barbados ?"

"Fucking boring as hell..and hot! Fuck, I'm like a strip of bacon! So where the hell are you? Still at Liz's?"

"Yeah." I answer, not giving her any more detail.

"How long are you staying?"

Shit.

"I think for good." I say, as if convincing myself. "I applied for a teaching position at my nephew's school."

"No shit! Good for you!" she gushes. "Shit, how's your dad taking it?"

"He's out here, too."

"Oh, thank God! Poor guy! He probably couldn't stand another minute without you. He's so cute. I love your dad."

"He's great. So, what are you doing now?"

"I'm just laying in bed. Just got back yesterday. Chris and I have been fucking like rabbits all night. We missed the shit out of each other." she chuckles. "How's your dad with Liz?"

"Fine. It's like thirteen years were erased."

"That's awesome. Tell her I say hi."

"I will when I see her."

"Where are you?"

Double shit.

"I'm at a friend's."

"Oh...who is she?" she asks nonchalantly.

Never lie to your best friend, never lie to your best friend

"It's a he."

There is a pause. "Whoa. Spill."

I lower my voice. "His name is Colton. He works with Liz."

Another pause. "It's eight o'clock in the morning. Did you spend the night? Wait...you spent the NIGHT!" she says, as if it's the most exciting piece of gossip she's heard all year. "Tell me you tossed out your nineteen-fifties morality and had sex with him!"

"I didn't."

"Ugh...Julia," her tone raises an octave, "What, is he ugly?"

I laugh, "Um, no, he's beautiful."

"So, is he like married? Gay? Fifty years old? What?"

"No, no and no."

"Okay, I give up. Was your dad there, too? What? What is the problem? Why are you so afraid to give it up? You're twenty-seven years old, Julia! Your father gave up caring about your virginity when you graduated from college!"

"I tried, trust me, I tried." I explain to her what happened.

"Wow. Chivalry isn't dead." Mary is impressed. "Sounds like you've got yourself a good guy there, Julia. And he's beautiful too?"

"Yep. All of him."

"Very good. There's just one thing wrong with this picture."

"What?"

"I haven't met him yet."

***

We pull up to Liz's place and I see dad's limo driver pull away. "Oh boy," I say nervously. "My dad's here."

Colton places a hand on my leg. "It's okay, Julia. Do you want me just to drop you off?"

"No, that'll make it worse. He's probably seen you already, and he'll want to know where I've been all night. I'm a terrible liar and I've never been able to pull one over on my dad."

"Not to worry. It's just like taking off a band-aid." Colton smiles, shutting off the engine. "He knows about John, right?"

I nod.

"So, there's no problem. We'll be honest with him, minus the...err...other stuff, and it'll be fine." He looks at me and winks, giving me an assuring nod.

My heart melts. "Okay."

He takes my hand once we're out of the car, giving it a rub with his thumb. He's wearing a pair of jeans and a blue plaid shirt that brings out his eyes. The way he walks is so sexy I feel like my insides have turned into hot wax. When we walk into the house, I say hello to my dad and introduce Colton.

"Dad, this is Colton. He works with Liz at Mingles."

Colton gives dad a firm handshake. "Pleasure, Mr.

Abbott."

"Gregory," Dad says with a warm smile, "I hear you have a horse ranch? Liz was just saying."

Okay, good, we're glossing over where I was last night.

"That's right." Colton says, following dad over to the kitchen table.

Liz widens her eyes at me and gestures with her head for me to come and sit down. "Thank you," I mouth to her, for whatever she said to dad to make him not ask uncomfortable questions.

"And you served as well, is that right?" dad continues.

"Yes, sir." Colton nods.

"Well, I appreciate you helping my daughters."

"Daughters, sir?" Colton is confused.

"You're a bouncer at the bar, right?"

"Yes, sir."

"Then you've protected both my girls at some point I'm sure." dad says with finality. "I hear that John came after you, did he?"

"Sort of, sir."

Dad shakes his head. "Calling me 'sir' is like putting an elevator in an outhouse. Please call me Gregory."

"Certainly," Colton says stiffly.

"So, John...what kind of trouble did he try to pull with you?"

Colton explains succinctly. "That's why Julia stayed with me last night. My horses let me know if there's trouble, and I have a neighbor who's better than a watchdog."

"You look like you can handle yourself, Colton. Tell me, what do you do for fun?"

"Colton is having a fundraiser this weekend, dad." Liz supplies.

"A fundraiser?" dad asks.

Colton explains about the events for the upcoming weekend.

Dad's face lights up. "Why I've never thought about

doing something like that at one of my golf courses, I don't know. That's a wonderful idea, my boy!" he pats Colton on the hand. "I'd love to help out. I'll double your contribution."

"That's very generous, Gregory. Thank you." Colton smiles. "I'll make sure that they put your logo on the materials."

"I'll have my assistant send it to you."

We are interrupted by a bang coming from the back of the house.

"What the devil is that?" dad asks.

Liz's face falls. "Nate," she says, running towards his bedroom. Colton and I are in tow, running with her.

"Nate? Nate?" Liz cries, knocking on his bedroom door before entering his room.

The room is clean, cleaner than one would think a thirteen year old's room should be. He has a small desk in the corner of the room, a pile of textbooks on the floor beside the desk, a single bed in the centre of the room against the middle of the wall, a tall dresser on the wall adjacent to the bed, and about a hundred posters of various sports figures from hockey players, baseball, tennis, basketball, and a couple of Star Wars posters.

There is a noticeable dent in the wall by his dresser, and his phone lays on the laminate floor, in pieces. On the edge of his bed is Nate, sitting with his head in his hands, evidently crying like his best friend just died.

"Nate? What's wrong?" his hair is disheveled as usual, and his sleeping pants are wrinkled, as is his white t-shirt.

"Nothing! Leave me alone!" he screeches, his voice cracks with puberty.

Colton sees the phone on the floor and walks over to it. I kneel next to Nate, mirroring Liz's position on the other side of her son. I see Colton pick up the phone, leaving the plastic pieces to the outer covering on the floor. He reads the display and looks at Nate. I'm not sure how well Colton and Nate know each other, but I know that they've both mentioned each other before.

"Ladies, you mind giving us a minute?" Colton says, smiling tightly.

Liz doesn't hesitate. She rises and I join her. We exit the room but leave the door open so we can eavesdrop.

Colton goes over to Nate and takes a seat next to him. "Hey, my man. I'm not sure what's upsetting you here, but I'll take a guess." Nate's head is still in his hands, as though Colton isn't even there. "Your dad split on you, and you were mad as hell at him for it, but now he wants to see you and you're afraid your mom is going to be upset. Am I close?"

"No." Nate says indignantly. "He screwed my mom and now he wants me to go live with him. Fuck that."

"So, if you've already made up your mind, why are you so upset? Your mom will be cool with whatever you decide."

"It's not about my mom. It's my dad. I'm pissed with him."

"And you should be." Colton says flatly. "But at least he wants to have a relationship with you. That's more than I ever got."

Nate lifts his head. "What do you mean?"

"My dad got tired of me when I was a teenager and shipped me off to the military."

"Really?"

"Yeah." There is a pause. "Got shot and everything."

Nate gasps. "And your dad sent you? And you got shot? That's....cold. What about your mom? How come she didn't stop you from going? My mom would kill me first."

"My mom split when I was little."

Another pause.

"Yeah,"

Colton is so great with kids. I can't believe he's sharing so much with him.

"So, don't begrudge your dad. You should feel lucky that you have a mom who loves you so much, and a dad who does, too." He clears his throat, "What happened between them has nothing to do with you. Sometimes parents work things out better on their own than together."

"So, what do I do?"

"Well, my man, I can't decide that for you. You're the man of the house now. It's time to make your own choices. Think them out long and hard and stick to them. You can't go wrong. People will respect you for that."

And that is the moment I fell in love with Colton Ford.

Chapter 33

Colton

Mr. Abbott is a good man. I like him already. He's a wealthy man, but that's the point: most wealthy men wouldn't part with a dime of their money, especially if it doesn't benefit them in some way. Gregory wants nothing in return for helping out for a worthy cause, and I admire that. It's something my dad never did. Julia's dad has a fine sense of people. He knows as well as all of us that John is bad news, and I sense he trusts me. There was no interrogation regarding last night; which is all the more reason why I'm glad Julia and I didn't let things go too far. The last thing I want is for him to look at me and think that I was the one who maliciously deflowered his baby.

When we return to the kitchen, Gregory is busying himself, making breakfast. "All is well?" he asks Liz.

"He's fine. Colton spoke to him. He'll be out once he's showered." Liz explains. She turns to me and winks her thanks.

"Well, I hope you're all hungry." Gregory says, "I'm not the best cook, but I've scrambled some eggs and started some toast."

"It smells great, dad." Liz says, joining him.

Julia approaches me as I enter the living room, about to sit on the couch. Wrapping her arms around me, she gives me a soft kiss on the mouth. My eyes widen as I look over to Liz and Gregory in the kitchen. Thank God their backs are to us. "Careful." I murmur softly, smiling at her.

She looks over at her family. "I think it'll be alright."

I can't say no to her touch. I wrap my arms around her and kiss the top of her head. "Whatever you say, sweetie."

We both take a seat on the couch. I drape my arm across her shoulders and she snuggles her head into my chest.

"So, Colton. Do you have any brothers or sisters?" Gregory asks. He looks over at me and doesn't flinch when he sees us nestled together on the couch.

Phew!

"Four brothers, three older, one younger." I answer. "Wade works at the bar with Liz and I, too."

"Does he?"

"Yes, he's the lead singer in a band."

Gregory chuckles good-naturedly. "Quite a diverse family you have, Colton. What do your other brothers do?"

"Two of them run an airline and the other one is a pilot."

"An airline? Which airline?"

I name it and he nods. "Oh, yes. That's right, you're Colton Ford. Your father was Wren Ford."

"That's right. It was my dad's airline. They took over the business when he passed."

Julia kisses my neck tenderly when I mention my dad. She nuzzles her nose into my skin, as if I need comfort. The contact is soft and warm, and I'll take it since Gregory's expression hasn't wavered. I lean my head into hers and rub her shoulder. If we were cats, we'd be purring.

"You seem to have done very well for yourself, Colton. Tell me, what do you do on the ranch?"

"I offer horse riding lessons mostly, and I teach self-defence and a little karate."

Julia lifts her head. "You teach self-defence? That explains why you were so good teaching me."

"That's a good skill to have, Julia." Gregory comments. "I'm sure with Colton's line of work, he has a lot of experience."

"He does." Liz nods her agreement. "Colton kicks someone's ass just about every night."

"I know. I've seen him in action." Julia adds.

Liz guffaws. "You've seen nothing, Julia. Trust me."

Gregory intervenes. "You should both be taking Colton's self-defence class. If you're both at the bar, you should be able to defend yourself. I don't need any calls from the Emergency Room...and I want more grandchildren."

"Where did that come from?" Liz laughs, shocked.

"Well I do." Gregory states.

"Don't worry, dad, Julia wants lots of kids, and I'd have more, but..." Liz trails off.

Gregory waves. "Oh, you're both still young, and who knows what the future will bring."

I get the feeling that Gregory said that more for Liz's benefit. Her face sinks, as if all hope has been flushed down the toilet the moment Grant left her.

"Julia's having a baseball team, dad, so you'll be tripping over the grandchildren before you know it."

I look at Julia, and her face is aglow.

"I'd be happier if I was a cat, so I can have a litter instead of just one at a time." Julia says, her smile shining bright.

And that is the moment I fell in love with Julia Abbott.

Gregory chuckles. "Oh, Julia, you make me laugh. Being a teacher, around all those kids day in and day out, is such a perfect profession for you." He grabs five plates out of the cupboard. Liz gets the cutlery as they set the table. "I remember once, when Julia was a teenager, I had her working summers at the golf course. My hope, of course, was that she would love the sport as much as I do and want to come work with me permanently. We had a family fun day one year where we set up a miniature golf course by the country club in Florida. Julia was supposed to be helping give out putters and tees, but she was too busy playing with all the little kids, trying to help them line up their putters properly and all that." Gregory waves, "I knew that day that she wasn't meant to work at a golf course. She told me not long after that, that she wanted to be a teacher, and I knew that was exactly what she was meant to do."

Liz begins scooping eggs onto the plates as we rise. I take Julia's hand as we walk to the table. Pulling her chair out for her, I kiss the top of her head before gently sliding her into place. "Thank you," she says. She steals a glance at my lips, and I want to kiss her badly, but Gregory sits right next to her, and I lose my nerve.

Breakfast turns into lunch and lunch into dinner, as we sit around the table chatting and playing board games. Nate even joins us for a couple games of Scrabble before he leaves to go hang out with friends. It's close to seven o'clock when we hear a knock at the door. Liz is busy washing the dishes, so Julia checks the peephole and a smile forms on her face as she opens the door. "Mary?! Oh my God, Mary!" Julia squeals, holding her arms out to her.

"Julia!" she cries. "Girl, have I missed you!"

"I guess so if you drove all the way here from Florida!" Julia exclaims, giving her a big hug. "What the hell are you doing here?!" she says, not hiding her delight.

"I...missed you, stupid!" she jokes. "Why the hell else would I be here?"

Mary spies Gregory first. "My favorite dad! It's been too long!" she walks to him, holding her arms out for him.

He returns the embrace with a huge grin. "Oh, my dear girl! How are you?"

"I'm great!" Mary answers, hugging him tightly. "I've missed you, too."

"Oh, you're such a doll." Gregory gushes, kissing her cheek. "Have you met Julia's new boyfriend, Colton?" he says, and my eyes widen.

Julia gives me a fleeting look, in complete shock. Liz divides her surprised expression between both of us, and Mary looks like she knows more about me than I want to know about, and she's enjoying it all the same. "No, I don't believe I've had the pleasure yet." She says, offering me her hand to shake.

"Lovely to meet you, Mary. I've heard great things about you." I say, laying it on thick. Julia did mention this girl is her best friend. Her handshake is firm and she smiles at me like the Cheshire Cat.

"Likewise, Colton." She winks. "I've heard a lot of great things about you, too."

I bet you have.

"Mary works with Julia at the school." Gregory supplies. "Are you hungry? We just finished dinner, but there is some left."

"No, I'm fine, thanks." Mary says, as we gather around her. She's wearing a pair of faded blue jeans and a sweater. Her skin is unusually brown from a dark tan, peeling in spots on her face. Her black hair is cut in a funny angle, and short in the front and back. "I could use a coffee though."

"I'll get it." Liz offers.

"Not without a hug first," Mary comments, lifting one arm to give her a one-sided hug.

"Long time no see, sweetie. How 'ya been?" Liz says.

"Can't complain. I just came back from Barbados." She announces to the room, as if her parched skin requires explanation. "Never do that in the summer. It's so hot the lizards won't even come out."

"And you begged me to go." Julia says.

"I begged you to go because my aunt and my mother are so damned boring, I needed someone to keep me entertained."

"So why did you go?" Gregory asks, finishing the dishes.

"Long story." Mary answers, getting the milk out of the fridge for her coffee.

"How long are you staying?" Julia asks, as we hold hands walking towards the couch.

"School starts in a couple of weeks, so I have to head back to class next week. When do you find out about the job?"

"Any day now. I already gave my notice, so I hope this goes well."

"It'll be fine, dear. Not to worry." Gregory says, the hope in his voice is reassuring, and Julia smiles.

"You can stay here with me if you want." Liz offers.

"Nonsense. Come stay with me." Gregory insists. "I

have a luxury suite available. Twenty-four hour concierge and all."

Mary lifts a brow. "Well that offer's too sweet to pass up."

"It's settled then." Gregory is satisfied. "I'll go make a quick call to ensure they turn the bed down and leave you anything you need."

"Oh, don't go to any trouble...wait, do." She winks.

Gregory lifts a finger and smiles. He's used to her quirkiness. Julia giggles; the sound is magical. We're back on the couch, snuggling. It feels like the most natural thing in the world. She looks at her watch. "I just have to go run an errand. Do you mind staying here with my dad and Liz?"

"Sure, is everything okay?"

"Yeah, I just need to pick something up."

Mary overhears. "My car is blocking yours. I'll take you."

I sense that there is a hidden message in this outing as I look out the window.

Mary's car is behind mine and Julia's car is in the garage.

Chapter 34

Julia

Mary starts as soon as the front door closes. "Holy shit! He's such a hottie, girl! I'm so bummed! He's even better looking than John! I got a woody just shaking his hand!" she gushes as she presses the key fob so we can enter her car. "And you didn't sleep with him? Are you nuts?"

"No, I'm not nuts." I laugh, feeling elated that she thinks he's hotter than John. That was about the only good thing about John; he was extremely handsome, but what he had in looks he made up for in his shitty personality. Colton is the whole package. He's beautiful, intelligent, caring, and strong both emotionally and physically. "Unlike you, I don't sleep with a guy ten minutes after meeting him."

"I did that *once*." Mary chides. "And I'm living with him, aren't I? It's not like it was a one-night stand."

"Fine, but still." I say as we enter the car and she puts the key in the ignition.

"So where to, chickie-poo" Mary asks, reversing out of the driveway.

"Just make a right out of the driveway and a left at the end of the street."

She does as instructed, "So you and Colton are pretty tight, eh? And did you see your dad? He likes him."

"Definitely." I agree. "Dad never asks questions if he doesn't like you."

"True." We reach the end of the street and Mary turns left, driving straight. "And he's so cute with you."

"He is."

"Have you heard any more from dick head?" Mary asks, as if the title requires no explanation.

"No. I think my dad said something to him to scare him off. Probably told him he'd tell his dad if he didn't go home. He's such a worm. Such a suck-up with my dad and his."

"So do you see this going anywhere? Has he made anything official? Your dad introduced him as your boyfriend...?"

"Yeah, no, nothing is official. I'm not sure if anything needs to be official though, I mean, that's so old-fashioned. We just love being together. That's all that matters, right?"

Mary looks at me and grins. "Look at you. My girl is growing up."

Which is ridiculous, because we're the same age.

I elbow her. "Shut up. Turn in here."

There is a small mini-mall up ahead, with a handful of stores and a twenty-four hour grocery store.

"So you're going to live here? For real?" Mary asks.

"Why not?" I shrug. "Liz is here, my dad is thinking of staying, but let's face it, he can come and go anywhere with his line of work. The only thing keeping me in Florida is you and the girls at work."

Mary lifts a brow. "And I don't mind coming out here to visit. Hell, if your dad's going to put me up in a five-star hotel, why not?" she laughs.

Mary had a hand in getting me the job in Florida. Ever since then, my dad has adored her and would do anything for her. If it weren't for Mary, I don't think I'd have had the guts to do some of the things I've done, even if they seemed wrong at the time. She may be a bad influence, but she's a good egg and I love her for it. "My dad would have a team of assistants show you a good time if it was required. He loves you."

She pats me on the leg as we pull up to a parking spot. "I love him to bits. He's such a cool guy...and sweet." She pauses. "This spot good? Where are we going?"

"Just over there." I gesture with my chin to a small bank of stores in the corner of the plaza. We exit the car and begin walking on the sidewalk towards the stores.

"Liz looks good. You'd never know her husband split on her."

"She's a survivor. Hasn't shed a tear to my knowledge. It's the anger I worry about. You think she's being nonchalant and then she starts spewing curse words.

"She'll be fine. That's her way of coping. I admire her. If Chris left me, I'd be a pile of shit for months."

"Please," I chide. "You'd be out at bars the same night. You're a survivor, too."

Mary shrugs. "Maybe. But I love him. For real. I think I'd truly be wrecked if he left me."

We approach a Safeway and Mary opens the door for me. "Thanks. Hey, you want to stay for Colton's fundraiser next Saturday?"

"Dunno. I might have to head back before then. Plus, I just got back from Barbados. Unless Chris takes care of it, I've got some shit I have to deal with before I head back to school." She looks around, following me. "What, are you out of tampons or something?"

"No," I laugh, as we head down the sanitary napkin aisle.

"So, what's the deal, missy? Are you going to send Colton to blue ball hell like you did to the dick head, or are you going to give up the goose and send him to Julia heaven?"

As we stop, I give her a knowing look.

She smiles, lifting a brow. "Ah,"

Chapter 35

Colton

We pull up to the ranch. Julia has had her hand interlaced in mine the whole drive. She's staring out the window with an impassive look on her face. "My dad loved you." She says as I shut off the engine. "Mary even said so. Liz, too."

"Yeah," I say nonchalantly. "Your dad's pretty cool. I can see why he's been so successful. He has great sense." I pause. "It's your turn this weekend. You'll get to meet all my brothers." I wiggle my eyebrows.

"So give me the low-down." She says as I shut the engine off. I walk over to her side and open the door. Rising from the car, she snakes her arms around my neck. My hands find her waist and I pull her to me, giving her a chaste kiss on the mouth.

"Na, you don't get to cheat." I say, kissing her, letting the contact linger.

"Can you be convinced?" she teases, dipping her tongue into my mouth, sending electric impulses straight to my cock.

"You don't play fair," I say when she breaks contact. "Besides, they'll love you. What's not to love?" I kiss her again, cupping her face with my hands. "Come on, it's freezing out here. Let's get inside."

The air has a bite to it, so I place my arm around her shoulders as we walk into the house. "You want some tea?" I ask, closing the door behind us.

"No," she says. There is a strange look in her eyes.

"What's wrong?" I ask, approaching her.

"Absolutely nothing." She says with a smile.

"Okay. Do you want to watch some television or a movie?"

She shakes her head no and bites her lip.

"Do you want to go for a ride with the horses? They haven't been out all day."

"Do they need to be ridden? Is there anything you

need to do for them?"

"No, I have someone who comes over and helps out if I'm not home. He's already been by. I sent him a text message this morning."

"Can we go see them?"

I smile. "Sure, if you like." I take her hand as we head back outside, towards the stables. Maya and Rebel are both calm. Maya is laying in a haystack, but still awake. Rebel is chomping on a blade of hay. When he sees me, he flicks his tail happily and lets out a small whinny.

"Whoa, boy. How are you?" I ask, petting his nose. Maya gets up and approaches me from her pen. "Hello, girl." I pet her nose, too. Julia begins petting and talking baby talk to them, just as badly as I do. We sound like we're recording an episode of Sesame Street.

"I wonder if they understand what we're saying to them." Julia inquires.

"Horses are smart. They can tell by the tone and volume what's going on. They can sense when something is wrong, too. Two of my brothers got into a fist fight once in the stables, and Rebel nearly took one of them out."

"What did Rebel do?"

"He reared up in the air with his hooves. If Wade had've been any closer, he would've been creamed. You should never fight around a horse, especially from behind. Horses freak out if you make sudden moves from behind them. I'd warned the two of them to stop, but they didn't."

"What about horses that are in western films and stuff? They see fighting all the time."

"And that's exactly why they remain calm. Horses need to be climatized to things otherwise they get stressed out and can get aggressive."

She pets Rebel on the nose and then strokes her flank. "I can't see either of them being aggressive. They're so good-natured."

"They are. They're my babies."

As I pat Rebel on his flank, Julia walks over to me and snakes her arms around my shoulders. "And how do they react to kissing?" she asks, planting a chaste kiss on my lips. I kiss her back, making a playful smacking sound.

"Well, I don't know, little lady." I say, making my worst John Wayne impression.

"You're so cute." She says. I don't know whether to take that as a compliment or not. Lowering my head, I kiss her, letting it linger. Her head turns slightly as she dips her tongue in my mouth. Hands in my hair, she pulls me closer to her face, kissing me deeply, plunging her tongue inside my mouth. My cock turns to steel immediately.

"I've been waiting all day to kiss you like that." Julia says. "That shirt brings out your eyes. It makes me hot."

"Remind me to buy a dozen of them then." I joke, tangling my fingers in her long hair.

The horses whinny happily, watching us make out like teenagers. I giggle when Rebel nudges his snout up against the side of my head. "She's mine, Rebel. Back off." I tease.

"Looks like you've got competition." Julia says, playing along.

"I smell better." I say, plunging my tongue in her mouth. A moan escapes from her throat, sending delicious thrills straight below my belt. "I love that sound." I breathe.

"I love it from you, too." She reaches my zipper, squeezing my cock. I make the same sound and she starts kissing my neck. "I can't get enough of this spot."

"Sweetie, you can have any spot you want." I say, cupping her rear in my hands, bringing her closer to my cock.

Breaking contact from my neck, she looks at me. Her voice is a breath, "When you do that to me, it makes me want to do things to you."

Lifting her ass with my hands, I drape her legs across

my waist, pressing her against the stall. At a precise angle, I lean into her, focusing on her most sensitive spot. "What about when I do this?" I ask salaciously, with my forehead almost touching hers. We're nose to nose, and her eyes close. Rhythmically, I begin slowly grinding into her.

"My God, it's like you're fucking me with my clothes on." She pants. The word 'fuck' out of her is hot. "Doesn't it hurt you?" she asks breathlessly.

"Not at all." I say, growing winded as all the blood rushes to my cock. I kiss her voraciously as she sucks on my lips, and I imagine the sensation around my dick. The horses have lost interest and have gone to lay down in their pens. "Looks like horses aren't much for romance." I comment, sucking her neck.

"They don't know what they're missing." She cries, "God, Colton, you're going to make me come. This is unbelievable." Her hips buck upward, taking in all the sensation. I speed up and her mouth opens as her head rears back. "God, don't stop, Colton. I'm going to come!" she hisses, then she cries out as her body goes rigid against mine. Maya and Rebel don't make a sound as she explodes against the stall. As I slow, Julia kisses me full on the mouth. "You're incredible." She whispers.

"*You* are." I say, my heart beating fast against her chest. "And for the record, I would never stop unless you told me to."

"Me neither." She says as I help her back to the floor. I divide my glance between her eyes as she cups my face in her hands, as if she wants to tell me something. Remaining silent, I let her say what she needs to say. Instead, she stays silent and kisses me tenderly, wrapping her arms around my neck in an embrace.

"Do we need to do anything for the horses before we go back inside?"

I shake my head no. "They're fine for the night." I love it that she worries about them as if they're children. With my cock still hard, we walk back into the house, bidding adieu to Maya and Rebel. Once we're inside, Julia doesn't let go of my hand. "Do you want anything?" I ask, gesturing with my chin towards the kitchen.

"Yes," she says, but she doesn't look at the kitchen, her eyes are on me.

I wait, but she doesn't answer immediately. "I'd like to go to bed." She says finally, taking her purse with her as she heads into the bedroom.

"Sure. You can have the bathroom first."

Locking the door and turning off the lights, I head to the bedroom, thinking that she's in the bathroom. So I'm surprised when I walk into the room and she's standing there in her lacy underwear and bra.

"Good God, Julia. You're a goddess." I walk towards her and slide my hand down her cheek. "Don't know what I ever did to deserve you, but I'll take it." I whisper.

"Maybe it was all those years in the service." She says, slowly unbuttoning my shirt, one button at a time, seductively glancing at me after each one. "And maybe it was all those years I spent in the wrong relationship that led me to the right one."

When she reaches the bottom of my shirt, she unbuttons my jeans and unzips the zipper, leaving my shirt hanging off my shoulders and my pants hanging open. My dick is hard; I can feel it poking up from my underwear.

"And you call *me* a goddess." She comments. "That would make *you* an Adonis. A gladiator. Hercules."

I laugh softly. "Whatever you like, sweetie. I'm just a man...standing in front of the sexiest woman alive."

Her hair is pooled around her shoulders, one side covering her breast. I slowly move the hair away from her body and kiss the spot.

"Colton." She says, lifting my chin up so we're nose to nose.

"Yeah," I whisper.

Her eyes search mine for a moment. "I...I...love you."

I kiss her softly on the mouth. "I'm head over heels

in love with you, too, sweetie."

She divides her glance between both my eyes. "Are you sure?"

I nod. "I must be. I never felt about anyone the way I feel about you, and I thought I was in love before." I pause. "*This* is love." I say, pushing the air downward with my hand for emphasis.

She reaches over to her purse, which is sitting on the bed, and pulls out a box of condoms. The look on her face has so much conviction it's almost intimidating. I dare not argue with her. "Well, well..." I breathe, taking the box from her. "I guess that's what you we're up to when you went with Mary earlier."

Her eyes are dancing. She's impressed with herself. "I bought a twelve pack." She jokes.

"I see that." I say, taking one out and tossing it on the bed. For a girl who told me less than twenty-four hours ago that she wants to wait for marriage to have sex, she sure seems eager to give her virginity away to me. "What made you change your mind?"

"Love." She says simply. "I'm in love and I want to be with you."

"We can be together in lots of ways, Julia. We've already done a couple." I comment. "You don't have to do this for me."

A look crosses her face, like she's scared. "Don't you *want* to have sex with me?"

Closing the gap between us, I place my hands on her shoulders and kiss her forehead. "I do. More than anything else. But not if it means messing up what we have already. Not if it means you having regrets and looking at me differently."

"I want to have that bond with you, Colton. That special bond that only people who make love have. I want to look into your eyes as you're coming inside me. I want to hear those three beautiful words come out of your mouth as we reach ecstasy together, in a way that nobody else can. I've never had that with anyone, Colton. I want it with you. Now. I don't want to wait, and I don't want to put that kind of pressure on you, either. I don't want you to feel like you have to marry me to feel like that with me."

"You've never made me feel pressured, sweetie."

"And you've never made me feel pressured, either, Colton."

I cup her face with both my hands and divide my glance between both her eyes. "I love you so much."

"I love you too, Colton."

I kiss the end of her nose and her forehead, before pulling my shirt off my shoulders and letting it drop to the floor. Julia leans forward and kisses my shoulders, inching her way up to my neck. I bend my head sideways to give her full exposure. My eyes close from her touch. Her lips are so soft and warm, and she's hitting the sensitive spot just below my ear, making my dick hard again. Nipping my earlobe, she grasps a handful of my hair at the back of my neck, and then sucks my neck in the same spot where she was a moment ago. "You're really good at that, sweetie. Almost too good."

"I love the skin on your neck. I can feel your pulse." She whispers in my ear, sending shivers down my spine. Cupping her breasts with my hands, I gently pull her bra up, freeing her breasts. She reaches back and unlatches her bra, letting it fall to the ground.

"God, you're so perfect." I say, taking one of her nipples in my mouth. I suck it first, so it hardens, and then I lick it, flicking it with my tongue. She moans and I grab her rear, kneading it with my hands. Licking her other breast, I reach down to her folds, and tuck one finger inside her panties. Her flesh is soaked and ready, turning my cock to steel. Inserting a finger, I rhythmically mimic what my dick would be doing to her, as I massage her clit with my thumb.

"Oh, God, Colton. I don't know how you do it." She breathes, pulling my jeans down. I stop for a moment, just to step out of them. Julia pulls my underwear down and her hand is immediately on my cock. "You have a beautiful dick, my love." She says salaciously.

"Why thank you. It's yours." I say as I take her breast in my mouth, returning a finger inside her folds. "You're so perfect, inside and out." I say, feeling the soft skin inside her. It's almost painful waiting to thrust my cock into her. Her body is hugging my finger she's so tight. I place another finger inside, thrusting it further in, feeling for the underside of her pelvic bone, where her g-spot is.

She gasps and I stop. "Are you okay?" I ask, suddenly remembering her virginity. "Sweetie, I'm sorry. Did that hurt?"

"No, baby, it feels fantastic." She groans. "Your fingers are amazing, Colton, but I want your dick inside me."

Her sex talk is such a turn on. Hearing the sexiest woman alive speak chosen erotic words to me makes my dick ache. Pulling my finger out of her, I take the condom off the bed, open the foil and place it on, while she watches intently. She removes her underwear and walks over to the head of the bed. I follow her. Her eyes follow my cock, as if mesmerized. "Are you okay?" I ask again.

"I've never seen one so big...or with a condom on before. It's so hot." She says, "I can't wait to feel it inside me."

As she lays down on her back, I lean over her, placing my legs inside hers, so they're slightly parted. "Once I'm inside I'll go slow. I don't want to hurt you. You tell me if something doesn't feel right, okay?" I whisper, staring intently into her eyes.

She answers by leaning up, enveloping her lips with mine. Her tongue plunges into my mouth and I meet hers with my tongue. We kiss voraciously, while she wraps her arms around my neck, pulling the hair in the back. The way she pulls is half pain half pleasure; an odd combination, but I don't want her to stop. We're breathless when our lips part.

"I want you, Colton. Now." She gasps, bucking her

pelvis upward to meet my cock. Our eyes are locked as I slowly slide inside her, watching her expression for signs of pain. When it doesn't go in all the way, her eyes widen a little.

"It's okay, sweetie. Just hang on." I kiss her nose. "I have to give one strong thrust to break through, okay?"

She nods and closes her eyes. I reach down and find her clit with my finger. Making circles on her clit, I watch her eyes close with pleasure. From inside, I can feel her tightening as she feels the waves of sensation, and I wait until she starts to move her hips, when I thrust quickly, making her gasp. I'm three quarters in and way past her hymen, when I still for a moment. "You okay?" I ask, still circling her clit with my thumb.

"Yes, mmmm....oh, Colton, it's wonderful." She smiles, touching my face with her hand. "You're so big. It feels so...full. It's...." unable to find words, she kisses me, plunging her tongue into my mouth. Her body is so warm and wet, and tight. It feels amazing, hugging my cock. Pushing in further, I slowly speed up, feeling the rhythm of sensation. She's beginning to meet my thrusts with her pelvis, and I feel her insides squeezing my cock tighter, making me grunt.

"Is it good, baby?" she asks, biting my lower lip.

"So good," I breathe, taking her lips and tongue with mine. We're both a mess of ragged breathing and moaning, lips and tongues. When I push in all the way, my mouth opens in delight.

"Oh, God, Colton!" she cries, lifting her chest and pelvis up. "Ooooohhhhh!" she breathes as I lift, pushing my cock all the way in, meeting her every movement with a quick thrust. Our skin is slapping together in the silence. "Come with me, Colton!" she says breathlessly, "God, I'm going to come!"

My balls slap her ass as I thrust in and out, feeling her orgasm on my cock. It throws me over the edge and I feel my seed shoot out of my body into her. My mouth forms an 'O' as I plunge in and out of her quickly, riding the wave of pleasure that rocks me all the way to my toes. As my cock empties, even the aftershocks feel amazing as I slow, breathing soft murmurs to her.

"I love you, baby." I pant, catching my breath, placing my forehead against hers.

"I love you, too." She whispers, as the pleasure subsides. I kiss her tenderly but full on the mouth once, twice, three times. I can't get enough of her. I kiss her cheek, forehead and her neck, and then I lean up, grasping the hilt of my cock and removing it from her slowly. The condom goes in the garbage beside the bed, and I snuggle in beside her.

"You okay? Sore?" I ask, spooning her from behind.

She shakes her head no. "Am I supposed to be?"

"Sometimes." I answer honestly. "You might feel a sting later."

"I'll be fine. You're so sweet."

I kiss her shoulder. "You want a drink or anything?"

"All I want is you."

"You have me. All of me. My heart and soul." I kiss her head.

"How did I get so lucky?"

"I was going to ask you the same thing."

Chapter 36

Julia

If that's what I've been holding out for, I'm an idiot.
But I'm willing to bet sex isn't ever that good unless it's
with someone you love. Now that I've had my first time
with Colton, I'm so glad I never had it with John. That
was the single most pleasurable experience I've ever had
in my life. Sex or not. Colton is so gentle but incredibly
sexy. The way he breathed and moaned and looked at
me, it sends shivers down my spine just thinking about
it. We fell asleep in each other's arms.

As I lay next to him, I watch Colton sleep. His long
eyelashes are so sexy, sweeping across his cheek. His
hair is curled around his face where he's sweat in the
night. Full lips are partly open as he breathes softly.
The blankets are only covering half his body, just
partially covering his butt. Firm muscle pokes out from
under the covers and I can see that sexy 'v' from his hip
to the center of his pelvis. Lifting the sheet slightly, I
peak at his penis, which is partially hard. It turns me
on instantly.

Pressing my body against his, I carefully turn him
over, and he wakes slightly, as I climb on top of him.
His grunt is sexy as he clears his throat. "Good
morning, baby." He says with a gravelly voice.

"Good morning." I say, sitting naked on top of him.
My wetness is at his pelvis, and I know he can feel how
ready I am for him.

"Well, well," he says, "this certainly is a great way to
wake up."

I can feel his dick harden and I lift, sitting on it with
my wetness. He immediately pulls himself up, holding
my waist, so both him and I are perpendicular to the
bed. We're nose to nose as he kisses me voraciously.
Grasping my nipples between his fingers, he kneads
them, making me moan. Then he sucks and kisses
them, while pushing a finger down to my clit. "Where

are those condoms, Colton?" I pant, wanting more.

He stops instantly and looks at me. "Almost forgot." He says breathlessly, looking around for the box. When he finds it on the nightstand, he reaches over with me still on top of him. He gets one and hands it to me. "You're gonna have to help out, baby." His muscles flex as he moves back on the bed. He's so sexy it kills me.

"Can I put it on?"

"Whatever you like." He smiles.

Tearing the foil, I rip the packet open, still sitting on him. His penis is so hard and it reaches right to his belly button.

"Just pinch the top and roll it on." He instructs, rubbing my rear with his hands.

I'm careful and slow but I do it right. When it's on, he grabs me by the waist so I gasp in delight, and impales me, letting me slowly insert his penis all the way in. "You okay?" he asks, watching my face.

"Perfect." I say, not trying to hide the wonder in my eyes. Colton takes my hands in his and places his hands on the headboard, effectively forcing me to be face to face with him. Then he lifts his pelvis and I bear up with my knees. Sucking my breasts from under me, he begins moving. The feeling is exquisite. He's all the way in and it's heady. "Oh, God." I breathe, as he hits the right spot inside. Speeding up, the mattress makes a rhythmic noise. I can hear Colton panting softly under me, as he works on my breasts. Taking his face in my hands, I kiss him voraciously, sucking his tongue.

"Mmm....Julia, I love it when you do that." He says between breaths.

We're meeting each other thrust for thrust, skin slapping in the silence. All we can hear is the soft murmur of the bed and our own breathlessness. It's so heady. Making love with Colton is my new favorite thing to do. I can feel myself climb with him, as my breasts bounce with our movement. Still grasping my hands, Colton leads me up, so I'm perpendicular to the bed again. He lets go of one hand and finds my clit with his thumb. I lean back, reeling in the feeling of his thumb circling my most sensitive spot. As I move, he keeps his thumb moving, making me begin to lose control. "Oh, Colton, that's so good." I moan softly. His dick fully in me and his hands working on my clit is incredible. Just when I thought last night was the best sex I've ever had, I'm proven wrong.

"Mmm...you're so....tight...and wet." Colton whispers. "I can't get enough of you." I look at him and he's watching me. "You're so sexy on top, baby."

"This is my new favorite position." I say, feeling closer and closer with each pass of his thumb. "God, you know exactly what to do to get me off. I'm getting close already."

"So am I." he says, although I can tell because his dick is impossibly hard inside me, and his breathing is becoming ragged. "Ooohhhh, you're getting so tight, baby. I can't hold on much longer."

"Let go, Colton." I say, "Come for me." I coax as I feel myself reach the edge. "Oh, God, Colton...don't stop!" I cry out, riding the waves of pleasure. "Oh, yes!" I say, feeling my orgasm take over, washing sensation all through my body. As I start to come down, I watch Colton. His eyes are wide open and focused, as if hanging on so I can come first.

"Come for me, baby." I say, tightening my Kiegel muscles, making him feel the strongest hug from inside me.

"Oh, Lord, Julia! Oh, God!" he cries before he shudders. I move faster for him, as his body ignites from under me. "Ooohhhhhhh!!" he murmurs as he comes. Seconds later, he stills and swallows, licking his lips. "That was so...wow." He breathes.

"It was definitely a wow factor for my morning." I say, lifting. Removing the condom, I hop off Colton and dispose of the condom in the garbage. When I return, he's made a spot for me inside the bed and is rubbing the sheets in a circular motion, indicating for me to join him.

The look on his face is curious. It's kind of a smirk. "What?" I ask.

"Nothing...it's just....you have sex hair...it's hot." He comments, nodding, satisfied. "It suits you."

I don't even bother to look. I have jungle hair in the morning, and I can't imagine how awful it looks after last night and this morning. "Do you still love me?" I tease.

"Of course, baby." He says, kissing me.

We lay there, basking in the afterglow, when suddenly we hear the front door burst open and loud voices calling from the other side.

"Colton?" a male voice shouts, and we hear footsteps coming to the door.

"Shit." Colton mutters, "Cover yourself." He says, pulling the sheets in front of me up to my chin.

"Maybe he's downstairs working out—" the same male voice says. The bedroom door is wide open, and a face that looks very much like Colton's appears. "Wait...err..." a laugh comes from his throat, "U...Wade, I found him....and a little something else."

"Nice, Garrett." Colton says, unimpressed, "You ever knock?"

"I will now," Garrett guffaws. "Well....aren't you going to introduce me?"

Garrett is tall and lean like Colton, but his eyes are green instead of blue, and he has salt and pepper hair. He clearly works out, but his arms aren't as big as Colton's and he has no visible tattoos from under his t-shirt. He's wearing black jeans and a blue t-shirt that has the band Aerosmith's signature yellow winged logo emblazoned on the front.

Colton leans up in the bed and rubs my back comfortingly. "Garrett, this is Julia."

"Julia?" We hear Wade's voice bark from the hallway, and he suddenly appears in the doorway, wearing the same expression as Garrett. They both look like they've caught Colton with his pants down...which they have, literally. "Twice in one week, Colton!" Wade snickers.

He points out the fact that we're clearly both naked, and boasts, "Now you can't tell me that this was all innocent this time." He points to my hair. "That didn't happen just from sleeping."

Garrett at least has the decency to turn his head and laugh. "Nice to meet you, Julia. I've heard a lot about you from Wade."

Wade points at Garrett. "You owe me twenty bucks. I told you he was porking her."

"Hey," Colton barks. "Take it easy."

They both lift their hands in mock defence. Then the front door opens again. "Hey, bro! You guys find Colton?" Two other footsteps come from the front door.

"In here." Wade is dying he's laughing so hard.

"Alright, that's enough." Colton says, placing his head in his hands in defeat as he sits up in bed. "God, don't you guys ever use a phone?" he hisses.

Two other men come to the bedroom door. "What the fu—" he says, before he reaches the door. "Oh, shit!" he laughs. "Jesus, Colton." He lifts his hand in the air, as though to stop himself from seeing the sight before him. The other guy says, "Whoa!" and purses his lips together to stop himself from laughing.

"Hardy har har," Colton says. "You guys get your sillies out now? Can we be grownups?"

"Well, I don't know, little brother. You're the one sitting there in your underwear." Garrett says.

My face is as red as a tomato. But seeing Colton's expression is priceless. I can tell he has a good relationship with his brothers, seeing as he's not hopping out of bed, beating the crap out of them. Although it would be difficult to fight naked.

"Can you give us a minute to get some clothes on please?" Colton spits. "I'm sure Julia would feel much more comfortable meeting you all with her pants on."

"Shit, Colton, until now we didn't know you were naked." Garrett teases. "Uh...Julia, is it?"

I roll my eyes.

"This is Jack and Dalton. In case you haven't figured

it out yet, we're Colton's brothers. The Ford boys."
Garrett motions to Jack first, who has long hair in a
ponytail, but is tall and built like a biker. "Don't let his
tough appearance fool you any…he's an accountant."
Jack smacks Garrett in the back of the head, but bows
as his brother introduces him. "And this is Dalton."
Dalton is the only one who looks different from the other
boys. Very refined, Dalton's hair is cut in a crew style
and he is clean of tattoos. Handsome nonetheless, he
has a baby face, even though he appears older than the
others. He also takes a bow, but then takes a few steps
forward and holds out his hand for me to shake.

"Sorry for the circumstances. Nice to meet you,
Julia." He winks and I can't help but smile. He has the
same wink as Colton. "We'll let you two get yourselves
together."

"Thank you, Dalton. At least one of my brothers has
an inkling of tact." Colton says.

The boys leave the bedroom and Dalton shuts the
door behind them.

"I'm so so sorry about that, Julia." Colton says, the
remorse dripping from his voice.

I rub his back. "It's okay, Colton. I had to meet
them sometime."

"I have to change the lock on my front door. All my
brothers have keys and this is clearly not going to work,
since none of them ever call before they visit."

"You don't have to do that, Colton. It's nice that they
come to visit you, and I know all this was in jest. They
didn't know I was here, after all."

He leans over and kisses me. "I love you."

"I love you too."

We hear the front door close and all is silent. "How
come the horses don't make all kinds of noise when they
arrive?"

Colton gets out of bed, walking around naked,
finding his clothes. "They know them all. Rebel and
Maya are very tame; they only cause a fuss if a stranger
comes along, especially when they sense something is

wrong. They're like my built-in alarm system."

I get out of bed and Colton smiles. "God you're a sight for sore eyes." he smiles at my nakedness. "If my brothers weren't here, I'd take you right here again."

"Oh yeah?"

"Oh......yeah," he says, wiggling his brows. "I'll go get your stuff from the car so we can get showered and changed."

Twenty minutes later we walk outside together, hand in hand. Colton's brothers brought all kinds of things in preparation for the fundraiser. They're all scattered around the pasture setting things here and there. Dalton had been on Colton's riding lawn mower, cutting down a parcel of grass. He removes the yellow noise-canceling ear cans and shouts, "Hey, Julia?" in an expectant tone, then they all, one-by-one shout out the same thing, until it is Wade's turn.

He says, "Hey...Julia, is it?" and winks that Ford wink that makes my toes curl.

Colton scratches his nose nervously. "Very funny, guys. What the hell are you all doing here at eight o'clock on a Monday morning? Don't you all have jobs?" he pauses, "Or phones?"

Dalton approaches and gives his brother a hug, slapping him in the back. "Sorry, little brother. I landed last night at around six and these idiots decided they wanted to come out here early. Garrett left Marcus in charge at the airport, so I took my vacation early. Wade was home so we crashed at his place last night. We figured you were up working out since we didn't see you out with the horses." He addresses me. "Sorry, Julia. It's great to meet you. Wade did give us a heads up that maybe our little brother here was seeing someone."

He leans over and gives me a hug, but I notice Colton doesn't let go of my hand. "Nice to meet you, too...Dalton, is it?" I play along.

"That's right. We'll wear name tags until you get used to us." He chuckles.

"Yo, Colton!" Garrett shouts from a corner of the pasture. "You're getting a dunk tank again this year, right?"

"It'll be here Friday." Colton calls.

"You gonna let them dunk you this time, or are you gonna be a pussy again this year?" Wade chimes in.

"I'll go if you go." Colton rebukes, interlacing his hand in mine.

"You hungry?" he asks, kissing me.

"Starved."

Colton yells out. "Any of you clowns eaten yet?"

With the mention of food, they're all ears. Wade actually drops the handful of wood he'd been carrying from the shed.

"Well, I guess that's settled." Colton shrugs.

We are about to head to the cars when one drives by that catches Colton's eye. The driver rolls down his window and my heart stops.

Chapter 37

John

I see the little pussy has his own army. How many Ford fuckers are there, anyway? That's alright, they all look as stupid as Colton Ford himself. He's keeping my Julia hostage in his horseshit smelling fucking petting zoo. I'll get him when he least expects it. He's such a dumbass. They all think I've skipped town, but I'm here. Oh, yeah, I'm here. Waiting. The right moment will present itself any time now.

His stupid fucking neighbor is a little busybody, too. He's seen me drive by so many times and stares at me like I'm some kind of fucking alien. It's my tinted windows, I know. Old fogies don't like the tinted windows, but I don't want the fucker to see me. It might be time for another disguise. Who knew I'd be so damned talented at that. Because of dad's business, I can get just about any car I want, when I want it. I've changed vehicles at least four times since being here. Stupid fuckers have no clue.

Like now, here I am, right up the street from Colton's house, and they have no fucking clue. As I drive past, I roll down the window and smile at my Julia. She hasn't forgotten about me, not even a little bit. He's got her by the hand, holding her to him like she's his fucking dog. It's disgusting. Colton, the stupid fuck, doesn't say a word to me, he just fucks me with his eyes, the asshole. Like I'm scared of him. Please. If it weren't for his stupid brothers all being there, I'd crush him like a goddamn bug right now. But I want to wait for the right moment. When he doesn't suspect it. When he's most vulnerable. He lets his horses out at night before bed, if his stupid teenage horse-nanny hasn't already. I'll get him when he's letting them out, when it's dark. When Julia's not with him. Oh, it'll happen. She'll get an out sometime and get away from the fucker. Then I'll get him. Then I'll take my Julia back. Rescue her from the fucker.

Gregory Abbott has no clout with my father. He tried to convince my dad that I'm some kind of serial killer. Like my dad would ever believe that. Dad called me yesterday and told me so. I laughed. He laughed. It was really funny. Dad asked me when I was coming home, but he wasn't overly worried. My brother is helping him with the business. I haven't had a vacation in so long, I was saving it for my honeymoon. Yeah, that. Julia and I will have a destination wedding, small, like fifty people, and then we'll celebrate together, alone.

Dad was more irritated that I left Toronto in such a huff as I did. I didn't even tell him where I was going. But when he found out that Julia skipped town and might be in trouble with her sister and some guy, he didn't hesitate to tell me that I can take all the time I need to do what's right. When I come back home with her safe, all will be well.

Her sister's a fucking idiot, too. I don't think she tells Julia when I call or go over there, looking for Julia. She keeps threatening to call the cops if I don't stay away, but her bark is worse than her bite. I've been over there a few times when Daddy Dearest is there, but I won't bother the old man anymore; he's obviously jaded, thinking his daughter is involved with this guy for some purpose. He has no idea his daughter is a prisoner. I'll save her, and then I'll be back in Mr. Abbott's good graces again.

The moment is coming soon. I can feel it. His guard will be down and I'll be there.

...I'll end him.

Chapter 38

Colton

It's a miracle Julia hasn't walked out on me yet. With not one, but two, morbidly embarrassing moments since she's met me, and she's still here, I credit her. Yeah, my brothers are a bunch of clowns, but we're all close, and we're all there for each other no matter what. I didn't even have to ask for their help getting prepared for the fundraiser. They just showed up. And they'll all be here for the week to help set up and take down. Best part is, they're not staying with me. They're all staying with Wade, camping out on his couch and floor, just like the old days. If Garrett sleeps in Wade's bed with him, I'll razz them both about it. Dalton will tell me so I've got some ammunition. It'll be fun.

Yeah, to my dismay, John the psycho is still here. He must be some kind of a drifter to be able to stick around for so long and do nothing. Part of me hopes he'll do something stupid so Julia can get a restraining order, but the other half hopes he'll take the hint and go home. We all thought he was gone, or at least we hoped. I bet he's been hanging around Liz's place, too, but if he is, she's not saying anything.

Last night and this morning was so awesome. The sex was out of this world and the fact that she loves me and I love her...that's a miracle. I never thought I'd be able to say those words to another woman again, or feel this strongly about someone. But Julia is so easy to love. She's wonderful. She means everything to me. I just hope like hell that she gets that job at the school. After all she's been through she deserves it.

When John the psycho does finally give up and goes home, I'm not sure if I want Julia to go back to Liz's house. I'm not even sure if I want her to go stay with her dad. I want her here, with me. But how do I tell her without sounding like a complete lunatic? We just professed our love to each other mere hours ago. Isn't it too soon? Won't she think I'm crazy? I may be, but I'm completely in love with her, and I don't want to miss a thing. I don't want to spend a moment without her. God, I'm an idiot...the way I'm thinking I might as well marry her. Jesus! She'll really think I've gone off the deep end!

As John drives by, I feel her fingers clench in mine, and I calm her by sliding my finger down the inside of her palm. The look on his face is a combination of a sneer and a dirty smile, like he knows something that none of us know or he's got something we want. But I know the truth. I've got something he thinks still belongs to him. Julia hates him and never wants to see him again. If I have my way about it, she'll never have to deal with that asshole again. He's played the wrong card and I won't let him get within feet of Julia.

I see Charles poke his head over the fence that surrounds my land and he gestures with his chin in the direction that John's car has gone. "You know that guy?" Charles asks.

"Yeah, unfortunately." I admit. "He been hanging around a lot?"

"I've seen him many times." Charles tips his head hello to my brothers. "He doesn't come right up to the ranch, but he comes close enough. What's his deal, Colton? He trouble?"

"I'm afraid so, Charles." I explain, looking at Julia, unsure of how comfortable she is with me sharing her personal life with someone she's never met. Charles sees mine and Julia's hands intertwined and a wash of guilt flushes through me. "Sorry, Charles. This is Julia, Julia this is Charles, my neighbor and good friend." I let go of her hand so she can shake his.

Being an old fashioned guy, Charles chastely kisses the back of her hand. "Pleased to meet you, Julia."

"Likewise." Julia gushes. "That menace is my ex-fiance. He came here all the way from Florida to stalk me."

A 'v' forms between his brows. "Well, if you don't

mind my saying so, if I'd lost someone as beautiful as you, I'd be doing much the same." He smiles.

"You're sweet. But John needs help. This isn't about chivalry, it's about possession and control."

My brothers pass me a look that says they understand. Wade's jaw tightens as he shakes his head in disbelief. "Why didn't you tell me?" he mouths, his expression saying he feels bad for his behavior, when the girl has problems she didn't earn. I shake my head no, as if to say 'not now, little brother'.

"Oh, I see." Charles says to Julia. "Well, you're in good hands with Colton here. He'll take good care of you."

She looks at me with twinkling eyes. "He already is."

Charles smiles and then looks at my brothers. "You boys here for the week?"

"Yeah," Dalton says. "For the fundraiser."

Charles nods once, satisfied. "That's what I thought. Come by for coffee. Let me know how I can help." He says. "I'll come by and tend to the horses."

"Sounds good, Charles. We're heading out for breakfast. You wanna come?" I offer.

The old man waves, turning his back towards the house. "Already ate hours ago. I'll catch up with ya later."

Jack shouts. "Come by for dinner. We'll have a barbecue."

"I'll be here." Charles calls.

Little do any of them know that in five days' time, Charles will be a hero.

...

The day was perfect. Julia got acquainted with the other three of my brothers, and everything went well. Any tension that had been there after they caught us in bed together had dissipated within minutes. Charles came to dinner and shared some more of his wonderful stories about his wife and their life together. Some funny and some I saw Julia getting misty-eyed over. But as much as I enjoyed catching up with my family, I couldn't wait to get Julia alone again. When my brothers left, the fire was still burning, and we sat there alone, basking in the heat.

"Tired?" I ask her, rubbing her back. We're sitting next to each other in the Muskoka chairs Wade pulled out from the shed.

She looks over at me, leaning her head on the back of the chair, with a look of contentment. "Not at all. I'm so relaxed. You have a wonderful family, Colton. I adore your brothers."

"They sure seemed to like you too." I say, stroking her cheek with my hand. "I think Charles has a crush on you."

Julia smiles, looking into the fire. The red embers reflect off her face, making her look like an angel. "Aside from my father, he's the sweetest man. He's so lonely, Colton. I feel bad for him."

"He's over here a lot. I keep him company."

"I'm glad." She says, clutching my hand in hers.

I have something on the tip of my tongue, and as much as it feels like the right moment, I'm so afraid to ask her, for fear of ruining things. Unconsciously I sigh and she picks up on the sudden tension. Looking at me, she sits up higher, the relaxed posture drifting away a notch. "Everything okay, Colton?"

"Yeah," I say, but I know my answer doesn't have much conviction.

She guffaws. "No offence, Colton, but you're worse at playing coy than Nate."

I can't hide the smirk. "Alright. I'm going to say something, and I just want you to think about it. Don't respond right away."

"Okay." She says, the relaxation returning a little as she sits back down and looks at the fire again.

"I know we haven't known each other for long, but I want you to think about maybe, sometime soon, err, moving...in with me." I swallow and continue. "I love you and I have lots of room and well, I feel like in the time that we've spent together, that it would work...err...us living together." I clear my throat. "But just think about it." I pause. "I'm not sure if you have some arrangement with your dad, but I just wanted to put this out there as an option."

Stop babbling, you moron.

A sound comes from her nose, like she's about to laugh.

"What's so funny?" I ask, almost offended, but the sound of her laugh is just too precious.

She barks out a laugh, and then she chuckles like a little girl. "It's just...I've never heard you say so many words so quickly before. You're adorable!"

"I'm glad you think it's so funny." I say, picking up the newspaper off the grass that I'd used to ignite the fire earlier, and playfully beating her with it. She lets out a gasp of glee, and laughs, shielding herself with her hands, from the paper. A second later she rises, and steps her foot over my legs, as she straddles me. The look in her eyes is intense as she slides her hands through the sides of my hair and leans in so we're face to face. Her hands are like silk and her scent is like coconuts.

"I love you, Colton Ford. And you're right, we haven't known each other for long, but what we have known of each other so far has been so right. I'm not sure if moving in together now is the right move, but I'm not sure it's the wrong move, either. So, I tell you what. We'll leave it up to fate." She cups my face with her hands. "If I get the teaching job at Nate's school, I'll move in with you. If I don't, I'll stay with my dad, seeing as I won't be able to support myself for the short-term anyhow." She pauses, kissing me chastely on the mouth. "How does that sound?"

"That sounds fair." I say, trying like hell to sound indifferent, but part of me wants to say move in with me anyhow, regardless of her financial situation. We both have money, so the point is moot. But I don't say anything further, partly because I don't want to rock the boat, and partly because with her straddling me, I'm fighting a severe hard-on and the urge to take her right now on the grass by the fire.

"Alright then." She smiles. Then her face darkens and she eyes my lips. "Do you want me to go sit back in my chair, or do you want me to stay here?" her voice is soft and seductive, like she knows what my answer is.

When suddenly I feel like we're being watched. "Why don't we go inside? It's getting cold out here."

"Sure," she says, and just as she says it, I hear Rebel stir. Julia hears it, too. "What is that?"

"I don't know." I whisper. "Just get in the house." I say, grabbing a plank of wood by the side of the fire.

"I'm not leaving you." Julia insists, rising with me.

"Julia, please, just go inside. Take the back way, it's ten feet from you." I don't mean to sound as firm as I do.

"Okay. Should I call the police?" she can't hide the terror in her voice.

"No, I'll let you know. Call Charles. His number is on the fridge."

"Okay." I watch her run to the back door and enter the house.

As I approach the stable, I hear shuffling. "Who's there?" I demand, holding the wood in my hand high, at the ready.

More shuffling. Rebel lets out a staggered whinny. Maya gets up from the haystack that she's been laying on.

"John, I know you're in here. My horses let me know when there's an intruder, so you might as well come out.

I hear a whimper and a thud coming from the feed room. "Damn!" a male voice says.

As I enter the room and turn the light on, I see a drunken Cheetah, apparently staggering to get up from falling into a hay bale. "Cheetah, what the hell are you doing in here, you asshole!"

"Who the hell's John?" Cheetah slurs. "Ain't no John

in here, unless you count the piss in the corner there."

I look, and Cheetah clearly relieved himself at the corner of the room. A line of urine streams from the apex of the wall all the way down to the center of the cement floor. Thankfully the feed room also has a drain so I can easily rinse the filth with water. "I'm going to kick your ass! What the hell are you doing! This isn't a toilet! How did you even get here, you're as drunk as a skunk!"

Hearing footsteps, I lift the wood plank into the air again. "Everything alright, Colton?" I hear as Charles' face appears in the feed room. I wonder how he got here so fast, but then I realize…Charles probably saw him coming. Charles sees and hears everything.

"Yeah, it's just this asshole again." I say, gesturing with my chin towards the drunkard leaning up against the hay, as if he's given up hope that he can get up on his own.

"What's your deal, Cheetah? Why are you here?" I ask.

"Just felt like it. Ball and chain kicked me out again."

Charles looks at me. "Can't blame her there."

"How did you even get here?" I ask, pulling him by the scruff off the bale.

"My friend…he drove me." He answers as I wave my hand in the air at his face, pushing the smell away from me. A repugnant look on my face.

"You don't have any friends, Cheetah."

"I do." He insists. "That guy…he knows you, too."

"What guy?"

"The guy…the one who gave me fifty bucks to piss you off."

Just as my face drops, I hear a blood-curdling scream come from inside the house. I drop Cheetah like a sack of potatoes and run for Julia. Hearing her scream my name, I dive for the front door, which is closest, and realize that it is locked. Running for the back door, I try it. It's locked, too. Looking in the back window, I can see John. He's facing the front door, waiting for me. He's got Julia by the throat; her back to his front. And it looks like he's got a knife to her throat.

Charles trots to me. "I'll run over to my house and call the police, Colton." He says, knowing that he's an old man, and he can't help stave off a psycho, who evidently has moved to attempted murder.

"Thanks, Charles." I say, as I take a step back, gaining leverage. When Charles leaves, I drop-kick the door, and it opens immediately. As I run to the front door, John turns. Julia's face is white with fear and her breathing is ragged with terror.

"You hurt her and so help me God." I warn, my tone low with wrath.

"And what? I've got a knife, Colton. And you're an idiot." John says, his satisfied smirk is enough to make me want to tear his throat out.

I begin moving, but he moves in unison. "There's no way out of this, Colton. I'm taking Julia home to Florida. I'm rescuing her since you've imprisoned her in this shithole, and we'll get married and forget all about you, pretty boy."

Biding time before the cops arrive, I start talking to him. "Oh yeah? You're sure she still loves you? I mean, she did skip town just to get rid of you. You're the idiot who followed her. Can't you take a hint? It's not like she's playing hard to get, asshole."

John's eyes slide down to Julia for a second. "Don't listen to him, Julia. He's high on horse shit. We know we love each other."

In that split second that his eyes are off me, I shake my head no quickly, hoping she'll get the message to keep silent. Anything she says will spur John on.

"Hey!" John says, catching the subtle reaction she has to my message. "No funny business here. I'm in charge. I'm just going to take her and we'll slip into my car and be off."

"You won't get far, John." I say. "The cops are on their way."

"Well then we best be going." John says as he starts to drag Julia towards the doorway. "You keep back or I'll slice her throat." He threatens, edging the knife on her throat. She lets out a cry that tears my heart in two. I'm half a second from drop-kicking him and grabbing the knife, when I hear the click of a gun filling its magazine behind me.

"Drop the knife, dick wad." Charles says, his voice flat. He's standing behind me, having come in through the back door. He's holding the gun in one hand, as if he's done this a million times before, and could probably do this while making breakfast. "Colton's right, the cops are on the way, so you might as well give up before you're charged with attempted murder."

"Bullshit, old man!" John is irritated. "I'm not dropping the knife, so you can go to hell."

Charles doesn't take his eyes of John, but he addresses me casually. "You think his head will look good mounted in my trophy room, Colton?"

I fold my arms across my chest. "I think so."

"Shut up, old man!" John says, as he pulls the knife closer to Julia's throat. It makes contact, and the blade is new and sharp, so it breaks the skin, immediately causing a droplet of blood to pour from the spot.

"That's it!" I say, "Let her go!"

My reaction spurs John on. His eyes light up like a Christmas tree. "Oh, you like that, do you, Colton?"

Suddenly the gun fires. I run for Julia, pulling her to the floor as she lets out a scream. John falls with a thud as blood spurts from the single gunshot to his forehead. The horses are crying out from the stables, and sirens are sounding in the distance.

"Are you okay?" I ask, my ears ringing from the shot.

She nods through tears, as she wipes at the blood coming from her throat. Her hand is completely soaked with red. I pull my shirt off and place it at her throat, being careful not to apply too much pressure.

Charles approaches. "You should get away from the body, kids." He suggests. "We shouldn't move it at all.

It pisses off the cops."

I give him a look. How he knows that...I don't want to know, but we oblige all the same. "Can you go out there and make sure Cheetah's still there? He'll need to give a statement to the police."

"Oh, I don't think he's going anywhere anytime soon. He passed out cold."

I look at John. Blood is pooling around him, and I grab Julia's head, cradling it towards my chest so she won't look at the sight. "Why didn't you just shoot him in the leg or something?" I ask Charles. "You didn't have to do that." I try to keep the judgement out of my tone.

"Ah, he had that look in his eyes, Colton." Charles nods, satisfied. "That kind of man won't stop until he gets what he wants. I've seen it many times." He explains. I can relate to that, and then I chide myself for forgetting that Charles served our country, too. "The cops'll see poor Julia here bleeding, and the knife in that dick wad's hand and that'll tell the tale. They'll have your complaint on record, too."

"Cheetah said he paid him to come on over here." I say, feeling Julia settle a little.

"A diversion." Charles adds. "He created a diversion so that asshole could get in the house. He's been hanging around here for weeks. I've been keeping my eye out."

"I know you have, Charles. And thanks."

"As long as Julia here is okay."

I look down at her. She's stopped crying, but her hands are still shaky. When the cops and the paramedics come through the door about ten seconds later, the rest of the night is a blur.

Chapter 39

Julia

As I walk out of the school, the smile muscles on my face are aching. Not just because I got the job, but because I get to say yes to Colton. We're moving in together, and the thought makes me glow. I wanted to say yes when he asked me the other night, but I was afraid of being too hasty and not thinking it through. I've done that before and it's never served me well. Something about Colton tells me that the more time I spend with him, the better my life will be.

I'm not at all sorry that John is dead. The only thing I'm sorry for is that his parents lost their son, and his brother lost his only sibling. They didn't deserve that. They didn't deserve the son that they got. But something tells me by the way his father reacted, that he expected something like this to happen. That made me think that he knew something was wrong with John the whole time, and then it made me angry because if he knew about it, why didn't he do something? And why didn't he try to protect me? I'm done with it. Time to move on. I'm just thankful that the hospital did such a fantastic job mending the slice in my skin so it wouldn't look so conspicuous when I went for the interview of my life.

As I pull up to the ranch, I see Colton in the stable with Rebel, giving him a bath. Maya is in the pasture; being ridden by a little boy I don't recognize. Charles is standing on the sidelines, watching the little boy with a huge grin on his face. "Who's this cutie?" I ask, walking towards the boy.

"That's my grandson, Guerin." Charles beams. "He's ridden Maya before and they seem to like each other."

I wave to Guerin. "Hi, I'm Julia."

Guerin is about eight years old. He smiles at me but he doesn't wave. He looks like he's a bit scared to let go of the nub.

"One last round, Guerin?" Colton asks, raising his voice as he approaches from the stable.

Guerin nods, not hiding his grin. Colton's t-shirt is soaked in spots from bathing Rebel. He approaches me and gives me a sloppy, playful hello kiss. "You want a bath next?" he asks, wrapping his arms around me.

"I'm good, thanks." I smile.

Charles's gaze goes to my throat. "Feeling better?"

"Fine. Just a scratch." I say, winking. "I'm sorry to have put you both through that."

"It's a small thing amidst something much bigger." Charles says, gesturing with his chin towards Colton. "To see that young man as happy as he is since you've come around, is worth it. What's happened is in the past now." He drops the subject. "So, Colton. You all ready for Saturday? I see you and your brothers have done a fine job here." Charles looks around at how groomed the pasture looks, and all the surfaces appear squeaky clean.

"Yeah, we're all ready. I've got all the props and boards in storage. Bringing them out Friday when all the rentals get delivered."

"Sounds like you've got everything under control. And this little boy gets to stay for the fundraiser, too." Charles addresses his grandson, who's almost finished his last run around the pasture.

"Oh, that'll be fun." I say. "Do you want to be in the dunk tank?"

Guerin shakes his head no and we all laugh. "Maybe your grampa will go in." I suggest.

"I can't swim." Charles jokes.

Colton unlatches the pasture and helps Guerin off Rebel. Guerin comes running to his grampa for a hug. "Can I go on again later?"

"If it's okay with Colton."

"Whenever you like." Colton answers.

"Thanks." Guerin gives Colton a hundred watt smile.

"Well, we won't keep you kids." Charles says. "Best get him home before his mother gets back from shopping." He pauses. "We'll see you all later. Thanks, Colton."

"No problem."

We watch Charles and Guerin leave, hand-in-hand. As soon as they enter Charles's house, Colton grabs me by the waist and dives, headfirst into the side of my neck, by my ear. He snorts playfully, gently nipping at my skin, being careful not to touch the bandage in the center. "Well, are you going to keep me in suspense?" he growls as I laugh. He's tickling me deliciously, and suddenly his tickling turns to kisses, making my thighs wet.

"Well, I didn't want to say anything with Charles here."

"And I can tell by your smile that things went well?" he asks, his hope showing.

"They went well." I kiss him. "I get to teach there starting in September."

He lifts me up high and spins me around, making me squeal. "Colton! Put me down!" I shout, but I'm only letting on that I want to be put down. His strong arms around me are fuelling my desire that started just a moment ago.

When he finally lets my feet touch the ground again, he kisses me fast, once twice, I lose count. "I'm so happy for you, baby. I knew you could do it."

"Thank you."

"We should celebrate." He says, kissing me one last time. I'm sad that he stopped kissing me, I was enjoying the touch, and I was about to make it more...interesting. "What do you say to dinner out? Wine? Cake?" he lifts a brow, waiting for my response.

Snaking my arms around his neck, I take matters into my own hands. We're nose to nose when I say. "I think we should make our own brand of celebration." My voice is low and flirty, and then I kiss him, dipping my tongue into his mouth.

His hands cup my face as he opens his mouth and takes mine in his, sweeping his hot tongue in my mouth, making me weak in the knees. We're breathless when he pauses to say, "Thank God. I've been dying to get you naked for the past two days." I'd stayed with my dad on Colton's suggestion, so the investigation and clean up could be completed without me witnessing any of it.

"I'm all yours, Colton." I say, the tone begging him to take me.

He lifts me, draping my legs over his arms, and he carries me into the house. Rebel is safely in his pen and Maya is grazing inside the gated pasture. He locks the door and applies the new hotel-style bolt that he installed as we head towards the bedroom. His kisses are tender yet hot as he carries me. I'm already wet and ready for him.

He wraps his arms around me and kisses me like it's our last kiss. His hands are rubbing my back, making me melt. "I.Love.You.So.Much." he declares between kisses.

"Colton." I pant. "I want to move in with you."

"I love you even more, if that's possible." He chuckles softly. "You sure know the right things to say at the right times." He goes to kiss my neck again, and hesitates. "Are you sure you're feeling up to this?"

With a salacious smile, I take his hand and place it under the waistband of my skirt, down into my panties, and let him feel how ready I am for him. He circles his finger around my clit and my eyes close. "I love it that you're always ready for me, baby."

Biting his lower lip, I say, "Always."

Unbuttoning my blouse, I remove my shirt as he watches with his finger moving. I then undo my skirt and it drops to the floor. Next, I take off my bra, gasping as I start climbing from his expert touch. He removes his hand to take my panties off. As he slides them down my thighs, he's trailing kisses from my breasts to my belly, and then as he reaches the floor, he dips his tongue inside my folds, making me moan.

Then I do something I never thought I'd do to another

man again.

Chapter 40

Colton

I can honestly say that I've never been so happy in all my life as I am at this moment. The woman I love is not only staying in North Carolina, but she found the perfect job, and she's agreed to move in with me. Life does not get much better than this. There's just one thing bothering me...does she want the same things as I do? The day I met her father, she made a comment about wanting to have a litter of kids, but the more I think about it, the more I realize that I can't base an assumption on that comment. I've made that mistake before and I won't do it again. If Julia and I are as serious as it feels, I want to make sure I'm not treading down the same path as I was in the past.

But it's really difficult to think about such things when the woman I love is naked, standing in front of me, unzipping my pants. The look on her face says it all...she wants me. I'll never get tired of that expression. As my jeans fall to the floor, I pull my shirt over my head and toss it on the bed. The condoms are in the nightstand drawer and I peer in that direction. "Let me just get the condoms so we're not scrambling in the heat of the moment."

She lifts a brow as she lowers my underwear and falls to her knees. My dick is like steel already and she's barely touched me. It's been two days. Two days. I'm like a lovesick teenager. It's borderline embarrassing. I know I'm going to come in under two minutes, especially if she does what it looks like she wants to do. She wraps her fingers around my hardened cock and licks the tip, like it's a popsicle. It's a new thing for her, and I'm loving it. Sucking in air slowly, I take in the sensation of her tongue trailing over the tip.

When she takes the head in her mouth, I draw in a deep breath and hiss it out. "Oh, God..." I breathe. The feeling is extraordinary. Every nerve ending in my dick is alive and at the surface. "Go slow, baby." I whisper, begging, not wanting it to end as fast as it feels like it's going to. When she licks it up and down, I rear my head back, not wanting to look. It's too hot. I'll look when I'm coming, by then it'll be too late anyway. My cock is glossy from her tongue as she stuffs the whole thing in her mouth and I lose control. I let out a cry that's more animal than human as I feel the tip touch the back of her throat. "Easy, baby." I whisper.

Her touch is perfect as is her rhythm as she pumps my cock slowly and then gains speed. A guy can never be sure if coming in a girl's mouth is proper sex etiquette, so I let her know it won't be long. It's like she doesn't hear me, so I say, "I want to come inside you, Julia."

She stops for a second and asks. "Do you want me to stop?"

It's as sexy as hell and I don't want her to stop, but I also don't want to do something I'll regret, so I take her hand and lead her to the bed, while grabbing the condoms from the nightstand. "Was I doing okay?" she asks, unsure of herself. "I haven't done that in a very long time." She admits.

Placing the condom on the other side of the bed, I cup my hands around her face. "Sweetie, it was perfect. Too perfect." I chuckle softly.

Climbing on top of her, I part her legs with mine. "I love making love with you." I say, kissing her hungrily.

"Me, too." She says between kisses. "Colton?"

"Yeah," I stop kissing her so I can listen.

"Do you want me to go on the pill....you know....so we don't have to use condoms?"

My heart sinks.

She lets out an embarrassed laugh. "I know this probably isn't the time to have this conversation."

"No, no, it's the perfect time." I say, placing my forearms beside her, cupping her body, so we're close enough to kiss but far enough away that we can talk.

My dick is still hard and sitting on her belly. "The answer depends on a question I've had in my mind since we met."

Concern spreads across her face as she brushes a lock of hair from my forehead. "What?"

"I guess it all depends on what kind of timeline you have on starting a family."

The ghost of a smile crosses her lips, giving me hope. "I was ready to start the moment I met you."

I try to stop my heart from doing flip-flops. "Well, I've been ready for the last five years, but sometimes in the heat of the moment, we lose our nerve. I've seen that before."

She kisses me and inches her way towards the other side of the bed. I turn my head to watch what she's doing, and with one finger, she flicks the condom off the bed. I don't hide my smile as I bury my arms under her and kiss her like there's no tomorrow. Her hips lift, meeting my cock as she opens her legs, letting it slide inside her. Without the condom, it feels like a million dollars. Not only because my most sensitive spot isn't sheathed in latex and I can feel her warm wetness in all its glory, but also because I know now that I'm truly with the person I'm meant to be with. The person who truly wants the same things that I do. Now and forever.

"I want a baseball team of babies, and if I want that, we have to start now." She says, meeting me thrust for thrust. Those words are music to my ears. "If I'm as fertile as my sister, we're in luck." She pants, tightening inside.

"Easy, easy, love." I say, wanting to savor the feeling of being inside her, skin-to-skin. It's heady.

"Sorry, I just couldn't wait to have you. I never thought two days would feel like this."

"Mmmm....oh, baby, this is sooo good." I breathe, kissing the tip of her nose. "I can feel every inch of you. You're....pcrfcct."

She digs her nails into my shoulders. "Your dick is gliding in and out so smooth, Colton. Oh God, yes!" she cries.

Slowing, I lean down and suck her nipples as she arches back, begging for more. My balls slap against her rear, as I push my dick into her to the hilt. She bares her teeth and hisses, as I feel her growing tighter and tighter. "Oh, God, Colton. Fuck me! Fuck me hard!" she cries. It's so hot when she swears in bed.

"Oh, baby, such dirty words." I chuckle softly, giving her what she wants. I can't help but smile, and then she tightens right up and I lean my forehead on hers as if in surrender. It's so good. I'm on the edge. I can feel my balls ready to empty inside her. My breathing is ragged as she begs me not to stop. As her body stiffens it's too much and I let go with her. We're both panting and pleading as we come together. It sounds like a porn movie as we cry out each other's names and say the Lord's name.

As we lay there in afterglow, our hearts still beating fast, she says. "That was completely amazing. I could actually feel you coming and it was hot."

"Ditto, baby. Sex without a condom is something to behold."

"We should do that again." She says, half-joking.

I bang my head against the pillow with a thud in mock exasperation. She laughs. "You're adorable." She takes my face in her hands and kisses me. "I didn't mean right now." Her eyebrows wiggle, "Well...maybe."

"You're insatiable. I love it." I grab hold of her waist and tickle her belly, making her bark out a laugh.

"I see you installed a bolt on the front door. You're a smart man."

"Well, I don't want the third time to be the charm. My brothers will never learn to use a phone, and I guess you're right...I don't want them to feel like they need to, either."

"You're such a good brother." She kisses me full on the mouth.

"You're a pretty good sibling, too, I hear."

She cocks her head sideways.

"Your sister told me you gave her your engagement ring to use to pay for her tuition."

"Well, what else was I going to do with it? Plus, she would never accept money from me or my dad." She pauses, "She got in, so I'm really glad for her."

"Oh, that's wonderful. She'll do well. Is she going to stay at Mingles?"

"I don't know. Probably. She won't take money from my dad, and how else is she going to support herself?"

"I have a few single, rich brothers..." I trail off, the insinuation clear.

She slaps me.

"What? It's just a thought." I shrug.

"I.Don't.Think.So." She says, feigning irritation.

Hey, you never know.

Chapter 41

Julia

Colton is sitting in the dunk tank. There is a roar of laughter as all his students gather around him, falling over each other for the opportunity to sink their riding teacher. But just as they begin to line up, all four of the other Ford brothers saunter up to the front of the line. They each take one hundred dollar bills out of their pockets and give them to Liz, who's collecting money and tickets for the attractions. Five tries costs just five dollars, but they contribute hundred dollar bills and make it very obvious, lifting the bills in the air. The laughter and clapping is hilarious. Colton folds his arms over his chest, presses his lips together and nods, as if to say 'Oh, yeah, I've been had'.

I walk over to him and try to contain the hilarity, but I can't. "You want a try, too?" he says, mocking irritation.

"Can I?" I joke.

"Go ahead, but I'll get you back...later." He winks.

"Alright, little brother. Bear down." Dalton says, taking his first shot. He throws the ball but it's an inch from the mark. The second ball hits the target but isn't strong enough. The third is nowhere near the mark. A little boy, clearly being coaxed by his mother, steps up to the mark and presses it, sending Colton plunging into the water below. Clapping and laughter are going on like it's a comedy club, not a fundraiser.

A soggy Colton emerges from the water and wipes his face with his hands. His soaked curls frame his face and his t-shirt sticks to his body, revealing all his tattoos and his muscles. He looks good enough to eat. I feel my thighs dampen immediately. "We've got to get a hot tub or a pool...or both." I say, wiggling my eyebrows at him.

"You like the wet look, do you?" he teases, getting back up on the plank.

"Oh, yeah,"

Dad approaches me, placing his arm around my shoulders. "You think Colton would mind if I have a try?" he asks, loud enough that Colton can hear him.

"Colton doesn't mind." My beloved says.

Charles is over making sure patrons can get on and off the horses, helping the regular hands who come and care for Rebel and Maya when Colton isn't home. A couple of the waitresses from Mingles are scattered throughout, helping Liz collect money and tickets, and Charles' son is helping kids in and out of the bouncy castle. Colton's brothers will be manning the barbecue once they're finished at the dunk tank, and I'm helping clean up, including cleaning the rented portable toilets that are in a bank of three at the back of the house.

The fundraiser is a huge success so far, with every neighbor in attendance. Neighbors, family and friends of neighbors, and people from all around the state, some even from out of state, have come to help raise money for a worthy cause. By the time the day is over, we raised over thirty thousand dollars. Dad and each of Colton's brothers add their promised share and Colton's shindig is an annual hit again. He's beaming with pride as we start cleaning up at the end of the night.

"Colton, we'll come by tomorrow and finish." Dalton says. "The rental company is coming by noon, so we'll have everything looked after by supper time."

Fortunately, there isn't a lot to clean. Clean up was done well all day so it's a matter of throwing out garbage bags, placing the props and boards back into storage, and putting everything back into place. "Good, 'cause I think we're beat." Colton sighs, placing his arm around me.

"My driver should be picking me up shortly, Julia. I'll say my goodbyes now." My dad says, embracing me. "You and Colton should come by for dinner tomorrow. I'm having Liz and Nate over, too."

I glance at Colton and he and dad share a look. "S..Sure," Colton hesitates. "That sounds great. We'll be there."

I haven't told my dad that I'm moving in with Colton yet, so Colton seems to be nervous around him. This gives me the perfect opportunity to announce the news. "Yeah, we'll see you then, dad."

Dad takes a step toward Colton and sticks out his hand, just as headlights pull into the driveway. "There's my driver." He shakes Colton's hand and pats him on the shoulder. "We'll see you tomorrow, Colton." He winks.

Colton returns the hearty handshake and smiles at him.

As his brothers start to shuffle out, Wade offers to give Liz and Nate a ride home. "Wait, where are they?" I say, not recalling seeing my sister for a while.

"She's inside cleaning up." Colton says. "I'll go get her."

Wade lifts a hand. "No, that's okay. I'll go. I'm heading that way, anyway."

"Fair enough." He gives Wade a handshake goodbye and we watch him walk towards the house. Two minutes later, Liz waves goodbye from the front of the house. "Thanks for your help!" I shout, and she lifts her thumb to both of us. Wade waves, too, and winks.

"What was *that* about?" I ask, looking expectantly at Colton, as if he knows something.

"What was what about?" he chuckles.

"That whole Wade wants to drive my sister home and he wants to go get her from the kitchen? What's that about?"

Colton's eyes widen. "I hadn't noticed."

I can smell a lie when I hear one.

"Bologna. Is your brother going after my sister?" I smile. I'll note the age difference, but in this day, years don't really matter.

Colton waves, "No, you're being ridiculous!"

"Has he said anything to you?"

"No." he guffaws as if it's the most ridiculous thing he's ever heard. "Come on, let's go in and have some tea. I'm dying for a warm drink and a bath. My bones are aching from all that dunking today."

I let the subject go. "Okay. I'll put the kettle on. What kind of tea do you want?"

"I'll come with you."

As we step inside the house, the back lights are on, but I notice the front lights in the living room area are off. The room is only illuminated by about a hundred candles. I look at Colton. "What's this?"

There is a huge bouquet of roses, about fifty red, long-stemmed ones, sitting in the most beautiful crystal vase on the coffee table.

He gestures with his chin. "Go read the card."

I walk towards the coffee table and bend down to pick up the card off the plastic holder in the center of the bouquet. The card reads, "Look behind you, my love."

When I turn around, Colton is on bended knee, holding a small square box in his hand. My hand goes to my mouth as I gasp. He hasn't even opened the box and the tears are pouring from my eyes. As he opens the box, I'm whimpering. His eyes are glossy with tears and he shakes his head slowly. "God, I love you so much, Julia." His voice cracks and a tear falls down his cheek. I bend down on my knees to meet his eyes. It pains me to see him cry, even though I know they're tears of joy.

I haven't even looked at the ring. I can't handle it. The moment is so emotional I'm afraid I'll burst. He continues. "I've never met anyone who's made me so happy so quickly." He wipes his eyes and sniffs, trying to stifle his emotions so he can get the proposal out. "There is nobody else for me. You're the only one. That's why I want to marry you....and I don't care that we've only known each other for about six weeks, I know...oh God do I know, that you're the one." He swallows. His hands are shaking as he pulls the ring out of the box. I'm a whimpering, sobbing mess of tears. I'm trying to say yes, but I'm hiccupping so hard that I can't get it out.

"Will you marry me, Julia?" he asks, holding the ring in front of me.

Still scared to look at it, I close my eyes, squeezing out more tears, and nod, mouthing the word yes. He looks at me from under the light, unsure and I bark out. "Yes! Yes!"

"God, if my brothers storm in right now I'll be pissed!" he chuckles, breaking the tension.

I bark out a laugh, wiping my nose as he places the ring on my finger. Feeling slightly more courageous, I chance a look at it. My eyes widen at the most beautiful diamond and emerald ring I've ever seen. It's not a huge diamond, making me smile. The emeralds circle the diamond as it glints in the candlelight. "I got you emeralds to match your eyes."

I shake my head in disbelief. "Colton, you've made me so happy." I sob.

He takes me in his arms. "Well, that's not convincing." He jokes, trying to make me laugh.

He sighs, holding me tight, as if taking in the moment. "I love you so much, Colton."

Pushing me forward so he can see my face, he says. "I love you more than anything, Julia."

He kisses me full on the mouth once, and then looks at me. "I'll never get tired of seeing that look of love in your eyes."

"You mean the look that you have right now?"

He thinks about that for a moment. "I suppose so." He says with conviction, and then kisses me again as we lift up off the floor.

I look around at all candles shimmering in the darkness. "So was it my sister who set all this up, when I thought she was in here cleaning?"

He lifts a hand in the air. "Busted." He smiles. "You don't actually think I could pull this off, do you?"

Laughing, I kiss him again. "Did Wade know, too?"

"Yeah, he knows."

I lift a brow. "Who else knows?"

He cranes his neck back. "Well, I had to tell my brothers, so they'd leave us alone." He growls in jest. "And I had to ask your dad because I'm an old-fashioned guy."

The tears start again. "My dad knows?"

Colton wipes a tear from my cheek. "He does. And do you know what he said to me when I asked?"

"What?"

"He said 'where were you three years ago', and 'give her lots of babies'." He winks.

My hands go to my cheeks as I cry tears of joy. "Oh, Colton. You have no idea how happy that makes me."

"It makes me happy, too. So we better have a quick wedding, because we haven't been using birth control and I don't know how your dad is going to feel if I get you pregnant and we're not married yet." He says matter-of-factly with a touch of humor.

"We can get married right here, Colton." I suggest, sobering. "This place can hold plenty of people, we saw that today. We can rent a tent in case it rains, and I can ride Maya down the aisle." My eyes are dancing with excitement.

He blinks. "Wow."

"Wow what?"

"I thought girls wanted the huge wedding with limos and all the bells and whistles and stuff."

"Well, what kind of a wedding do you want?"

"As long as my brothers are there, all that matters is that we get married. We can do it in the living room for all I care. I'm just shocked that you don't want the classic princess wedding."

"Do you want that for me?"

He wraps his arms around me and looks up at the ceiling, in deep thought. "I want whatever you want, Julia. If you want a wedding here, we can do that. As long as I get to take you far away on a romantic honeymoon where I can have you whenever I want, wherever I want, I don't care if we get married over the internet."

"A romantic honeymoon, eh? Where do you want to go?"

"Somewhere where I can do this," he kisses my neck, hitting the sweet spot just below my ear, "and this," his lips trail down my neck to my chest, where he pulls down my shirt and kisses the flesh just above my breast. "and this," he pulls my shirt off, unhooks my bra and sucks my nipple, making me moan. "Wherever I want, anytime I want."

"Mmmm....so you mean like a secluded island in Bora Bora or something? Where we have our own spot and nobody can see us. We can make love in the water or on the beach all hours of the day and night..."

"Now you're talking." He smiles on my skin as he kisses my other breast, nipping at the flesh around my nipple. "You know it's amazing." He says between kisses. "That we get to do this every day for the rest of our lives?"

"I'm looking forward to it." I gasp as he sucks on my nipple, and then licks it, flicking his tongue over the erect skin.

"Me too. But you know what I'm really looking forward to?"

"What's that, my love?" I moan, taking in the sensation of his tongue teasing my nipples.

"People calling you Mrs. Ford."

"Mmmm...."

"And calling you my wife." He kisses me full on the mouth, dipping his tongue in to find mine.

"And calling you my husband." I say breathlessly.

"And you telling me you're having my baby."

I look at him and smile. "You being a daddy."

The look he gives me is so tight with conviction. He divides his glance between both my eyes and kisses me like it's his last kiss, leaving my chest heaving. He pulls my jeans down and off, grabs the blanket on the back of the couch, and lays it on the floor. Taking my hand, he guides me to the floor, and I lay down. Pulling his shirt off, Colton tosses it in the pile where my clothes are, and takes down his jeans. He is gloriously hard as his underwear comes down and his body is fully on me.

Candles alight, our naked bodies intertwined as if we are one, Colton enters me, looking at me as if I'll disappear if he doesn't. "What's wrong?" I ask.

"I forgot to ask if you like the ring."

Leaning my head back on the blanket, I let out a little giggle. "It's only the most beautiful piece of jewelry I've ever seen."

He leans his forehead against mine. "Thank God."

"As if it would matter, Colton." I whisper. "I'd marry you if all you gave me is a pipe cleaner for an engagement ring."

Sliding his hands across my brows and into my hair, he kisses my nose. "I'd have given you the Hope Diamond if your sister hadn't talked me out of it. Or the world. I'll give you anything you want, Julia."

"You already have, Colton." I slide my hand to his chest. "You've given me your heart. That's all I'll ever want. That's all I'll ever need."

"You have it. All of it."

"You have mine, too, Colton."

Chapter 42

Jack

Two Years Later

Knee deep in paperwork, my desk is piled high with financial reports, spreadsheets, files, you name it. There is weeks worth of work here, and at this point, I'm lucky to get out of the office before midnight. If I didn't have to go babysit Wade at Mingles tonight, I'd work well into the wee hours of the morning. Colton is away in Afghanistan, expected home in a couple of weeks. Dalton, Garrett and I are holding down the fort at the airline, while Colton completes his training on how to design commercial aircraft.

We need to have a leg up in this industry, as dad always taught us, and having an in-house aircraft designer, capable of making en pointe decisions, cutting through red tape, is just the edge we're looking for. Especially someone who is directly invested in the business and is family. Back when Colton was married to Pam, this advantage was never on the table, but since he and Julia married, she has done nothing but support his military career with the caveat of knowing that he will carry on with his military knowledge here on U.S. soil.

After being away, off and on, for the last six months, Colton has not been in touch with Wade and his shenanigans the way that I have. It pisses my new girlfriend Kelly off that I have to constantly head to Mingles, and then work my back off during the day, which leaves little time for her. But she's stuck around for a couple of months, which is more than I can say for any of the other girls I've dated. Having an assistant is an idea that I've played with for a while, and it's long overdue, but in the meantime, I answer my own calls, and there is one coming in right now.

"Jack Ford." I answer a little too tersely, as I am

admittedly annoyed by the interruption. I'm too lazy to check the caller ID, and it's always corporate coffers calling me anyhow.

"Jack...Blake here, from Mingles."

I smile. "Heyyyy...there's a voice I didn't expect to hear."

"Hope I'm not catching you at a bad time or anything. I know you're a busy guy."

"I'm always busy, but it's never a bad time for you, buddy." I'm still grinning, leafing through a report, trying to find a figure that has been a head-scratcher since earlier, when I made an adjustment. "What can I do for you?"

"Colton's expected back soon, is he? I thought I heard Wade say that he's coming home in a couple of weeks."

"As far as I know. Julia's itching to have him back. I think it's to a point where he's home long enough for her to remember what he looks like, and then he's gone for another few weeks to a month. This back and forth stuff can't be easy for him, but it's the only way that he can get proper training and retention when he's learning all this aircraft stuff."

"I hear ya there." A chuckle. "I'll be glad to have him back." A pause. "Listen, I won't take up too much of your time, Jack, and I ran it through my head several times if I should call Colton, but the number he gave me he said it was for life or death, and only to use if you, Dalton and Garrett were all dead, and if Wade was on his way out, too."

I snuffle a laugh. "That's Colton."

"But anyway, I've been keeping my eye out for Wade, as I always have, and I think that boy's in some serious trouble, frankly."

"Oh yeah? What kind of trouble?" I crane my neck back in disbelief. Wade hasn't said a word to me about anything, and I'm usually the first to hear.

"Well, aside from him having some trouble with this one girl who came in here last night with a bunch of girlfriends…on some…bachelorette thing, um, this other girl came in, coming after Wade like nobody's business." A pause. "Now, I didn't say nothing to Wade, trying to mind my own business, and I wouldn't have bothered you if I didn't think it was any real problem, but Wade called me about it just now, and by golly, now I'm really worried about him."

I put the paper down. "Well, what did these girls want from Wade?"

"Well, the one just looked like he'd struck her the wrong way is all, but the other, well…Jack, she was…pregnant."

My stomach drops. "Shit."

"Now Wade says it ain't his, and I want to believe him, see, but Jack, you know how Wade does with the ladies. Now he swears he's careful and all, but, you just never know."

"Oh, man. This is the last thing we need." My voice is flat.

"Yeah, especially with the way she came at him from what I heard." A pause.

"Did she like…hit him?"

"Naw, nothing like that. But she looked none too pleased. Now, I know them pregnancy hormones are quite the thing and all, and she looked just about ready to pop any day now."

"Shit," I put my face in my palm.

Blake's voice is blunt. "Jack, that ain't even the worst of it."

"Fuck, is it too early to drink?" I sigh.

"Well, I'm a bartender…ain't never a time not to drink."

"Go on,"

He draws in a deep breath and releases it. "Wade said she served him papers."

I lift my head. "What?" my voice has raised an octave.

"That's what he was calling me for." Blake says reasonably. "He's too afraid to tell you, Garrett or

Dalton, and since Colton's away, he talked to me."

"What kind of papers did she serve him?" My tone is demanding.

"According to Wade, she wants compensation."

"Like...child support?"

"Worse...she's suing him."

"For what?" I shriek.

"Wade couldn't say." I can hear the shrug in his voice. "Says the wording in the document is so riddled with legalese, he can't tell what she's asking for other than money. He can't decipher the justification."

"Is it like a sexual harassment suit?"

"Dunno. But Wade says he ain't got the money to take it to a lawyer, and like I said, he's too scared to tell the family, so I told him to try one of them pro bono lawyers."

"Jesus Christ." I mutter. "He'll be drained dry. Those lawyers don't know shit." I hit the desk, palm flat, with my hand.

"Jack, now he made me promise I wouldn't say nothing to nobody, so you can't tell him you know."

"Yeah, I get it." I cut him off. "Jesus Christ, what was he thinking?"

"Well, if you pardon my saying so...Wade don't think about much except music and women. Now, don't get me wrong, he's an incredible talent and a hard worker, and the women seem to just love him. But it only takes one, Jack. And he's found the one to get him down."

"And I'm not supposed to say anything to him." I say, showing my irritation.

"Well, you know your younger brother, Jack. He stops trusting me for blowing the whistle on him, he'll stop playing here, and his career goes in the toilet."

"That isn't true, and you know it." I point out a little too bluntly. "He'll play somewhere else. He's got the balls for it."

"I don't doubt that, but he ain't got the connections, and neither does Chuck, I'm afraid." Blake says fairly. Chuck is Wade's manager. "This is Wade's home base.

All his fans are here, you know that yourself, this place is packed with people and standing room only when he plays here." A pause for emphasis. "I wouldn't want to have him sacrifice any of that for something he may be able to figure out on his own."

"And what if he can't?" I'm almost yelling. "Wade's a whiz with lyrics and a guitar, but he's not very street smart. He'll go see this shitty lawyer and get eaten alive."

"I'm begging you, Jack." Blake's voice is even. "Please." Another pause. "I only told you in case things get really ugly, and I'm sure that you'll be the first to know if and when it does get ugly."

I sigh.

"I'm sure your number will be the first one he'll dial if this lawyer goes south. I just want you to be aware and keep an eye and an ear out for him. He needs it with Colton not here."

"I wish I'd have been there last night when this all went down." I lick my lips. "We wouldn't be having this conversation."

"Not much can be done now. Don't beat yourself up about it. I'm sure you're up to your elbows in work over there."

I look at my desk. "Well, you're right about that."

"I'll let you go, Jack."

"Thanks for the call, Blake."

Despite the mountain of paperwork on my desk, I rise and grab my keys. Part of me wants to go straight to Wade's house, but I know that that would be a mistake. Sometimes having a big family comes in handy, and this is one of those times. Fastening my seatbelt, I start the car, and activate the Bluetooth. Glancing at my watch, I decide that this time it's important enough to make that call to Afghanistan, even though since my brother left a couple of weeks ago, all my instincts have told me not to dial the number.

The international ring sounds very foreign, but when I hear Colton's voice on the other end, he sounds like he's sitting right next to me. "Colton Ford."

"Hey, big brother...have you fried out there in the desert yet?"

A chuckle. "Not exactly. But it was like a thousand degrees today. Luckily, there's some air conditioning in certain parts of the building."

"Excellent. Hey, I think Julia's got some kind of to-do thing planned when you come home this time."

"She better." He answers flatly, but good-naturedly. "I'm coming home for good this time."

"Sure?"

"Oh yeah. I've garnered all the intel I can from here. At this point, I can build a plane with my eyes closed."

"I'm counting on that."

"Good. So, what's up? I don't hear from you much. Garrett calls me every day or so. What's *your* excuse?" Garrett and Colton share a lot of notes, since Garrett is a pilot.

"Wade." I say, as if no further explanation is required.

"What's he done?"

"It's not a 'what', it's a 'who', evidently."

"Shit. Alright. This must be important, otherwise you would have waited until I got home, I'm assuming."

"It's also time-sensitive."

"Oh, man. Alright, dish."

"Just got off the phone with Blake. Apparently, our little brother knocked some chick up and she's suing him."

Colton never swears. "Fuck...me."

"And the worst part of it is, he confided in Blake about this, so my hands are tied."

"So, she's ready to deliver any day, I'm guessing." Colton follows along.

"That's what Blake says."

"And he won't tell any of us because he's ashamed."

"Yep."

"Fuck...I knew this would happen one day." Colton spews. "The little punk can't keep his dick in his pants.

We gave him the birth control speech. He's not stupid."

"All evidence is proving otherwise right now."

Colton is silent as I continue driving on the highway.

A few moments later, he sighs. "This is going to *kill* Julia."

"Shit. I never even thought of that." Julia and Colton have been trying to have a baby since they got married two years ago.

"Not just because of the obvious, but also...well, you know how close they are."

"Yeah,"

"She thinks the world of him."

"Yeah, he's her favorite."

"Pretty much."

"So, what do I do, man? I'm in my car right now, and I'm headed towards Wade's house. But Blake begged me not to say anything; but to keep an eye out, just in case."

Colton is silent for a moment, and I'm about to ask if he's still there, when he continues. "Turn the car around."

"What?"

"You heard me."

"So...don't go pound on him and chaperone him to my lawyer?"

"No. Blake's right. Even if you explain it to Wade, he'll take it personally with Blake. That kid is so goddamn independent and stubborn, he'll pack his bags and move on to some armpit of a bar to play there. You know never to cross Wade. He'll never trust you again."

"So, instead, we watch him get creamed?"

"Give him some credit, Jack. We don't know the whole story."

"Something tells me that pulling into his driveway will reveal all that."

"I'm telling you to turn the car around, man." Colton's voice has raised an octave. "You called me, looking for my opinion, and now you have it. Wade might be a little green, but he isn't going to be knowingly taken advantage of by anybody. Just wait and see."

"I hope you're right, big brother."

"Just...wait and see."

Read about the next Ford brother…Wade. All the brothers make an appearance in each novel, by the way.

Enter at Your Own Risk

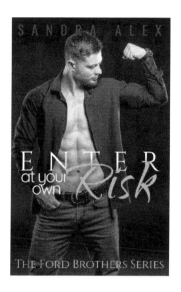

Kendra can't stand Wade. The feeling is mutual. Until someone changes the rules.

This has been an epic trashy week. I'm studying to write the bar exam, and my best friend is getting married soon. As much as I hate it, my friends and I take her out for a bachelorette party. There's a live band playing, and the lead singer just drips cocky attitude. The guy literally crashes into me in the bathroom hallway and he acts like it's *my* fault. With his rudeness and course language, it takes everything in me not to clock him the way that my father taught me when I was a little girl. And then, when I don't think that my week could get any worse, he shows up at the law firm the next day...and he's my new client.

***

What a horrible night. Normally, every chick in this place gives me bedroom eyes, but this one redhead, if looks could kill, I'd be dead. She's like a disgruntled librarian with a bun in her hair so tight it's like a facelift. We all but duke it out after she ploughs into me. Then this other chick shows up later, none-too-pleased, claiming that I fathered her unborn child! I should wear a sign that says, 'Newsflash: I'm the only Ford kid that doesn't have an inheritance, so back off!'. That should do it. But the message never gets across. I mean, what can you take away from a man to hurt him, when he already has nothing? Truth is, there's plenty, especially after tonight...

HEA (Happily Ever After)
Hate to love romance
Rock star romance
Military romance
Medium heat
Course language
Mild cliffhanger ending
Second book in a complete 5 book standalone series

Read the FREE sample of 'Enter at Your Own Risk' at the end of this book

Keep in Touch!

Join my free newsletter and be the first to know when I have a new release out!

It's absolutely free, there are no strings attached, your information is completely confidential, and you can unsubscribe any time.

All you need is an email address.

To subscribe to my newsletter, visit www.sandraalexbooks.com.

Extended Epilogue

Want to know what Colton and Julia are up to in two years? Flash forward and check it out! Find out in this FREE **exclusive** Extended Epilogue that's <u>not available for purchase</u>.

To get your exclusive FREE Extended Epilogue, visit www.sandraalexbooks.com.

Enter at Your Own Risk - Sample
Chapter 1

Booksie

Live the life or die trying

Just as I begin to think I've got a leg up for my team, a bullet hits me in the back of the head. My helmet shudders and I can't help but laugh when the paint drips down the back of my neck. It'll be a gooey load in the washing machine tonight. I hear Jenny, my best friend, yell, "Booksie! Run for the yellow hub! Nobody's watching it! We're going to gang bang them!" Jenny's such a sucker for paint ball. It was her turn to choose what to do for girls' night out, and this was her first choice.

With twenty points over our opponents, Jenny is satisfied when the game is over an hour later. "You wanna go for another round?" Wendy, Jenny's sister, asks. We give her a look like she's just sprouted an extra head. "Well, that only killed an hour and a half...what else are we going to do with the rest of the night?" We're standing in the parking lot of the paint ball warehouse; what's left of our team, anyway. The other three girls went home. Wendy looks across the street, about half a block down. "Shit. Did you guys know there's a strip joint here?" her eyes bug out.

"Forget it," I say, flat out. I have a boyfriend at home, and I'm sure he wouldn't be pleased knowing I went out to watch naked guys prance around in a poorly lit environment.

"Why not, Booksie? We have to check one out before Jenny's bachelorette anyway, right?"

Shit, she's got me there.

"I wanna go." Jenny says matter-of-factly. "Why don't you want to go, Books?"

My friends have called me Booksie forever. It's a playful poke at the fact that I'm always at home reading or studying. The point is that my nose is always in a book.

"Why do I need to go to a place like that, anyway? I have Mark at home."

Jenny places an arm around my shoulders. "Which is precisely why you need to go. I love you, babe, but Mark is more of a nerd than you are. Don't you want to go somewhere where the hot guys beg for your attention, and make your toes curl? Does *Mark* make your toes curl?"

"Does Brandon make *your* toes curl?" I ask too quickly.

"Hell, yes!" Jenny answers, which doesn't shock me. Brandon is so dreamy I kick myself for not introducing myself to him first. "Now, quit arguing. Mark isn't expecting you home until after midnight. We have hours to kill. Let's go."

"I really don't want to go." I whine. "We look like a bunch of freaks with all this paint in our hair, and I've sweat like a pig under the paint ball gear."

She gives me a look. "I have a brush and a deodorant stick in my car. We're going."

"Seriously?"

"Seriously. And it's my car so you're shit outta luck, Booksie."

I knew she'd play that card if she got desperate. Jenny means well. But ever since she and Brandon got engaged, she's become Bridezilla. Just the mention of something to do with the wedding, and she's all over it.

Ten minutes later, after a deodorant bath and us each taking a turn with Jenny's wedding makeup samples, we enter the strip joint. All of us wore interchangeable clothes to paint ball, not knowing exactly what we'd be doing afterward. Never dreamed we'd end up at a place like this. An arrow, or at least what I thought was an arrow, instead it was a crooked neon penis, led us to the upstairs portion of the building, where the naked men are. The downstairs is a sex toy shop...shocker.

At least the music is promising. As we enter the club, paying a handsome fee of ten dollars per person, I see the dance floor is full. There are no strippers in sight yet, to my relief. It's just a load of girls dancing and having a good time. *Perhaps this won't be as bad as I thought.* "You want me to the be the designated driver, sis?" Wendy asks Jenny thoughtfully.

"No, I want to check this place out with a clear mind."

Eye roll.

"I need a drink." I say, surprising myself.

"I'll get us white wine?" Jenny offers.

"Sounds good."

Two minutes later I've finished my first drink. "Go get her another." Jenny instructs Wendy.

"It's not like you to drink, Books. I like this side of you." Jenny elbows me. "It's about time you unclenched for five minutes."

"You should do the same." I say, taking my second drink from Wendy. We're standing by the bar, which is not much bigger than my walk-in closet. The whole club is no bigger than a small church. The dance floor is a square at one end of the club, with an archway covered in glinting beads being used as a makeshift door on the wall end. The dance floor is flanked with old wooden chairs that look like they've been bought at a garage sale. The round tables are slightly warped but appear clean. The floor isn't sticky, and neither is the bar, which is a plus, considering I thought this place would be one that you'd have to wipe any surface off first before touching it.

Jenny is about to rebuke when we hear an announcer come over the speakers. He asks us all to take our seats as some hottie is about to grace us with his presence. And he's not kidding. Some guy dressed as a firefighter suddenly appears from behind the beaded archway. He's decked out in everything, including the oxygen tank, impressing me. *Maybe he's a real firefighter and he does this on the side.* I let myself think that as the second glass of wine takes effect. "Woohoo!" I screech as Jenny and Wendy exchange a look. They're impressed, too.

He comes out, at first just grooving to *The Bee Gees' 'Stayin' Alive'*. Making his appearance throughout the whole dance floor. When the song reaches the first chorus, as it goes 'Stayin' aliiiiiiiiiive', he pulls off his jacket slowly as the stage lights flash. A few girls whistle, encouraging him to remove more. Underneath his jacket is a tank top over a set of wicked pecks and memorable shoulders and biceps. He looks oiled up under the lights. He continues, wiggling his eyebrows and pulling at the suspenders holding his pants up, which I notice are a couple sizes too big on him. His short blonde hair is slightly curly, and his green eyes sparkle in the light.

It's not long before he's wearing just his tank top and a pair of shorts. He leaves his fireman's hat on while he gyrates to the extended version of the popular disco tune. I can't take my eyes off him. He's beautiful and toned and has the moves that suggest he's a god in bed. When he finally rips off his shorts, the audience roars and my eyes go straight to his, well...you know. He's well endowed. He fills the G-string very well. My thighs are instantly damp and warm. Ten seconds later, he rips, and I mean literally, rips off his tank top from the center of the dance floor, under the stage lights. He's so hot my insides melt.

"Here, I grabbed some bills from the bar." Jenny says, handing me a bunch. "Go see what he'll do to you with that."

"What? Why me?" I bark, thinking I'd rather just sit here and drool, the wallflower that I am.

"Please." She says flatly, "What happens at the strip joint stays at the strip joint. Go have some fun. You deserve it."

"What about Wendy?"

"You can both go."

I look at Wendy and she shrugs and gestures with

her hand for me to go ahead.

Girls are hovering around him. One of the bouncers brings him a chair. He's lifting his leg up and dancing provocatively, I gather so his manly bits will look more pronounced....as if they need to be. He's more man than I've ever seen. As Wendy and I approach, we have to almost push through the throng of horny women vying for his attention. He's doing his thing; dancing and bulging out his biceps and abs so the girls can drool over him. With a G-string covered in bills, he walks towards the tables that aren't abandoned, spreading himself around.

"I guess we'll catch the next one." Wendy says. Just as she says that, the tune changes to Donna Summer's 'Hot Stuff', and another stripper appears. This one is in a white tuxedo complete with tail and top hat. He's steaming hot; tall and built as well as the fireman, but this one has an olive skin tone with deep blue eyes and short hair. I can't believe they make men that look like this. It's almost like a fairy tale.

Wendy guides me back to our table and we notice the fireman is making his rounds at each table. "Maybe he'll come back to ours." She says. "You want another wine?"

"Sure." I say, watching tuxedo man remove his jacket and drape it over his shoulder like he's a runway model. Hell, I'll take it. He looks good enough to eat. His dress pants are snug around his rear, which is also tight. I have to supress the urge to go over and take a bite out of his ass. It looks like two scoops of ice cream. My underwear is soaked, and I have to cross my legs to try and slow the blood flow. We stay in our seats this time as we wait for tuxedo man, who is slowing becoming tuxedo-less man, come our way.

His shirt barely contains his biceps as he undoes the buttons. When he stands there in just his suit pants, I count his six pack abs, drooling over each one. I want to touch them, kiss them, suck his hard nipples. God, this is the hottest thing I've ever seen. Wendy hands me another drink and I take a slow sip of it as I watch tuxedo man come closer to us. He rips off his pants, which I now realize are tearaways, and I look...there. Holy fuck. He's bigger than the fireman. This place is doing things to me. These men are doing things to me. This wine is also doing things to me.

Next thing I know, tuxedo man is standing within a foot of me. I take a dollar bill and blindly place it in his G-string, not taking my eyes off his. He's a monster compared to me. But he has such innocent eyes. "Go ahead, I won't bite." He says as I tuck the bill in. He touches the side of my face with his hand and my insides turn to syrup. As he dances away from me, I realize my mouth is wide open.

"Are you okay?" Wendy says, half-laughing. "You look like you're going to puke or something."

I shake my head no and toss down the rest of my wine. "I think I'm in love." I say, not meaning to say it aloud.

Jenny barks out a laugh. "Me, too, sister. This place is definitely on the list for my bachelorette. I've gotta find out the names of these guys and make sure they're here that night."

"I'll be there." I say, still entranced.

"Totally." Wendy says.

When another stripper comes out, I'm numb. I've never seen anything like this before. It's like 'Let's Make a Deal' of penises. I'll pick whatever door any of these angels comes out of. I watch the fireman make his way towards us. "Hey, did you know there's a VIP room in this place?" Wendy says. "I asked the bartender." She looks at me. "You wanna take one of these hotties to the VIP room?"

"Why? Does Jenny want me to test it out?" My tone is intentionally facetious as I speak like my best friend isn't sitting right next to me.

"Go." She ignores the jibe, chuckling. "You won't last sixty seconds in a room alone with one of these guys."

"Oh yeah?"

"Yeah," she guffaws, almost spewing Pepsi out of her nose.

"Is that a dare?"

"Double dare."

Chapter 2

Booksie

The first last time

'I'll show them', I say inside my head, as fuzzy as it is. Rising, ever so clumsily from my chair, I stick my tongue out at both Wendy and Jenny and get a laugh. Walking over towards the fireman, I see that he's standing, talking to a woman who looks old enough to be his mother. *Maybe it is his mother.* And I just about lose my nerve, when he sees me and smiles. "Hi, can I help you?" he asks in an Australian accent, which makes my toes curl. *God, could he be any hotter?* "Wha...aaa....are you busy?"

"Naw, not really, love. I don't go back on tonight. What can I do for ya?" His reaction surprises me. I have no idea how this strip joint industry works.

"Oh, okay. Well, I don't want to bother you." I say, walking away.

"Did you or your friends want the VIP room?" he looks at me blankly, as though he offered me a slice of cheese from a cheese platter he's holding. My hesitation is obvious, and he smiles. "Come on, I'll take you." He grabs my hand, making my insides like hot molten lava. Leading me through the throng of horny women, we end up at a small bank of pods, almost like changing rooms that you see in a department store. Inside each room is a small cushioned seating area fit for two (or one and a half, really) in cheesy red velveteen. The walls are painted the same dark red.

I almost have to laugh at the décor, even though I should talk; my couch at home is canary yellow and I still have my Judy Jetson bedsheets on the bed in the spare room. "Classy enough for ya?" he winks, inviting me to have a seat. The music from the stage carries well into the area, but it is muted enough that one can have a conversation. He smells lovely; like wood and spice.

"It's fine." I say, not knowing what to say next. It's

surprisingly difficult to talk to a guy who's sitting next to you in a G-string. "Should I pay you?"

He waves. "Not to worry. My name is Dan." He offers me his hand to shake.

"Booksie." I shake his hand. This feels like a sexy job interview.

He rises, standing over me. His package is almost in my face and my heart jumps out of my chest before I realize he's going to squat so we're at eye level. *Phew!* "Well, you can relax, Booksie." He strokes the side of my face with his hand, looking at me like I'm an angel. "I'll be gentle." He kisses the side of my neck, sending shivers down my spine. The stubble on his face lightly scratches my skin deliciously. He then kisses my collar bone and pulls back to look at me. "Do you mind if I kiss you on the lips?" he murmurs. The tone is sexy as hell.

I don't even blink, but I shake my head no and close my eyes. At first, he kisses me softly with just slight contact. I don't respond right away until I feel his warm hands on my face, cupping me gently. My heart is racing, and I can feel my heartbeat...there. "Just relax." He whispers against my lips, before opening his mouth, gently forcing his warm tongue inside. I let my body take over, forgetting I have a boyfriend at home...for a minute.

As his mouth makes love to mine, I feel like I've suddenly turned to pudding. I couldn't pick Mark out of a lineup. He gently pushes me against the wall, as his hands go to my breasts and I begin to rear up, letting him have full access. My head is spinning with wine and hormones as my nipples bud from his touch. He uses his hand to pull my hand to his...stuff, and it feels like a steel rod begging to be released from its prison. His hand keeps my hand in place. I don't dare move.

I'm in a tailspin of drunkenness, hormones and confusion when voices blurt into the area, interrupting us. Giggles and girly squeals are heard, entering, and then they stop when they see the curtain between us drawn. When they leave, Dan, my sexy guest, takes a seat and rakes his hands through his hair. "I'm not supposed to do all this to ya anyway, love. I'm just supposed to dance for ya."

"Oh, I'm sorry. I'm new at this." I get up and adjust my shirt, and then sit back down again.

"Me too. This is my first week."

"Oh," *Gee, you'd never know it. Was he just born sexy?*

"Yeah," he chuckles. "Boss man finds out I'm out here makin' out with you it could be my last week, too."

"Do you want to go back to the other room?"

He waves and shakes his head. "Not really."

I feel brave, suddenly. Like finally I'm not the only person who doesn't know what they're doing. "Do you like it here?"

"Not really, no. But I have to do something to pay the bills. I used to be a bus boy and a host at a restaurant, plus I worked nights hauling bags of grain," he points to his bulging biceps, "that's how I got these. But I couldn't make nearly what I'm making here holding down three jobs."

"Don't you have an education?"

"I was working on it back in Australia, but some unexpected things happened, and I had to move here and give up school for a while." He presses his lips together. "I'll be going back once my troubles are settled here. This is just temporary."

"What are you going to school for?"

"Engineering. I'm working on my master's degree."

"Jesus." I'm shocked. "Well, I hope I didn't get you in trouble. I won't tell anyone. Besides, I've got a boyfriend at home, so the less I say the better."

"You're sweet." He grabs my hand. "C'mon. I'll take ya back."

As we're walking, the alcohol is beginning to wear off, and I have a burning question. Before he bids me adieu at the entrance door, I hand him the money I owe him and ask, "How come you wanted to...um...blur the lines...with me?"

He smiles. "You mean how come I took a risk with you?"

"Yeah,"

He leans in and holds both my hands in his. "Whoever this boyfriend of yours is who's at home, without you, I hope he knows how lucky he is." He winks and walks away, looking back to salute me farewell.

As he walks away in his G-string, all I can think of is...wherever he's going, I sure hope they have pants for him.

An hour later I'm sober and walking towards the front door, arriving home good and horny...and two hours early.

...and I walk into the biggest shock of my life.

***

The house is quiet and dark, and I think how perfect this is. I'll get into the bedroom, find my sexy negligee and surprise Mark in bed. Inwardly I know I'll be picturing Dan the whole time, but how is Mark going to know that? He'll have the best sex of his life, so he won't complain. Tiptoeing through the door, I don't even bother to turn on the kitchen light. Closing the kitchen door quietly, I place my purse on the table. My paint ball bag I left in Jenny's car. I'll get it from her tomorrow.

Removing my shoes, my bare feet tap gently on the linoleum floor. The living room lights are all off, and so are all the hallway lights. A small, sensor light that doubles as a flashlight is illuminating the hallway, and as I enter the bedroom, the room is lit with about six pillar candles. At first I think this is the moment I've been waiting for; Mark and I have been together for two years and while saving for a house, we rent this one so I can finish my studies and so he can help save up for a down payment. So, it wouldn't be at all strange to come home and find our bedroom filled with candles and Mark waiting for me on bended knee, asking for my hand in marriage.

...except that this is not that moment.

My loving boyfriend is on his back, in our bed, and some blonde tart is riding him, rearing her head back in the ecstasy I've always craved and never received from him. They're so into their sexy escapade that they don't even hear my gasp. On impulse, I take the candle closest to me and throw it at Mark, causing the fire and hot wax to instantly burn him. He screams like a girl, jolting up so quickly he knocks his slutty friend over and she falls onto the floor with a big thud. She's not even pretty; she's slightly overweight and bigger than me, with mussed up shoulder length bottled blonde hair, mascara smudged across her eyes and smeared lipstick. With another candle conveniently inches from my hand, I lift it a whip it at her. She raises her hand defensively and rises from the floor, naked.

Glaring at my beloved, I say nothing, as he quickly runs around, dick whittled down to nothing, and snuffs out the candles. He grabs his underwear off the floor, helping the slut gather up her clothes. I don't wait for him to give me some lame excuse. "I hope she gives you gonorrhea." I seethe as I walk out of the bedroom, grabbing my book bag off the floor in my wake.

Chapter 3

Wade

Worst Night Ever

I'm hitting the high notes bang on tonight. Who would have known the acoustics in a trash can like this would be so awesome? Normally I wouldn't play in a dump, but it's been slow at home in North Carolina, so I took the gig for the bread. The chicks here dig me, so it's cool. The guys are grooving to the tunes as well, so it's all good. It should be pretty easy getting action tonight, too, based on the looks I'm getting. It's never a challenge for me in that department. Being a rock and roll artist is a turn-on for most women.

My brothers, all four of them, hate it that I'm a singer. Well, not so much that I'm a singer so much as the fact that I play in armpit establishments. But it's all I've got. That's what it takes to make it in the industry. You've got to do your time before you hit it big. Like a rite of passage. I'm cool with it. Hell, I've been at this for years now, since I was seventeen and fresh out of high school. It's all I've ever done. It's all I've ever wanted to do. Yeah, my basement apartment's a hole, but it's *my* hole. At least I'm doing it on my own, without any help from my rich siblings. I've never asked them for a dime and I never intend to, either.

This one chick is all but flashing me in the audience. She's got long blonde hair and legs up to her neck. It doesn't look like she's with anyone, but I'll find out in a minute when I play the next song: a slow ballad. The boys hate it when I change the routine for the night based on what the chicks are doing. But hell, I'm the captain of this ship. As we change gears and play a cover of *Jeff Healey's 'Angel Eyes'*, I wiggle my finger in the air, looking straight at the blonde, indicating for her to come up to the stage. Obliging, this sexy woman approaches. I stick my hand out to help her up on the stage, and I place my free hand around her waist.

She laps it up, snaking her arms around my neck, making love to me with her eyes as she dances with me and I sing to her. She's running her hands through my hair, like we've known each other for years. Most women love this kind of shit. Looking around, I see some of the other single girls turning green with envy. It's kind of heady. When the song comes to a close, the blonde kisses me on the lips and winks at me. Before the next song starts, she whispers in my ear "You going on a break?" her expression says she wants to do more than dance.

Removing the mic from my face I answer, "I can go for a break anytime I want, darlin', I'm the lead singer."

"Storage closet." She mouths as I help her down off the stage.

The boys are ready for a break, so I announce it while pre-recorded music starts playing from the speakers.

Following the blonde, I see her open the storage closet door. I enter the dark room as she turns on the light. There's a lock on the door, which she engages. Then she grabs me and kisses me, tongue and all, until I can't breathe. "Easy, easy," I say, almost laughing.

She's wearing a black minidress with spaghetti straps. Her high heels are black with a gold heel so tall I'm not sure how she keeps her balance. While salaciously gazing at me, she lowers one of her spaghetti straps, revealing herself. When she takes down the other one, both her tits are sticking out, hard nipples and all. My dick turns to steel. They're small but real, and so pert I can't help but want to suck on them.

"Well, are you just going to stand there and stare or are you gonna touch them?" she asks, purring.

I've never had sex in a storage closet, nor have I ever wanted to. Especially this one; which has smelly garbage bags and various chemical cleaning products in it. I just figured we would make out; I had no idea this chick was going to start undressing. "You don't...like...charge by the hour, do you?" I joke.

She lowers herself and reaches for my zipper.

"Whoaaa," I say, "Hey, take it easy. I'm not getting naked in here. What's your deal, anyway? Are you a hooker?"

"I'm whatever you want me to be, baby." She winks. *Fuck, I'm outta here.*

"Uh, yeah, thanks, but no thanks." I say, unlocking the door, not waiting for her to pull her dress back up.

Walking by a bouncer, I point the blonde out. "Get her out of here, man. She's a prostitute."

He nods as I step back on stage and watch her get politely escorted out.

I see my brother Jack walk in the front door. He lives a half hour from here, so he said he might show up. Usually Colton, one of my other brothers, comes with me to gigs—he's a bouncer—but he's away right now.

Jack waves at me and takes a seat by the bar, as we start back up with a fast tune on stage. I remove my hand from the standing mic so I can wave back. A brunette approaches Jack and asks him to dance. He's a pretty decent guy so I'm not surprised. He has a ponytail and tattoos, and hey, he works out, so there's not much challenge for him with the ladies, either. Problem is, he's stupid and lets the women find out he has money. When that happens for me, I'll *never* tell.

A pack of girls enters the bar. One is wearing a banner across her body that says, 'Bride to Be', and the others are wearing matching t-shirts labeled with their position in the bridal party. *Oh, goody...another bridal party.* Chicks that are getting married, and their friends, are loud, cheap and obnoxious. And usually already drunk, so they barely drink anything, which pisses the owner off. There is no cover for women here, and it works like a magnet. They choose a table in the back, away from the crowd. I watch them. There's one chick that looks so pasted together, like she spends every cent on plastic surgery. Her eyebrows are tattooed on. Another is really overweight but has a pretty face. The bride is hot, kind of a Courteney Cox look alike, with dark hair and blue eyes and a body. They're all looking at me with goo-goo eyes from the table, except the last one, a redhead, who's rolling her eyes, looking unimpressed.

The waitress stops and takes their drink orders. The redhead gets up and walks to the bathroom. I watch her. She's staring at the floor with each step. Her hair is tied back in a bun and she's got black pants on and her t-shirt says 'Bridesmaid', and she's got long, dangly earrings that glint under the bar lighting. When she finally looks up, I wink at her. A sour look crosses her face, as if to say, 'what the hell do you want, asshole?' as she pushes the door open to the lady's room.

My drummer signals to me that he needs to take a break. I announce to the crowd that we'll be back in ten minutes, and pre-recorded music starts playing from the speakers again. When I put the mic back on the stand, I realize I need to use the bathroom pretty bad. I see Jack lined up at the bar and I signal to him to get me a beer. He nods as I walk into the men's room. After I relieve myself, I head into the green room beside the washroom, knowing Jack will come back there, and as I walk to the room, I bump straight into the redhead.

"Oh, shit, pardon me." I say.

"Why don't you watch where you're going?" she says, and then recognition comes to her face as she realizes who I am. "What's the matter? Being up on stage, you lose your balance when you're back on the floor?" her tone is condescending.

"Hey, look, I said I was sorry. What's the problem?" I lift my arms in defence. *What's wrong with this chick? PMS?*

"There's no problem. I just don't like being molested when I walk out of the lady's room."

"I didn't *molest* you, lady. I accidentally bumped into you. I said I was sorry."

She guffaws. "What's the matter? Are you so used to women throwing themselves at you, you can't handle it when one doesn't *like* your attention?"

I lift a brow. "Look, lady. I don't know if you've got

PMS, if you're some kind of man-hater, or if you've just been recently dumped—can't imagine why," I cock my head sideways in mock disbelief, "but like I said, it was an accident, and I've apologized. What more do you want? What, you want me to buy you a beer? Buy your friends a round of drinks? What?"

"Don't flatter yourself," she says, just as Jack approaches.

"What's the problem here?" he says, carrying our beers.

"Oh, great, pretty boy has an army." She comments sarcastically.

"Not that it's any of your business, but this is my brother." I say, taking my proffered beer.

"Yeah, I bet you have lots of 'brothers'." She air-quotes.

This chick is psycho

I take a sip of my beer. "I do, actually. Four if you really care to know."

"I *don't* care." She spits.

"You must care seeing as you're still standing here." I spit back. I've just about had enough of this shit hole.

"You're an asshole."

"You're a bitch." I chuckle. "Or a dyke, one of the two."

"For your information," she stops herself, lifting a hand. "Never mind. You're not worth it."

"Apparently I am, since you're still here, fighting with me." I laugh sarcastically. Jack is enjoying this. He's smiling as his gaze goes from me to the redhead, like he's watching a tennis match.

"God, where do assholes like you come from, anyway? Your kind seems to follow me everywhere." She says to herself, as if she's taking stock.

"North Carolina, you?" I ask, playing along sardonically.

"Oh, that's great."

"Why? You from North Carolina, too?" I laugh, almost feeling sorry for this crusty chick.

She rolls her eyes. "Fuck."

"Oh, she's got a potty mouth, too." I say, spurring her on. "Well, I tell you what…" I trail off, gesturing to her with my hand, testing her to see if she'll tell me her name.

"Kendra,"

"Yeah, sure, we'll call you Kendra. I'm sure that's your real name."

"Mine's Bob." Jack supplies, lifting his beer with a wink.

"Well, Kendra, you stay away from my side of town," I tell her where that is, "and we'll get along just fine." I laugh. "By the way, I'm Wade…Wade Ford." Jack and I are killing ourselves laughing, knowing that our real names sound like stage names, when they're not. Colton, Dalton, Jack, Wade and Garrett Ford…how much more stagey can names get?

"Fuck you," she says as she stomps away, huffing.

Jack takes another sip of beer and places an arm over my shoulders. "You'll be married to her in six months."

After the women I've run into tonight, I'll never get married.

Little do I know this is just the beginning.

Chapter 4

Wade

The night just keeps getting better

I laugh at Jack's joke and guzzle my beer so I can head back on stage. For the next hour I sing my heart out and the dance floor is full. Jack salutes me goodbye as I take another break. Bitchy girl and her clan are gone, too. But a whole new set of patrons have filled the place. There are still a couple of hours left to kill as I check my watch, downing another beer on my break. One of the bouncers calls my name, "You're Wade, right?"

I nod, "Who's asking?" *God, what now?*

The bouncer gestures to a girl; I can only see her head through the crowd. When she approaches, I notice she's sporting a pregnant belly. She has short, wavy brown hair, glasses, and is wearing a sour expression on her face. I have no idea who she is or what she wants with me, but she tips her head sideways expectantly. "Let me guess...you don't know who I am." It's not a question.

"As a matter of fact, no, should I know you?" I ask, trying for equally cocky and condescending.

She looks around for a moment. "Do you think we can go somewhere private and talk?" her tone is cutting.

"Can you tell me who you are first?" I guffaw.

"Not that it would make a bit of difference, but I'm Priscilla. The last time I was here was about six months ago, which was around the same time you were here last." She rubs her swelling belly, and the hairs on my arm stand up on end.

"Err...we can go in the back room." I say, leading her. The bouncer stares at me and mouths 'you okay?'; the same bouncer that escorted the hooker out earlier. I nod yes. He nods his understanding but remains there, folding his arms across his chest.

When we arrive in the green room, I close the door. "So, what can I do for you, Priscilla?" *This ought to be good.*

She doesn't sit on the couch, probably because it looks like it might be infested with some sort of vermin. And I don't offer, either, since I don't even want to sit on it.

"Do you remember me, Wade?" her tone suggests she's irritated.

"Nope. Why don't you refresh my memory?"

She looks at the couch, "I used to have long black hair? I was about thirty pounds lighter?" she points at the couch. "I believe we christened that couch a few times, and the wall, and the floor?" she says, clearly not proud of it.

"Not ringing any bells, Priscilla."

A hand goes to her hip. "Jesus, how many women do you screw a night?"

"I don't think that's any of your business."

She puffs out a breath of air, "Well, remember me or not, I'm carrying your child, Wade."

My neck cranes back. "Bullshit."

This chick is nuts! What is it with this place? Remind me never to come here again! Jesus Christ, this place should be called 'Enter at Your Own Risk'!

"Deny it if you like, but it's yours." She is matter-of-fact. "And since there are dozens of Fords in South Carolina, I couldn't find you. Until I heard through the grapevine that you were playing here tonight. That's why I'm here."

I wasn't about to share with her that I don't live in South Carolina, that I live in North Carolina. The least this psycho knows about me the better.

I look at my hands, trying to buy time. "Well, I can tell you, Priscilla, that I didn't sleep with anyone when I was here last. This place is about as clean as a dumpster and despite what you *think* you know of me, I have standards."

I'll admit I was considering doing the blonde in my car later, before I knew what her deal was, but not now, and not in this dive.

"Well, like it or not, Wade Ford, you're going to owe me...big time." She says, handing me a manila envelope. "I'll see you in court." She speaks to me like I'm a joke and walks out of the room.

When I open the envelope, my eyes widen. Despite her telling me that she couldn't find me, she'd somehow tracked down my address and phone number.

For the life of me, I don't remember this woman. But something tells me she's going to be in my memory for a long time.

Chapter 5

Wade

Just when I think it's bad, it's worse

Having barely slept, I stare at this piece of paper that has now become my nightmare, and I have to fight the urge to tear it up. The legal jargon looks legit, but how the hell would I know? The only piece of paper I ever saw that had anything legal on it was my dad's will after he died. Even that was thoroughly explained by the Estate Attorney who dealt with my dad's last wishes. I don't have a lawyer; my brothers do, but I've never had a need for one, being the only Ford boy who doesn't have any inheritance. That's a long story. I don't like to talk about it.

If I tell my brothers about this, they'll think I'm a fool. I've never as much as touched a woman without having a box of condoms handy. Yeah, I know, birth control isn't one hundred percent effective, but hell, I'm careful. And there's no way in hell that I knocked this chick up. I remember every girl I've ever slept with. Guaranteed the name Priscilla is not on my list. I can't even decipher what she's trying to get out of me from this document. Good luck, because I've got *nothing.*

I quickly Google lawyers in the North Carolina area and realize I'm kidding myself. There's no way a decent lawyer is going to give away free legal advice. I can't ask any of my friends for help; they'll razz me worse than my brothers. There's only one person who can help me who won't judge me.

...

The phone rings at Mingles, the bar where I sing at in North Carolina, and I cross my fingers that Blake, the bartender, is there. He picks up on the third ring, slightly winded.

"Hey, Blake. It's Wade. Am I catching you at a bad time?"

"No, I was just sweeping the floor in the back. Had to run for the phone." He answers cheerily. "What can I do for you?"

"Hey, can I ask you something? And I need you to keep this between us."

"Sure. What's up?"

"Last night I was playing at that armpit of a club out in South Carolina."

"Aw, shit. That place? What are you going there for?"

I sigh. "Just...let me finish."

"Alright." He says reasonably.

"Well, this pregnant chick comes up to me, says I'm the father of her child, and hands me this legal document, and walks away." I pause. "I don't know what to do."

I then explain that I'd never seen her before in my life, and I don't know anyone named Priscilla.

"What's the document say? She suing you? Shit, the kid's not even born yet. She ain't even given you the option for child support."

Fuck...child support?

"Oh, man, you're scaring me, Blake." I say honestly.

"Well, Wade, it ain't no secret that your family is rich. Anyone who looks the name Ford up in the North Carolina area will see who you are. I'm surprised this hasn't happened sooner, frankly."

"But I don't have a dime!" I slam my fist on my thigh.

"Well, she don't know that."

I sigh. "What the hell do I do?"

"You have a lawyer?"

"No," I whine.

"And I'm guessing you can't afford one, and you don't want to tell your brothers, which is why you're asking me."

"Yep." I make a popping sound with the 'p', marking my 'I'm so screwed' attitude.

"You ever heard of 'pro bono'?"

"What the hell's that?"

"It's when a lawyer does cases for free."

"Why would they do that?"

"Some do it for charity, and for some it's like volunteer work to get experience. They're out there."

"Really? And they're legit?"

"Sure. Look it up. You just need one for legal advice at this point. For all you know this document is fake. Was it done on letterhead with a logo and all? Mind you, someone can copy that off the internet and paste it if they're real clever. You'd be surprised what kind of documents people can muster up out there. Some real slime balls in the world, Wade."

"Jesus, Blake. How do you know all this stuff?"

Blake chuckles. "When you've worked in a bar for as long as I have, you learn things."

"What I don't get is how she even got my contact information. She said she couldn't find me, that's why she came to the bar when she heard I was in town."

"Ah," Blake grumbles. "That was for dramatic effect. If she was serious, she'd a had you served by a dude carrying a clipboard. You'd a had to sign for the envelope and everything."

"So, you think this is phony?"

"Probably. But I'd still get an opinion on it. If for nothing else for protection. Be one step ahead of people like that. There'll be lots of them for you boys especially."

"Thanks, Blake. Hey, remember to keep this between us, eh?"

"I'll take it to my grave, son."

Other Books in this series

The ex-military pilot. The bewitched single mother. The plane crash that saves their lives.

Getting pregnant by the wrong man and trying to make it right didn't serve me well. It's been years and we're not any closer to where we should be. Working night and day in an I.C.U. doesn't bode well for a relationship, either, but I'm doing my best. Tonight, the most beautiful man walks into the hospital. He's here for his father, who was just rushed in with a massive heart attack. If the man lives through the night, I'll be surprised. His son, Garrett Ford, is a pilot, and he's dressed like one. It's difficult to focus on my job with a man who is larger than life, and dressed to kill, with piercingly blue eyes and full lips. What's more, he's very polite and professional, which gets me. When his father wakes up for just a second and thinks I'm his estranged wife, Garrett looks at me in a way that I'll never forget.

***

She's hands down the most beautiful woman I've ever seen. Nora could stop traffic. What's more, she's smart, hard working, independent, and she's the best single parent I've ever met. Her kid's dad is a pill, but I have to turn the other cheek with him around, even though I know he'd rather see me crash and burn than see Nora and I together. I soon learn what lengths he'll go to to remove me from the picture. We'll see how far he gets. Trouble is, Nora sees him through a different set of eyes, and there is no convincing her that he is what he is. It's tough being the outsider in this three person relationship, and sometimes I feel like Nora's daughter Missy just puts up a front for me. I mean, what kid wouldn't want her natural father and mother to be together? Soon, it's clear just how much that is true...

HEA (Happily Ever After)
Second chance romance
Medical romance
Military romance
Medium heat

Course language
Mild cliffhanger ending
Third book in a complete 5 book standalone series

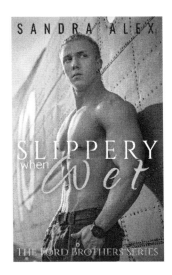

An underloved widower. Her younger, sexy, CEO neighbor. The move that changes more than her address...

Moving to a new neighborhood is never easy. But after Aaron's accident there wasn't a choice. He's a stubborn man, a hard-working man, and now he's a disabled man. Marriage is never easy, either, especially when we got married so young. We both traveled down different paths, and what we both wanted then isn't necessarily what we both want now. A new friend helps me see that, but he also helps me see that I deserve those things that I still want. It may be too late. Lots of things I think I've grown too old for suddenly come to light when Dalton shows me what I think I've missed out on. He also shows me that I haven't missed out, that my time is coming. He also comes to my rescue one night when both Aaron and I are helpless. Sometimes the kindness of strangers can be severely underrated.

***

Kathy, my girlfriend, there's something up with her. Amelia, my new neighbor, sees right through her, and helps me pick up the pieces. Her husband I'm not sure of. Never met him, but he watches me when I walk her home one night. There's something up with him, too. When I learn that our paths crossed once before, it makes Amelia see me in a whole new light. She's almost ten years older than me, but she acts as though it's more like a hundred. What she doesn't realize is that she's incredible, beautiful, intelligent as hell, and she is no more outdated than I am in so many ways. It takes a tragedy for her to see that, and it takes a miracle for her to believe it. And it takes a hard lesson from me for her to learn that everything happens for a reason, and it's more than just Aaron that brought her to me...it's fate.
HEA (Happily Ever After)
Second chance romance

Best friends to lovers romance
Medical romance
Military romance
Medium heat
Course language
Mild cliffhanger ending
Fourth book in a complete 5 book standalone series

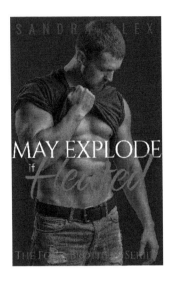

A tarnished Russian genius. A blinded CFO. A shocking interview that opens more than Jack's eyes...

No, really, I'm not afraid of anything. Born and raised in Russia, I've seen things. I've experienced things that I'll take to the grave. After our parents died, my sister and I began another life...in America. Seems men aren't much different in the land of opportunity. And when a once in a lifetime career choice pops up on my radar, I go for it, despite the fact that the CFO of the company looks like he wants more than just my list of references. When Jack Ford turns his back, I ready myself, but instead of taking a piece of what's being offered, for the first time in my life...a man surprises me.

***

Kristina's resume is unfounded. She looks great on paper, and she's even better in person. Her articulation is at a level of professionalism and passion that is unsurpassed, and she can demonstrate that ability easily when given a sample task. This first interview goes off without a hitch. And then I find her later in a place where I would never expect her to be. My brothers instantly veto me bringing her in for a second interview, but something draws me to her, despite that. But when the second interview ends in a shocking and unforgettable twist, I walk out of there shaking her hand, not realizing that I'm in the presence of a woman who will help me a hundred times more than I will ever help her.

HEA (Happily Ever After)
Second chance romance
Medical romance
Military romance
Office romance
Medium heat
Course language
Mild cliffhanger ending
Fifth book in a complete 5 book standalone series
Sneak peek into 'Crossing Boundaries'

Did you enjoy this book? You can make a big difference.

Do you know what the difference between an author that sells a few copies of their book a month and a New York Times bestselling author is?

<u>The answer is clear and simple</u>:

REVIEWS

Don't believe me?

Take a look at any NYT bestselling author and a regular author (like me) and see the difference in the number of reviews.

<u>The fact is clear</u>: **reviews lead to sales. Sales lead to bestseller charts.**

One other simple fact is that many advertisers *won't look at a book* unless it has a <u>minimum of 50 book reviews</u>.

That's where you come in. **I need your help**.

Honest reviews of my books help bring them to the attention of other readers.

If you've enjoyed this book, I would be very grateful if you could spend <u>just five minutes</u> leaving a review (it can be as short as a like).

Thank you very much.

Sandra Alex

Author's Note

Thanks so much for reading *Proceed with Caution.* I'm so excited about writing a new genre!

Want to know when I have a new release? Sign up to my newsletter for new release updates. Visit www.sandraalexbooks.com for details.

Thanks so much for your support!

~Sandra

Printed in Great Britain
by Amazon

84302176R00160